SAM

(Th

Jean C. Joachim

Moonlight Books

8/14

Sam's Decision

PUBLISHER

Moonlight Books

Dedication
To the late Michael Magness

It is with deep gratitude that I honor my friend, consultant, and critic, Michael Magness. Michael gave unselfishly of his time and immense knowledge of history to help me construct an accurate picture of Colonial America and a compelling story.

He acted as a sounding board. Michael made many great suggestions and held my feet to the fire to justify plot points, character qualities, and dialogue. He helped me make this book the best it could possibly be.

And that doesn't even come close to the great authenticity he gives this book by his guidance on the facts of Colonial America. He was my source, my guide for historical information. He always had time to consult with me on any point of history, what people said, wore, ate, and could you get a divorce in Colonial America. Turns out, you could.

His fondness for Fitch's Eddy – a town he helped create – kept it alive for me. I plan to write one more story as history has come alive for me through this series – thanks to Michael.

My one sadness is that Michael didn't live to see the publication of this book. He passed away over the winter. However, I know that he would have wonderful things to say about the book and criticisms, maybe ways it could have been made better. That was Michael, interested only in producing the best book. possible

Thank you, Michael, for your help, listening, guidance, and unwavering friendship.

Jean C. Joachim

SAM'S DECISION
Chapter One

itch's Eddy, Fall, 1790

F With his dog, Lucky, by his side and his musket tucked under his arm, Sam Chesney slipped quietly out of the Inn right before dawn. Legally, he owned the Inn, because women couldn't own property, but his grandmother ran it. She provided him with a comfortable bed and excellent meals. In return, Sam chopped wood, pumped water, lifted heavy objects, supplied fresh game for her table, and fed the livestock. He couldn't wait until his little sister, Lizzie, and his half-brother, Jem, were old enough to take over those chores.

He trekked a short distance through tall grass toward the woods and the old oak tree where he'd join up with his brother-in-law, Benjamin Fitch.

They met there to hunt. The image of his grandmother's roast duck got his mouth to watering and made his stomach growl. He reached in his pocket and pulled out a day-old biscuit and bit off a hunk. It would have to do for his breakfast until he returned.

Sam respected waterfowl, and their uncanny ability to hear him creep through the woods, no matter how soft his footfall. He enjoyed the challenge of sneaking up on them. If Sam got the jump on a small flock, he almost always bagged one or two.

Often, Benjamin Fitch would brag about his hunting skills. Thus, a friendly rivalry grew between them. Sam crept along, feeling his way.

"Psst! Sam! Over here."

In the slowly rising sun, Sam recognized the outline of his friend's hat.

"Ben? That you?"

"Who else would it be?" Ben appeared from behind the tree, flanked by his brown-and-white dog, Patches.

Sam chuckled.

"Where's Josiah?" Ben asked.

"Aw, he's a tenderfoot," Sam said, making a gesture. Though Josiah Quint was Sam's best friend, he didn't cotton to hunting. Since he took his meals at the Inn, he didn't need to outfox wild animals.

"Come on. You're late."

"Don't think no ducks are gonna complain, do you?" Sam asked.

Ben laughed.

"Shh!" Sam put his finger over his lips. Even the slightest stirring in the underbrush would alert their prey.

Together they parted the dense brush and moved as silently as they could. The dogs, friendly with each other, trotted along behind. When they reached their favorite spot ten yards from a pond, they knelt down. Something solid banged against his thigh. Dipping his hand in his other coat pocket, Sam discovered a piece of raisin bread wrapped in paper. He figured his grandmother must have slipped it into his pocket before he got dressed. Grinning at her thoughtfulness, he pulled it out and offered half to Ben.

After taking the bread, Ben tore off a piece and gave it to Patches, who gobbled it up. Ben pulled out two small croissants from a small bag hanging from his belt. He offered one to Sam, who shared it with Lucky.

The sun took its time rising over the horizon, sprinkling daylight through the trees. Sam rested back on his haunches. The young men trained their gazes on the water. Suddenly, Sam straightened up.

"What?" Benjamin asked.

Sam put his finger to his lips, then pointed. Half a dozen ducks swam silently from one edge of the pond to the other, ducking from time-to-time to scoop up a tasty fish. The men cocked and shouldered their muskets.

The clicks alerted the birds. They picked up their heads and spread their wings. With a cacophony of quacks, they took off, flying across the water. Sam and Benjamin aimed and fired. Two ducks fell into the pond. Seconds later, the men took aim again. The ducks were farther away but they each managed to hit a second one.

"Lucky! Fetch!" Sam called, gesturing.

"Patches! Duck!" Benjamin said, pointing.

The dogs sprang into action. The men sank down, reaching for their pouches of cider while the dogs chased down the fallen birds. After a long drink, Benjamin leaned back to rest against a tree.

"Your sister's with child." He took a long draught.

"What?"

"You heard me." Ben put down his drink.

Sam swallowed then gazed at his friend. "It's about time, Fitch. Guess you finally figured it out, eh?" Sam grinned.

While he laughed, Benjamin took a swipe at his friend's shoulder. "At least I'm doing it; you ain't. Are you?" Benjamin cocked an eyebrow.

"Watch it, Fitch. She's my sister."

Ben snickered. "And she's *my* wife."

Sam was raising his arm to slap his friend, when Lucky and Patches interrupted. They dropped the ducks from their mouths and raced back to the pond to get the last two.

Sam stuffed his duck in a sack. "Anyone else know?"

"My mother and father. Your ma and Caleb. No one else. You're the first. Outside of my family. You and Doc." Benjamin shook his head. "I wanted to wait. Be sure. Ya know? But Sarah insisted."

"Now you're sure?"

Ben nodded. "She'll probably be mad I told you."

"She'll get over it." Sam stuck out his hand. "Congratulations, Ben. You're going to be a father."

A wide grin spread across Benjamin Fitch's face. "Yep."

"Bet your mother and father are happy."

"Happy? They are plumb loco about it. You'd think we'd invented the wheel or something. Geez. People have children all the time."

"Yeah, but now ol' Elijah's got an heir."

"If it's a boy."

"True." Sam nodded. "And if it's a girl, I guess you'll have to keep trying."

Benjamin laughed. "Fine by me."

Sam punched Ben playfully. "My sister. Careful."

"Yeah, yeah. You're gonna be an uncle."

Sam grinned. "That's right. I'll teach him how to hunt."

"I'll teach him. He's my son."

"If he's a boy," Sam teased.

"I almost forgot. My dad said to tell you to come around and see him today or tomorrow. What's that about? What have you got to do with my father?"

"Never you mind. My business. You'll find out soon enough." Ben shrugged.

The dogs returned with the last two ducks. The young men packed up their kill, shook hands and went their separate ways.

WHEN SAM RETURNED TO the Inn where he lived with his grandmother, Martha, and his little sister, Lizzie, he laid his kill on the kitchen table.

"Oh, good. Duck for supper. Here, Sam," Martha said, handing him a buttered corn muffin.

No one made muffins and bread as good as Martha, except maybe his sister, Sarah. He bit into the tender, warm confection and wiped the dribble of melted sweet, creamy butter from his chin. Between bites he blurted out Sarah's news.

"Well, shear my sheep! It's about time that young woman got busy. Land sakes, I thought this would never happen." Martha grinned.

"Ben said she told Mama already."

"I wondered why Abby had a sly look on her face and avoided me last night with a flimsy excuse." Martha shook her head. She looked down to see three-year-old Jem Tanner, her newest grandchild, tugging on her skirt. "More little ones in my kitchen!" She picked up a muffin, slathered it with butter and handed it to the little boy. "Here you go, Jem. Don't go getting the butter on your shirt, now. Sit at the table and eat proper-like."

Sam lifted his littlest sibling up on a stool and ruffled the boy's hair.

"Sam," the child said, between bites, staring with big, adoring eyes at his half-brother.

"Gotta go, Grandma. Jem, be good." Sam walked to the door. He had things to do before meeting with old Elijah Fitch. Was it too early? He looked up at the sky and determined the general store would be opening up soon. He had to talk to Becky. Had to get things settled between them before he approached Old Man Fitch.

He sat on the bench outside the store. The sound of someone stirring inside drew his attention. The door popped open, and his girlfriend, Becky Rhodes, daughter of Daniel Rhodes, who owned the general store, stepped forward, sweeping the pile of dust and dirt outside.

"Oh! Sam. I didn't see you." When she smiled, a becoming blush stole into her cheeks, blending her freckles together. Her hair the color of fire sparkled in the early morning light.

"Howdy Miss Rhodes." Sam removed his hat. "Mind if I speak to you a minute? In private?"

"Of course, come in." She swept the last remnants of dirt out the door, then stepped inside, leaving the door open for Sam. He entered and followed her up to the counter.

"What can I do for you?" She donned a white apron with a ruffled hem.

"Don't need nothin'. Want to talk about you and me."

"Oh?" She raised her eyebrows and the pink in her cheeks deepened.

Sam took her hand in both of his. "I have plans, Becky. Big plans. I want to have my own farm, like my pa did. I'm gonna get one from Old Man Fitch."

"But you have a good job with Caleb. You're learning smithing and doing fine, so I hear."

Sam lowered his gaze. "Yeah. I know. Caleb's been good to me. I don't mind smithing, but I'd rather have my own place. Run things myself. I'm a man of the earth. I want to grow my own crops. Have cows, maybe even a horse someday."

"You have Sunshine."

Sam snorted. "A goat. And she belongs to my sister. She's not mine. I want my own animals, my own place." He raised his gaze to hers. He loved her bright red hair, and her intelligence. "You're smart, Becky. I'm gonna need a wife. One who is not afraid to get her hands dirty. I'll need a woman to help me run the farm."

"You could just hire a farmhand." Her lips compressed into a fine line.

"This ain't comin' out right. You know what I mean."

She removed her hand. "No, I don't, Sam Chesney. Seems to me like you should put up a 'farmhand wanted' sign outside the store." She turned her back to him to attend to something on the shelf behind her.

"Becky. Come on. You know what I mean. I'm getting all confused here."

"I'll say you are. If you're expecting me to be a farmhand. You're darn confused." She turned her attention back to the shelf.

Frustrated, Sam stepped behind the counter and turned her around to face him. "Becky Rhodes, you know what I mean."

Shooting him a cool look, she said, "I don't, and you're not supposed to be back here."

He grabbed her upper arms and jerked her to his chest before he brought his mouth down on hers in a hard kiss. Becky leaned into him, resting her hands on his shoulders. He broke suddenly, stepped back and stared at her with hot eyes.

"You know what I mean, Becky. I love you. I want you to be my wife."

Her mouth fell open slightly and her eyes widened. "You what?"

"You heard me. Marry me, Becky."

"And be your farmhand?"

"Be my wife, my partner on my farm. I need a smart wife, like you."

"I don't know nothin' about farmin', Sam."

"I'll teach you. You can milk a cow, can't you?"

"And a goat, too. And shear a sheep."

"See, you're ready." He took her hand again. "It'll be you and me. I love you. I'll take good care of you. You won't be a farmhand, you'll be my beautiful wife."

With wide eyes, Becky withdrew her hand. "No."

ADJACENT TO THE GENERAL store, in the shadows by the open window, out of sight of Sam and Becky, stood retired sheriff, Abiel Wilcox. He held his breath momentarily as he listened to the conversation between Becky and Sam.

When Sam stormed out of the store, slamming the door, Abiel jumped, but hung back. So Sam Chesney was looking for a wife? Abiel stroked his chin. His granddaughter could do worse than hitch up with a Chesney. Even if he didn't run the Inn, he owned it and if Violet married him, someday it would be theirs. As he neared home, his nose picked up the scent of something apple and cinnamon baking.

He opened the door. "What's that I smell?" he asked, interrupting a heated conversation between his daughter-in-law, Hope, and Violet.

"I just don't feel well. My stomach. Must have been somethin' I et," Violet said.

"Don't think you can pull the wool over my eyes, Violet Wilcox! I know. I know what's going on."

Violet dissolved in tears. "I'm sorry, Mama. I'm sorry. I didn't mean to."

"I know, child. I know. Thank God your daddy isn't here to see this." Hope embraced her daughter and stroked her hair. "Never you mind. You ain't the first girl in this situation."

Abiel stopped. "What did you say?"

Hope's face reddened. Violet hid her face in her mother's shoulder. Abiel cocked an eyebrow.

"You might as well know now. You'll find out eventually anyway. Violet is with child."

"Zeb Gates! That bastard!" Abiel smashed his fist down on the table. He turned angry eyes on his granddaughter. "What did I tell you? I knew that rotten peddler would lead you astray!" Shame and disgrace connected with his good family name tore through him. "I told you he was no good! But nobody listens to me in this house! Nobody!" He stomped out, forgetting about the delicious aromas coming from the kitchen.

Worry soured his stomach. His throat went dry. He rubbed the back of his neck and headed for his favorite path in the woods to think things out. What could they do? They'd have to leave. Move again. Make up some story about the child and start over. But Abiel didn't want to move. He had the perfect set-up – a job that put a roof over their heads and paid him a small stipend. Where else could he get such a sweet deal? Nowhere. No, they'd not move. There must be another way.

As he stepped over fallen, rotting tree trunks, and through prickly raspberry bushes, a plan hatched in his head. Might be the perfect solution and solve two problems at once. As he fleshed out the idea in his mind, he turned around and quickened his pace toward home.

It seemed too simple to be true. Sam Chesney needed a wife, and Abiel's granddaughter, Violet needed a husband. Abiel counted on Sam's being too naïve to know all about how a child came about. Maybe the lad knew the basics, but Abiel would bet he didn't know nothing about timing.

Now he'd have to let Hope and Violet in on the plan. He hoped Violet wasn't still too stuck on that low life Zeb to make eyes at Sam. Abiel smiled. Violet was a beautiful young woman. Once she set her cap for Sam, he'd never be able to resist.

Thoughts of Zeb returned to the old man. The charming vagabond had hung around Violet behind Abiel's back. If he hadn't been a lawman, he'd have made up an excuse to shoot the man. He knew exactly what that scoundrel Zeb was up to. Poor trusting, naïve Violet. He'd taken her in completely. When Abiel had cornered the man and suggested marriage, Zeb had hot-footed it out of Trumbull, vowing to return in the new year, With amazing speed, Abiel whisked Violet and Hope away to Fitch's Eddy before Zeb returned.

Violet had cried and resisted, carrying on for days. She even threatened to run away. He hardened his heart to his granddaughter's pleas and firmed up his decision to save his family by leaving Connecticut. He knew Elijah Fitch from years ago. Fitch had encouraged Abiel to settle his small family there, even offering a home in town to the Wilcox family in exchange for Abiel acting as Sheriff, when necessary. Though it wasn't official, no one told Abiel he couldn't do it. He dusted off his rifle and pistol, packed up Hope and Violet, and hightailed it out of Trumbull before Zeb returned.

Sullen and complaining, Violet had no choice but to move with her mother and grandfather to Fitch's Eddy. With no money, no profession, and no way to reach Zeb, Violet resigned herself to leaving Trumbull.

Abiel had considered waiting for the baby's birth then moving again, but he needed the job and had taken a shine to Martha Chesney. He resolved to remain in Fitch's Eddy.

This new solution would solve all his problems and allow him to pursue a new relationship of his own. He grinned to himself as he hurried home. Now he had to convince his granddaughter to go along with his plan. Even Sam would come out ahead by acquiring the farm wife he sought. Bursting with pride at his cleverness, Abiel entered his humble home.

"Hope, Violet! Come here," he said.

The urgency of his command produced an immediate reaction. Both women scurried from the stove where they had been making stew to the table, where Abiel sat, perched like a well-fed magistrate.

"Yes, Father, what is it?" Hope asked, her brows drawn together, her hands twisting a corner of her apron. She always called him "father" even though he was only her father-in-law.

Violet plopped down on a chair and stared with wary eyes.

"I have the answer!"

The women glanced at each other, then at him with questioning looks. Hope raised her eyebrows, her gaze searched her daughter's. Violet turned away from her mother and grandfather.

"What can you do? Make the child go away?" Hope asked.

"No. I have a better idea," He said.

"You do? Did you find Zeb?" Violet's eyes softened, her voice eager.

"No. Better," he replied.

"Can't I just have the baby quietly?" Violet moaned.

"No unmarried mothers in the Wilcox family! Don't you know how bad this is? You'll be shunned. So will your mother and me. And

all for that no-account scoundrel, Zeb. I won't have it. I've led an honorable life and I'll not have it sullied by a few moments of madness with
an irresponsible drifter!" He banged his fist on the table. "And we'll fix
it. Save the Wilcox reputation, and find her a husband to care for her."

"But where will you find a husband?" Hope asked.

"Zeb's coming back?" Violet asked, half-rising from her chair.

Abiel's expression clouded over. He scowled. "Don't ever mention
that scoundrel's name again in my presence! No. You will have an honorable husband."

"And where will you find such a man?" Hope asked.

"Right here in Fitch's Eddy," Abiel said, his expression changing
back to sunny.

"And who might that be?" Violet asked, fists on her hips, defiance
in her eyes.

"Why, Sam Chesney, of course. That's who." Wearing a smile of sat-
isfaction, Abiel leaned back in his chair.

SARAH CHESNEY FITCH stood in the kitchen watching the
French cook prepare pastry dough for baking. Benjamin entered by the
kitchen door, followed by Patches. Sarah knelt down to greet the dog,
scratching him behind the ears.

"Patches! Oh, Patches, did you help our Benjamin today?"

Ben frowned. "You greet the dog before your husband?"

Sarah sprang up. "I'm so sorry." She threw her arms around his neck
and pushed up on tiptoe to give him a long, sweet kiss.

"That's better."

"It's just that you know how much I love you and Patches doesn't
know I love him."

A soft chuckle from the baker drew Sarah's eye. "Well, it's true.
How many did you get?"

"Two for me and two for your brother." Ben leaned over to whisper in her ear. "And I told him about your condition." He straightened up and briefly rested his palm on her belly.

"Oh, Ben, I wanted to tell Sam." She frowned.

"What difference does it make? Soon everyone will know or they will think you are eating too many of Giselle's eclairs," he said. "Where should I put these, Giselle?"

The baker wiped her hands on her apron. "I'll take them," she said, heading for the small side room used for preparing meat.

Left totally alone, Benjamin took Sarah by the waist and pulled her up against his chest. He leaned down to give her a long, passionate kiss. She melted against him. When he stepped back, he spoke in a husky voice. "On my way back, I thought of you."

Sarah arched an eyebrow and shot him a knowing look. "You're always thinking of me *that way*, Ben."

His face colored. "Can I help it if I love my wife?"

"Love?" She raised both eyebrows.

His lips formed a salacious grin. "Don't tell me you never think of me that way."

"Well," she lowered her gaze as heat stole up her neck. "Maybe."

He picked her up and twirled her around. "My passionate bride!"

"Shh. Someone will hear you. Giselle is only a few feet away."

He laughed. "You want privacy?" He put her down and took her hand. "Come." He hustled her over to the back staircase.

"Now?" she asked.

He stopped at the bottom step, faced her, and raised his eyebrows. "Why not?"

She grinned, her gaze connecting with his lustful eyes. "Why not." She giggled as he swept her up in his arms and climbed the stairs.

After they made love, Benjamin left Sarah resting in bed while he got dressed.

"I can't be late today." He pulled his shirt on over his head.

She smiled as she watched him dress. He raised his pants up and faced her.

"You do like it, don't you?"

"Making love?"

He colored slightly but nodded.

"It's the one time I have you all to myself. The only time we are completely alone. And I can talk to you without anyone else hearing."

He raised his eyebrows. "Is that the only reason?"

Heat flooded Sarah's face. "No, of course not."

He grinned. "Tell me." He buttoned his waistcoat.

She shook her head. "A lady never talks of those things." But she shot him a flirtatious glance.

He laughed. "Ah, my beautiful, funny Sarah." He walked over to the bed and bent down to kiss her. She caressed his cheek.

"I'll bring your supper today."

He paused to stroke her belly. "Soon you will be too big to bring me food."

"I suppose." She shifted onto her other side.

"Then I will come home to eat."

"You will? Why?"

"Because a midday meal without the company of my bride would be a sad one." He cupped her cheek.

She ran her fingers through his hair, pushing it off his forehead. After one more kiss he strode to the door and was gone. She yawned, stretched, and swung her legs over the side of the bed. It was time for her to get up and go to the Inn. She still stopped off there to help out as there wasn't much for her to do in the Fitch mansion.

As she finished getting dressed, there was a knock on her door.

"Come in."

Ann Fitch swooshed into the room. "We have so much to do, Sarah. Now that you're expecting, we have to get ready. Sit down, my dear. Don't tire yourself. You must remain in perfect health."

Sarah's mouth fell open. She stared, wide-eyed as her mother-in-law blathered on about Christening clothing and cradles. If Sarah had no idea what kind of whirlwind she was caught up in, she'd learn soon enough. A new heir to the Fitch fortune was huge for Elijah and Ann Fitch. And soon to be a topic of conversation throughout the town.

DETERMINED TO HAVE his way, Sam returned to the store the next day to try all his charm and persuasion on Becky. Before he could argue with her, several customers entered the store. She brushed by him to wait on them. He tried to catch her eye.

"Can we talk?"

"I'm busy Sam. No time for jawin' now. Mrs. Austin, what can I get you?"

Pushed aside and ignored, Sam stepped back, out of the way. When Becky avoided meeting his gaze, he left. He stopped to lean against the building and get his bearings.

That didn't go anything like he'd planned. He'd expected Becky to be overjoyed he'd asked for her hand. Lord knows she'd been hinting about it enough! Not only did she turn him down flat, but now she wouldn't even give him a chance to broach the subject again. Maybe he'd better think things through once more. He needed to try a different approach.

He plucked a licorice root from his pocket and stuck it in his mouth.

"Mornin', Mr. Chesney," came a soft, lilting voice.

He looked to his left and spied Miss Violet Wilcox stopping at the threshold of the store.

"Mornin', Miss Wilcox," Sam said, grabbing the licorice and shoving it back in his pocket. Straightening up, he tipped his hat and slapped a big grin on his face. Miss Wilcox wore a dark purple frock, most becoming with her sky-blue eyes and dark hair. Maybe she didn't have hair like fire, but her peaches 'n' cream complexion and long, dark lashes could melt a man's heart in an instant.

"Not buyin' anything?"

"Changed my mind. You?" No way would he admit his real reason for being at the store.

"We need sugar and flour."

"Baking something?"

"Why don't you stop by before supper?" Violet adjusted her hat, shifting it toward the back of her head, revealing more of her pretty face.

"What ya makin'?" Sam raised his gaze to hers. He leaned forward slightly.

"You'll see. Guarantee you'll like it." She shot him a dazzling smile, then moved into the store.

Sam nearly swooned. Damn if that young woman didn't have the flirtiest way about her. Becky Rhodes wasn't the only attractive female in town. Now he'd come to think of it, Violet Wilcox might even be a mite prettier.

Sam hitched up his pants, then headed toward Fitch's logging office. He wasn't quite ready to make his move. But he planned to secure the promise of land and then recalculate. Becky had thrown a wrench into his plans. No way could he take over even a small farm without a wife.

A chilly wind foreshadowing the coming of winter whipped around his legs. Sam pulled his hat down over his ears and raised the collar of his coat. Harvest season was almost over, and winter would be settlin' in soon. This would be the perfect time to get his land and make his plans, so he could be ready for spring planting. He moved quicker, taking bigger strides. The notion of his own place got his heart beating faster.

All he'd need was one cow, or maybe one goat. Two oxen would speed up plowing. But if he only got one, he'd make do. He'd need a couple of chickens. Maybe his grandmother could spare one or two chicks.

As he made his way up the hill, his mind ran through the list of vegetables he wanted to grow. Potatoes were always good. They'd last a long time. Carrots and squash were easy, then cucumbers and onions. He might plant a few pumpkins, too, if he could find seeds.

With his imagination in full flight, the trip passed quickly. Before long, he found himself at Elijah Fitch's door. Sam swallowed, then raised his fist and knocked.

"Come in!" shouted Elijah.

Sam opened the door gently and stuck his head in. Ben was bent over a table reading some papers. He looked up.

"Who is it, Benjamin?"

"Sam Chesney."

"Send him in."

Ben smiled. "You heard my father. Go on in."

Sam walked quickly to the back of the building where Elijah had his office. He pushed open the door and took off his hat.

"Come in, come in, Mr. Chesney. You're going to be an uncle. Did you know that?"

"Yes, sir."

"Going to have the finest nephew in the state of New York."

"But what if it's a girl?" popped out of Sam's mouth.

"Sarah wouldn't do that. Disappoint her father-in-law, would she?"

Sam simply stared at the old man. Was he off his rocker? For his sister's sake he hoped she'd have a boy.

"Take off your coat, young man. What do you want? A job? Smithing not paying enough?"

"No, sir."

"Sit down." Elijah gestured to the one chair facing him. Sam eased down, never taking his eyes off Elijah Fitch. Caleb had warned him that

Fitch was a sly, crafty man who always ended up with the fat end of any deal. Sam had better be careful.

"Not a job? What then?"

"Land. A farm."

"You want to be a farmer?"

"Yes, sir. Like my father."

"We may be related now, in a manner of speaking, but I don't just hand over land as a gift." Elijah narrowed his eyes.

"I know, sir. I didn't mean that. I mean when a farmer goes belly up. If he can't handle the farm. I'd like to take it over and pay it off in crops and butter and cheese."

Elijah cocked an eyebrow. "And who will you have with you to help you work this farm?"

"I plan to get me a wife. A good, smart one. She'll help."

Elijah laughed. "Gonna turn your wife into a farmhand? Can't imagine too many girls in Fitch's Eddy signing up for that proposal."

"No sir. Not yet. As soon as I can pay something, I plan to hire a real hand. I just need her to help tide me over. Just until the first harvest."

"I see. Got it all planned out, do you?" The older man cocked an eyebrow.

"Yes sir. No sir. Well, maybe. Sort of."

"And what crops do you plan on planting?"

"Carrots, peas, potatoes, beets. Cabbage?"

"You askin' or tellin'?"

"Cabbage," Sam said, his voice firm.

"That's a mighty lot of work to put all those in the ground right after the last frost."

"I know, sir. I don't mind hard work."

"Fixin' to get married before you move to the farm, I reckon." Elijah picked up his pipe.

"Yes, sir." Sam shifted his weight.

"Who do you have in mind? Becky Rhodes?"

Sam swallowed. That's exactly who he had in mind. But now that didn't look good.

"Well, maybe not."

"She turn you down already?"

Sam nodded

"Mighty fickle, if you ask me. It's all over town about you and Becky being sweet on each other."

Sam changed the subject. "So do you have some land I can work?"

"I might. Promised to let my man on the near forty by Morgan's Creek go back East. Said I'd forgive his debt. He didn't owe much anyway. He's been promised a job there with family. He's not much of a farmer and his wife keeps having children. They're better off. And so am I."

"Forty acres would suit me just fine."

"You'd best look at the land first before makin' promises. You'll have to keep up your payments to me or lose your farm. You understand that, don't you? I need some payment before I turn over the land. In good faith. Before I trust you."

"Yessir. I have money saved up."

Elijah snickered. "Really?" He lit a match and held it to his pipe.

"Yep. All my winnings from the harvest festivals. And the money I earn working for Caleb."

"He pays you?"

Sam nodded. He reached into his back pocket and pulled out a soft leather pouch. Loosening the rawhide drawstrings, he turned it over, emptying a mound of silver coins on Fitch's desk. What he'd thought was a lot looked paltry on the massive surface.

"Doesn't look like much." Elijah eyed the coins as Sam separated them. "I'll take half," he said, reaching for the coins.

Sam clamped his hand over the money. "Ain't seen the land. We ain't closed the deal yet."

Elijah's face darkened, then he laughed. "Good for you. Protect yourself. You're right. You look over the land and let me know. I'll send Benjamin to show you the way." The older man picked up a piece of paper and bent over it to read.

"All right, Mr. Fitch." Sam scooped his money into his hand and returned the coins to the pouch. He sat there, fidgeting, until Ben caught his eye. He motioned.

"Come on. Meeting's over," Ben said, taking two steps to the door and holding it open.

Sam scooted out ahead of his friend. When the door was closed, Benjamin turned to Sam.

"You sure you want to do this?"

Sam grinned and wiped the sweat off his brow with his sleeve. "Yep."

"You taking Becky Rhodes as your wife?"

"Nope."

"She turn you down?"

"Yep," Sam said, shaking his head. "I didn't expect it."

Benjamin stopped and stared. "Who then?"

"I don't know."

Benjamin laughed, then proceeded to lead Sam to the near forty.

Chapter Two

Sarah Chesney Fitch, remained at the table with her mother-in-law, Ann Fitch. Though breakfast had finished an hour earlier, a plate with buttered French bread remained on the table, along with slices of apple pie.

Sarah, just beginning to show her pregnancy, eyed the bread. Hunger grew in her belly.

"Eat, child. A new one is growing inside you. You need food." Ann picked up the plate and offered it to her daughter-in-law.

Sarah took two pieces. One she put on her plate, the second one, she brought to her mouth for a big bite. "I love this bread. So much better than mine." She chewed, marveling at the soft texture as contrasted with the crusty exterior. And the butter! Of course, it was the same as the butter at the Inn, but why did it taste so much better? Giselle must have put something special in it. Or maybe they fed the cows differently? Everything seemed to taste better at the Fitches' grand table.

"Names. You must name him Benjamin Hammond Fitch, Junior."

"What if it's a girl?" Sarah hid a smile behind her hand. Amused by her in-laws' insistence she would give birth to a boy.

"A girl? You wouldn't dare have a girl." Ann waved her hand to settle the matter.

Sarah laughed out loud. "It's not up to me."

"Well, pish tush. If you have a girl, you'll just have to have more until you have a boy."

"For a girl, I'd like Elizabeth Chesney Fitch, I think. We could call her Betsy."

"Hmm. Elizabeth is nice. But Chesney? If you want to use one of your names, why not Wolcott? It's so much more refined. After all, who was Chesney?" Ann Fitch dabbed at her lips with her napkin.

"Who was Chesney? My father. The man who died saving my life. That's who." Sarah sensed a burning in her cheeks.

Ann Fitch reached over and patted her arm. "Oh, yes, dear. I'm so sorry. I didn't mean to be rude. He was a very brave man. And we are grateful to him for saving you. But you must admit that Wolcott will be recognized throughout the state."

Sarah eased her arm away. "Then we can name my second child Wolcott. Maybe even Wolcott Fitch. If it's a boy."

"Goodness, no! That would never do. First born son should always be named after his father."

"You didn't name Ben after his father."

Ann Fitch blushed and cast her gaze to her hands. "That's true. To be honest, I didn't care much for the name Elijah. Benjamin is so much nicer, don't you agree?

"I do agree. Everything about Ben is nicer than Elijah." Realizing her frankness, Sarah covered her mouth with her hand.

Ann Fitch laughed. "You do speak your mind, don't you, my dear?"

"Most of the time. It's the way I was taught."

"You mother and father did right by you. We're pleased to have you in our family."

Sarah blew out a breath. She hated sparring with her in-laws but refused to be bullied by them. When she got pregnant, they were overjoyed. Their enthusiasm bubbled over. She suspected she'd have to fend them off from trying to run her child's life.

"A cabinetmaker is coming to Fitch's Eddy. Elijah has already commissioned him to create a cradle for the baby."

"Oh?"

"Yes. It was Elijah's design and it's magnificent. Fit for a king, or a Fitch!" Ann laughed.

"Don't you think I should have a say in the design for my baby's cradle?"

Elijah Fitch walked into the parlor.

"Sarah! Just the person I wanted to see. Micah Edwards made a cradle for baby Benjamin. It will arrive in a fortnight."

"Don't you think you should have asked me?"

"Ask you what? A splendid bed made by a master craftsman. What could be better? You do your part, give birth to a healthy boy, and we will do the rest." Elijah stared at her belly.

Feeling blood rushing to her neck, Sarah turned away. "Stop staring at me."

"Pardon me. Just an eager grandfather." He bowed.

"This is my baby. We don't know if it's a boy or a girl. And it's mine! Not yours."

"We will be the child's grandparents," Elijah said.

"But I will be his mother."

"Aha! You said 'he.' You know it's a boy, don't you?" A triumphant gleam lit up Elijah's eyes.

"I know no such thing!" Sarah pushed to her feet and flounced out of the room. The sound of Elijah's laughter echoed down the hallway.

AS THE SUN ROSE IN the sky, Sam finished inspecting the land and talking with the farmer. He was late to work, so Sam hurried toward the blacksmith shop. He'd best be there before noon. First, he had one task to do at the Inn.

"Here you go. Fresh from the oven," Martha said, handing him a buttered biscuit. "Come on, Lizzy. Time to peel apples."

Martha shepherded the young girl back to the kitchen. The pretty nine-year-old plunked down on a stool by the oven and picked up the peeler.

"Peel apples. Knead dough. All I do is work. I never get to see Sunshine," she whined.

"Oh, hush. We need two more pies. Then I'll give you the cores to take out to your goat."

"Yes?"

Martha nodded. "Sam, where have you been? Caleb was looking for you."

"I had some business. I'm heading to the shop now," he said, then took a bite of the biscuit. "I swear, Grandma, no one makes biscuits as tasty as yours." Sam ducked into his room and stowed his money pouch under the mattress.

"Go on, Sam Chesney, you flatterer." Martha waved her hand, but a becoming blush stole up her cheeks.

Sam laughed. He slipped through the door and ran all the way to the blacksmith shop. Huffing and puffing, he entered quietly and took his seat.

"Sorry I'm late, Caleb."

"Where you been?" Caleb, Sam's stepfather cocked an eyebrow and stared at the young man for a moment.

"Business. Personal stuff," Sam said, picking up a hammer as he approached the forge.

"Oh, Becky Rhodes, eh? Off courtin'?"

"Not exactly."

"Then what, exactly?" Caleb stopped pounding and took the tongs. He picked up the knife he was working on and dunked it in the quenching bucket.

"Nothin'."

"All right. Guess a young man's entitled to some secrets. Here. Elijah Fitch wants this axe fixed. And he wants a kettle tipper, too."

Sam took the implement. "Make him pay. Next time he'll treat his tools better," Sam muttered.

"Fitch pays a pretty penny. Don't you worry."

The two men worked side-by-side in easy silence, each respecting the other. Sam could hardly keep his mind on his work.

His thoughts wandered back to the near forty at Morgan's Creek. The land looked choice. Of course, you couldn't tell the quality of the soil, or how rocky until you started digging.

The man there had already harvested half the acreage. A short man with silver strands mixing with his dark hair. Several children moved about, toting water from the well to the small house, or tossing hay to the goat. One young girl washed a baby in a bucket. The infant fussed and kicked.

My family's not gonna be like this. All sixes and sevens.

Sam kept his thoughts to himself.

"So you're the young man who's fixin' to take over this place?" Even though it was chilly, the man wiped sweat from his brow with his sleeve. Sam raised his eyebrows.

"How'd you find out?"

"Fitch's son told me."

"Yep. The land looks fine," Sam had said, casting his gaze across the fields.

"Looks that way, but it's mighty rocky in places."

"Ain't you gonna miss farming?"

The man gave a short, mirthless laugh. "No way in Hell. Can't wait to get back East. My cousin's got a general store in Connecticut, and he's desperate for help. It'll be a mighty nice respite from farmin'. Workin' inside in the winter. Plenty of food for my family. An easy life if you ask me. You got a wife and children?"

"Not yet."

"You'll need 'em to run this place. Always work to do here," the man said. "Never enough hands."

"I'll manage."

The man frowned but nodded. "Come back to the house for some tea."

"Much obliged," Sam said.

Once in the house, the men had discussed what the farmer would leave behind and what he'd take with him.

"I ain't gonna have need for the plow, hatchet, axe, and most of the other tools. You're welcome to 'em."

"Thank you. I can pay," Sam said, jingling the pouch in his pocket.

The man put his hand on Sam's forearm. "Keep your money. You'll need it. I'm taking the goat, cow, and the oxen. I'm takin' the chickens with me, too. We'll need the eggs and milk for the trip. The house belongs to Fitch, so it's yours to live in."

"Understood. Happy to have the tools."

"There are a couple of wild turkeys livin' in the woods. Plenty of ducks, too. You a good shot?"

"Yep."

"Then you won't starve. I wish you better luck with these acres than I had," the man said.

"Thank you." Sam pushed to his feet, shook hands with the farmer and headed back to town. His mind filled with plans for the farm. Strategies to get Becky to agree to marry him also occupied his thoughts.

As he worked on old man Fitch's axe, he recalled Violet Wilcox's words, *"Why don't you stop by before supper?"*

His stomach growled at the memory. She'd hinted something tasty would be waiting for him. As they took a break for a meal, Sam quickened his pace. The sun slowly inched down, leaving a gorgeous artist's palette of pinks and oranges streaking across the sky. He looked up. It meant the next day would be a good one. He'd have to take note of the sky every morning if he wanted to farm. He remembered his father's words.

"Bright sky at night, sailor's delight. Looks like a fine day ahead for us tomorrow, Abigail. Good for plantin'," George Chesney had said, drawing his wife to his side. Sam's heart ached for the touch of his father, tousling his hair, patting him on the back for a job well done. And his wise words. Sam thought his father was the smartest man in the world. Smarter even than old Elijah Fitch!

As the sun set, Caleb and Sam closed up shop. The smith headed toward his cabin, wife, and son, while Sam sauntered toward the Inn. As he passed by, he noticed a glow from candlelight in the windows of the modest Wilcox house. Sam picked up the pace and closed the distance to their house in no time. As he approached, the aroma of butter, apples, and cinnamon met his nose. Walking had boosted his appetite, and his mouth watered in anticipation of a delectable confection created by the lovely Violet Wilcox. He knocked on the door. Abiel Wilcox answered.

"Sam Chesney, by gum. Come in, come in, young man," Sheriff Wilcox said, taking Sam's arm and coaxing him inside.

The sweet scent of apples grew intense. Sam's stomach rumbled again.

"Sit down, sit down. Violet, a dumpling for this hungry lad," the Sheriff gestured to his granddaughter.

Violet placed two large, lightly-browned dumplings on a dish. She added a knife and fork, then brought it to the table.

"Much obliged," Sam said.

Her violet eyes met his dark ones. A warm smile graced her lips. Sam cut the dumpling in quarters, then took a piece with his fork. It melted in his mouth. The medley of flavors on his tongue; the tartness of the apple, the sweetness of the sugar, and the spicy cinnamon seduced his tastebuds.

"This is...wonderful!" he said, shoveling another large bite into his mouth.

"In Old Trumbull, where we lived before, Violet was known for her baking," the Sheriff said.

Violet poured a mug of cider for Sam and brought it to the table.

"I can see why," Sam said before digging in again. "Does she know anything about farming?"

"She's a quick study," Abiel said.

Sam nodded. Perhaps Becky Rhodes wasn't the only smart, accomplished, pretty girl in Fitch's Eddy?

Chapter Three

About an hour before dusk, Sarah sat at the window seat in the parlor, sewing. Despite her rise in status and wealth, she still liked to make dresses and do embroidery. Creating with fabric and thread entertained her. And she proudly showed off her even stitches. With a cloak thrown over her shoulders, Ann Fitch entered the room.

"Elijah has business in town. We're dining at the Inn. Giselle is preparing dinner for you and Benjamin. I thought you'd like to dine with him at the office.

"Oh, yes. I would. How thoughtful. Thank you." Sarah placed her sewing carefully in the basket, smoothed her skirt and pushed to her feet.

"You don't mind taking it to him? If it's too heavy, I'll have Charles accompany you."

"Oh, no. I don't mind. I'm sure it won't be too heavy." She smiled at her mother-in-law.

"Do you have any idea what your grandmother is serving at the Inn today?"

"Sorry. I don't."

"I hope we have Abigail's apple pie. The bread will have to do, since you aren't there to make it anymore." Ann sighed. "Guess I can't have it both ways – you about to give birth to my grandson or at the Inn baking bread."

"Giselle's bread is far better than mine."

"Don't under value your baking skills, my dear." Ann patted her hand and left the room.

Sarah grinned. Dinner alone with Benjamin would be a treat. She barely got to spend time just the two of them, except at night in bed. She'd spied Sam leaving the office early. What was her brother up to? She had to know. Eager to see her husband, she wrapped a heavy shawl about her shoulders and hurried down to the kitchen.

Giselle laid a pretty cloth over the basket.

"What do we have for dinner today?" Sarah asked. The aromas of cooking and baking made her mouth water. It seemed her appetite had increased threefold since she'd been carrying Benjamin's child.

"Two small venison pies, apple dumplings, cheese, bread, corn fritters and cider. Can you manage it, Missus?" Giselle picked up the basket and handed it to Sarah.

It was heavy, but Sarah flexed her muscles gained from kneading dough and carting heavy containers of milk and cider.

"I've got it." She smiled and made her way slowly to the kitchen door. Giselle opened it and Sarah stepped out.

The sun still shone bright. It warmed her face and shoulders. Relieved to note that the path to the office was mostly downhill, she skipped along, making the journey go quickly. She spied Benjamin standing by the window watching.

He opened the door and stood in the entry, legs spread, hands on hips, grinning. When she neared, he reached out for the basket. He put it down and slung his arm around her waist, scooping her up into his arms. He swung her around the room.

She wound her arms around his neck, threw her head back, and laughed. When he stopped, he pulled her to his chest and leaned down for a passionate kiss. When they broke, she fell back a step, raising her hand to her lips.

"You're hungry for more than dinner, Mr. Fitch," she said.

Desire glowed in his eyes. "Yes, but dinner will have to do. I have work to do."

"Can't you take dinner with me?"

"You brought food for two?"

"Yes. Your mother and father are dining at the Inn tonight. I was hoping you'd stop and eat with me. We get so little time together." She cast him a wistful glance.

"Of course." His gaze slid down her body, stopping at her belly. He reached out his hand to rest his palm gently on the slight bulge there. "I can still pick you up."

"Oh, yes. But maybe not for much longer."

"I'll always be able to lift you, you're so slight."

"Will you still love me when I get big?"

"You'll always be my beautiful bride. My Sarah," he sighed, running his thumb down her face.

Heat rose in her cheeks. He rarely spoke so sweetly. Only without others present. When family or friends were around, he was more formal. Warmth surrounded her heart. "Oh, Ben, I love you so much," she said, throwing her arms around his chest and kissing him.

He stroked her hair back from her forehead and gazed into her eyes. Her mother had told her it was the look of love and Sarah could always tell how Ben felt by looking into his eyes. Her reverie was interrupted by the rude rumbling of her stomach.

"We must eat. You must not deprive my son of nourishment," Benjamin said, picking up the basket and putting it on the small table. "What did Giselle pack for us today?"

"Oh, lovely things." As she rattled off the list of items, she took each one from the basket. They sat together on a bench, their legs touching as they tucked into their repast.

"I saw Sam leaving the office today. Why was he here?"

"You should ask him. It's not my business to tell," Ben said, taking a bite of his meat pie.

"Come on, Ben. I'm your wife. Shouldn't we share everything?" She picked up a fritter.

"He's my friend. He asked me not to tell anyone."

"But I'm not anyone."

"Granted, you are my wife, but you're also his sister. And if he wanted to tell you, he would," Ben frowned, turned his attention to his food. He picked up a goatskin bag of cider.

Sarah drew the corners of her mouth down. "All right then. Don't tell me. See if I care." She pushed to her feet, took one last bite of meat pie and picked up her shawl.

"You're leaving?"

"You won't talk to me." Her eyes filled.

"I will. I will! Don't leave." He closed his fingers around her upper arm.

"You and Sam keep secrets from me all the time. I don't like it. If he was a girl you would have married him instead of me!" She crossed her arms over her chest.

"Sarah, how silly!"

She stuck out her lower lip. "I don't like being left out."

Benjamin took her in his arms and rubbed her back. "Sarah, Sarah. Silly girl. Men talk about things with each other they don't tell their wives."

"Sam doesn't have a wife."

"That's for sure. And he's not likely to," Ben said.

Sarah looked up. "Really? Has he asked Becky yet?"

Benjamin's face reddened. He picked up an apple dumpling and moved to the window, turning his back to his wife. She followed.

Lowering her voice, she placed her hand on his forearm. "Did he ask Becky?"

He whirled around, "Yes! And she said 'no,' and that's all you'll get out of me."

Sarah gasped, drawing her hand to her mouth. "She turned him down?"

Ben nodded and finished eating his dumpling.

"Foolish girl," Sarah said, shaking her head. "I know she's sweet on Sam. She'd be lucky to marry him. He's hard-working and fun." She frowned.

"I agree."

"Why would she turn him down?" Sarah asked.

"You'll have to ask her. Now do we have to spend all our time together talking about Becky and Sam?" Benjamin smiled and drew Sarah closer. "I can think of better things we could be doing," he said, lowering his mouth to hers.

Sarah slid her palms up his chest and tipped up her chin to receive him. Warmth flooded her veins like it always did when he kissed her. As if she stood in front of a roaring fire, heat for her husband traveled her veins, consuming her, driving all rational thought from her mind.

His woodsy scent of pine and sweat teased her nose. The hard feel of his strong muscles pressed against her breasts. His hands gripped her hips and held them fast to his. Overtaken by desire, she could deny him nothing.

"Yes," she mumbled.

She curled her fingers over his powerful shoulders to steady herself as he lifted her up and carried her into the small back office. After shutting the door with his foot, he eased her down on the desk and made love to her.

AFTER THE FOOD WAS eaten and their thirst for each other quenched, Sarah smoothed her skirt, straightened her bodice and picked up her shawl. Benjamin pulled a pin or two from her bun to secure stray locks loosened by their passion. He kissed her forehead and held her close. When she reached for the basket, he stayed her hand with his.

"I'll bring it."

"Thank you."

He cupped her cheek, "You're a good wife, Sarah."

She smiled. "And you're a passionate husband. I hope I make a good mother, too." She touched her waist.

"You will, sweetheart, you will."

With one more lingering kiss goodbye, and a sigh, Sarah set out to return home. As she walked, a cool late afternoon breeze chilled her. She wrapped her shawl tighter as she hatched a plan to find out what Sam was up to. If Benjamin wouldn't tell her, she knew who would.

When she arrived home, the house was quiet. Ann and Elijah Fitch were still in town. Sarah yawned, then took her knitting to the most comfortable sofa in the large sitting room and stretched out. She was asleep before she could craft more than a dozen stitches.

She awoke to the chiming of the large grandfather clock in the entryway. It was seven o'clock. Ann Fitch sat quietly reading on the upholstered lounge chair across the room. Sarah yawned, stretched her arms up and stared at her needlework.

"Oh my goodness, so late and I'm almost out of thread," she said, peeking from under her lashes at Ann Fitch. "I'll get some at the general store," she said.

"Tomorrow morning. I have a list of things we need. I'll send Moses with you."

"Thank you."

Sarah took the book she was reading, bid her mother-in-law goodnight and headed for the bedroom. Before she finished one chapter, Benjamin crept in quietly.

"I thought you were asleep," he said.

"No, reading."

Benjamin took the book and read the title. "A Sicilian Romance, by Ann Radcliffe. You're still reading this?" he asked.

"Every time I sit down to read, I fall asleep. I'm not making much progress."

Ben smiled. "I guess making a baby is tiring work."

"What did you do today?" Sarah asked, sitting up and bending her knees. She wrapped her arms around her legs and gazed up at her husband.

"Nothing exciting. I took stock of early harvest. Oh, yes. And I wrote a contract for Mr. Edwards. He's the cabinetmaker moving here soon."

"A contract? What for?"

"Boards that Josiah is making at the sawmill. Mr. Edwards sent me his order."

"It's exciting to have a cabinetmaker here. The town is growing," Sarah said, reaching for her book.

"Yes. And father has had a letter from a mason."

Benjamin undressed and slipped into bed next to his wife. She snuggled down against him. She leaned over to blow out the candle. Ben raised his hand to her shoulder to stop her.

"Wait. Read from the book."

"Aloud?"

He nodded.

"You want to hear about *A Sicilian Romance*?"

"Yes. Then we can fall asleep together."

Sarah lay back against the pillows and opened the book. Ben tucked her up against him. As she read, her eyelids grew heavy. Ben licked his fingers, reached over, and pinched out the candle. He wrapped his arm around his wife's middle and was soon asleep beside her.

IN THE MORNING, SARAH rushed through her breakfast, anxious to get to the general store. Curiosity burned in the chest of the young woman.

"I hear you're going to town this morning," Elijah Fitch said, spreading creamy butter on a slice of French bread. "It's cold."

"Take the carriage. Be sure to take your heaviest shawl. I'll tell Charles to bring out the warmest blanket," Ann said, pushing to her feet.

"Thank you so much."

"We must protect you and our beloved grandson," Ann muttered, almost to herself.

Sarah eased up and hunted for her warmest cloak. When she found it, she met Charles in the vestibule.

"Here, miss," he said, opening the door and allowing her to exit first. He helped her into the carriage. Moses the house servant joined her. He lifted the warm blanket and spread it on her legs. Once settled in and snug, she gave the go-ahead to Digby, the driver. The carriage lurched forward and proceeded down the dirt path to the main road.

"What you aimin' to buy, Mrs. Sarah?" Moses asked.

"Thread. And you?"

"I've got Mrs. Fitch's list of goods, and one of them cherry suckers for me," Moses said. He jingled the coins he had in his pants pocket.

But that wasn't all Sarah was aiming to get at the general store. She planned to worm the truth out of Becky and why she turned Sam down. While the vehicle bumped along, Sarah thought up her strategy. Becky would never know Sarah had no clue about what Sam was up to, right? She'd probably figure Sarah knew everything because she was Sam's sister. Hah! Perfect. Sarah would play along, and Becky would spill the beans, unwittingly.

The carriage pulled up in front of the general store and the footman helped Sarah down. Moses followed. There were other customers in the store. Busy filling orders for sugar and cloth, Becky had her head down. Hope and Violet Wilcox stood at the counter. Elizabeth Austin corralled her sons, William and Matthew.

"Look, Ma. It's Miss Chesney," Matthew said, pointing.

"She's Mrs. Fitch now, boys. Address her proper," Mrs. Austin said, smiling at Sarah.

The boys bowed at the waist, took off their hats. "Howdy, Mrs. Fitch," they said in unison.

Sarah bent down and grasped them together in a hug.

"I suppose now you've got one of your own on the way, you're too busy. And," Mrs. Austin cleared her throat, "too well off to be takin' students."

Sarah straightened up. "Haven't they found a new headmaster yet?"

Elizabeth shook her head. "No. And my boys need to learn their readin' and writin.'"

"Let me talk to my husband, and I'll see what we can do."

"I'd be much obliged," Elizabeth said.

"Can we see Sunshine?" William piped up.

Sarah chuckled. "I don't know. I don't live at the Inn anymore. You might ask my grandmother. I'm sure if you do a few chores for her, she'd be happy to let you visit Sunshine." Sarah picked up two cinnamon candy sticks and gave one to each boy. "Becky, please add those to my order," Sarah said.

"For me?" William piped up.

"Yes," Sarah said. Matthew hugged her.

"Thank you."

"Much obliged, Mrs. Fitch," Mrs. Austin said.

It pleased Sarah to have the money to buy a treat for those boys. She missed her days with the lively Austins. They'd made her laugh and tried hard to learn her teachings.

Moses set the list down on the counter, then went to the candy sticks to find his favorite flavor.

"Nice to see you, Sarah," Becky said, picking up the list. "Is this for Mrs. Fitch?"

"Yes."

"I meant the other Mrs. Fitch," Becky grinned.

"I can't get used to being Mrs. Fitch," Sarah confided. "Oh, and I need some thread."

"Go pick your colors. I know, Sarah. What's it like to be a married woman?" Becky slowed her work filling the Fitch order so she could chat with Sarah.

"It's heaven. Seems to me you might be tryin' that out yourself before long," Sarah said.

"Me? Whatever makes you say that?"

"Didn't my brother make his intentions clear to you recently?"

Becky's face turned as red as her hair. "Word sure travels fast in this town."

"I heard you turned him down," Sarah said, moseying over to the thread and sorting through the colors.

"That's my business," Becky said, speeding up her work.

Sarah put her hand on Becky's forearm. "You can't get rid of me that easy. I want to call you sister. Why did you turn Sam down?"

"Sam doesn't want a wife. He wants a farmhand." Becky sniffed.

"What do you mean? He's a smith, not a farmer," Sarah said.

"Not for much longer. He's fixin' to get a farm from old Mr. Fitch."

Sarah gasped. So that's what Sam was doing at the Fitch office!

Becky turned a sharp eye on her friend. "Didn't you know? You're his sister."

Now it was Sarah's turn to blush. "Of course, of course, I did," she lied.

"You're mighty surprised for someone who knew," Becky said, before going in the back room to fetch two jars of molasses.

Sarah covered her mouth. She bet her mother and Caleb didn't know of Sam's plans. She plucked a licorice candy stick from the assortment on display and tucked it into her pocket. When Becky returned, Sarah said, "And add two cinnamon sticks and one licorice to my order, please, Becky."

"Sure thing."

Sarah lowered her voice, "You sure you don't want to marry Sam?"

Becky drew her eyebrows together. Her eyes filled. "I don't want to be no farmhand. I want to be a wife."

"A wife's gotta do a lotta different things, besides cook and sew," Sarah said.

"I don't know nothin' about farmin'. I'd be like a servant, not a lady."

"But you'd be with Sam. You know he loves you."

Becky raised her gaze to Sarah's. The redhead's face clouded over, anger spit from her eyes. "He didn't say nothin' about love. He talked about all we'd have to do."

"Oh, dear. I'm sorry, Becky."

"So am I. Here, Moses, is Mrs. Fitch's order. I added in your thread, too, Sarah. Good day to you." Becky flounced through the door and into the back room. Sarah heard soft sounds of crying.

"Come on, Moses. I've done enough harm for one day," Sarah said, hurrying out the door before Becky's mother poked her nose in to see who made her daughter cry.

THE NEXT MORNING, SAM arrived early at the smith shop. He finished fixing the Fitches' axe before Caleb arrived. As he started work on the kettle tipper, he thought about the farmland that would be his in the spring.

Surprised the farmer had not planted potatoes, Sam spoke out loud to himself. "Anybody can grow potatoes," he said.

"Anybody who?" Caleb asked, his large frame filling the doorway.

"Nothin'. I finished the axe."

"Why don't you take it up to the Fitches? You can see your sister, and maybe she'll ask you to stay for supper."

"They set a fine table up there," Sam said, his mouth already watering at the idea of Giselle's French bread, tarts, and stew.

"Go on, then." Caleb shooed the young man out of the shop.

Sam raised the collar on his jacket against the cool morning breeze. Leaves changed colors, harvesting was half over, and winter would be upon them soon enough. He balanced the goatskin sack carefully on his shoulder. The axe weighed a bit, and the edge was as sharp as a razor. He smiled at the thought of the fine job he'd done restoring the tool. It looked brand new. Even Caleb had complimented him on it, and the man didn't often waste words.

As he got closer to the big Fitch mansion, he spied his sister stretched out on a divan reading a book.

"Sarah!" he called between cupped hands. He noticed a flurry of activity on the other side of the window as he approached the door. He raised the heavy gold knocker.

Charles answered the door.

"Yes?"

"Got Mr. Fitch's axe," Sam said.

"I'll take that," Charles said, reaching for the bag.

"Sam!" Sarah called out from the hallway. "Charles, it's my brother, Sam. Please, let him in."

"I gotta deliver this personally," Sam said, tightening his grip on the sack.

"Very well," Charles said. "Come in. Mr. Fitch, senior, is down at the office. He'll be home shortly. You can wait in the parlor."

Sarah threw her arms around her brother's neck and hugged him. "Did you come to see me?"

"Nah. I'm delivering an axe I fixed for your father-in-law."

"Oh," she said, crestfallen.

"But since I'm here, I can stay to visit a while," he said, cupping her cheek. "You're looking right plump."

"Can you stay for dinner?" she asked. "We're having venison stew."

"Sure can. Thank you." Visions of the meat, roasted potatoes, and freshly baked cake danced in his head.

"Charles, please tell Giselle we'll have another at the table," Sarah said, taking her brother's arm. "And please tell her we'll have tea in the parlor now," she said.

"Yes, missus."

Charles turned toward the kitchen while Sarah guided Sam to the spacious room. He looked around with wide eyes. Their house was beautiful. No expense had been spared to create a luxurious home with beige brocade silk covering the walls and Persian rugs on the floors. Finely carved wooden cabinets, tapestries, and comfortable sofas graced the parlor. A fire burned in the large fireplace, which bore hooks and ironworks so it could be used for cooking as well as heating.

Sarah flopped down on the largest sofa and patted the seat next to her. Sam joined her.

"I was in town today," she said.

"Oh?" Sam raised his eyebrows.

"Yes. Had to pick up some things at the General Store."

"You saw Becky?" Sam shifted in his seat.

"Yep. We had a good long talk."

"Oh?" Sweat beaded on Sam's forehead. "What did she tell you?"

Sarah slapped his shoulder. "What do you mean about getting a farm? Asking Becky to marry you just to become a farmhand? Huh? You're doing so well at the smith shop. Why would you want to have a farm?"

"It's my dream," Sam said, jutting out his chin.

"You have forgotten how hard papa worked – night and day, just to put food on our table."

"But we ate good, didn't we?"

"We got by, that's all. We all worked on the farm. Without a family, how are you going to make it work?"

"I don't need a family. I ain't plowin' and plantin' all forty acres. I'll plant only what we can manage. We only need enough food for ourselves. Being two people, how much can we eat?"

"What happens when you become three?"

Sam's eyes glittered at the prospect of what becoming a father entailed. Then his expression sobered. "We'll manage."

"Who's we? Becky ain't gonna marry you."

"She ain't the only woman in this town!" Sam bolted up from his seat. "You're pretty high and mighty now that you got a rich husband. Who are you to be telling me what I should or shouldn't do?"

"I'm sorry, Sam. I just want you to be happy. And I don't think you'll be happy married to anyone but Becky."

"She got pretty high and mighty, too. What's got into all the females in this town, anyway. Think they can push a man around? I make my own decisions."

Sam jammed his hat on his head and pulled his jacket closer. "I best be getting' back."

"But you just got here."

"I wore out my welcome fast, didn't I?"

Sarah took his hand. "Please don't go. It's lonesome here. Don't tell the Fitches. I miss the Chesneys. Stay. Or you'll miss the best meal you'll have all month."

The prospect of fine food got his mouth to watering. A cool breeze drew his attention. Old Mr. Fitch had returned.

"Boy. What you got there?" he asked Sam.

"Your axe, sir. As good as new. Better even," Sam said, handing the satchel to Elijah Fitch.

The older man opened it and took out the tool. He gently ran his calloused thumb over the blade.

"Sharp enough to skin a goat. Good. Thanks, Sam. Your mother's new husband got you real schooled in smithin'. You stayin' to supper?" he asked, returning the tool to the satchel.

"I've invited him, Elijah," Sarah said.

"Good." The old man took a sidelong glance at the lad. "Looks like he could use a good meal. We have the finest table in all the Catskill Mountains," Fitch boasted.

"I don't doubt it, sir. Thank you for the invitation."

A bell tinkled from the kitchen, signaling the meal was ready. Elijah, Sam, and Sarah quickened their pace to the dining room. Sam's eyes lit up when he saw the sumptuous repast laid before him on the sideboard.

There was a large pot of venison stew. Then buttery mashed potatoes. Next was a platter of boiled turnips, glazed carrots, and roasted onions. Two loaves of perfectly browned bread sat next to a dish of sweet, creamy butter and a small pot of jam.

"Get your plate and help yourself," Elijah said.

Sarah pointed to the place setting next to hers, and Sam picked up the fine china dish decorated with small blue and yellow flowers. Ann Fitch joined them.

"Hello, Sam. Nice you could join us today," she said, picking up her plate and strolling to the sideboard.

Sam heaped his plate with food. Sarah poked him in the ribs.

"Don't be a pig," she whispered. It was loud enough for all to hear.

"Don't want to let good food go wastin'," Sam said, slipping onto the chair next to his sister.

Elijah laughed. "Darn right, Sam!"

Benjamin blew into the room, followed by a gust of cool air. He filled his plate and joined his wife, taking the seat on her other side.

While Elijah and Benjamin talked about business, Sam chowed down. The meals at his Grandmother's place were hearty and tasty, but nothing like the Fitch table. Four vegetables for one meal was unheard of at his grandmother's table. And two loaves of bread for five people? Never.

Happy to listen and learn about the logging business and how their tenant farmers were doing, Sam ate his fill quietly. The cook brought out two plates of freshly baked sweets and placed them on the sideboard. She took the empty jug of cider and returned to the kitchen to refill it.

Stuffed to his ears with food, Sam struggled to find room in his belly for the fine French pastries and cakes tempting him.

Sarah picked up the dessert plates and brought them to the table.

"You're not going to stop now, Mr. Chesney, are you?" Old man Fitch asked.

"I'm mighty full, sir."

"I bet you can squeeze in one more thing," Elijah said.

"What do you recommend, Mr. Fitch?" Sam asked.

"I always find her eclairs to be my undoing," Fitch said, patting his stomach.

Sam eyed the rich-looking confection and turned to his sister. "Will you take half?"

"Yes." Sarah cut the chocolate covered dessert in half and scooped Sam's portion onto his plate.

When they finished eating, Sarah walked Sam to the door.

"You sure are lucky to live like this, Sarah," Sam said, standing at the entrance to the grand house.

"I am for certain."

"I hope you appreciate it." Sam knitted his eyebrows.

"I do. I hope Lizzy can find a grand place to live in comfort."

"Me, too."

"And a wonderful husband like Benjamin," she added.

Sam scowled. "He'd better treat you right. If he doesn't, you tell me. I'll fix it." He fisted his right hand.

Sarah laughed. "Don't be silly."

"I mean it, Sarah. You're my kin. We Chesneys stick together."

She handed him his hat and he went on his way, unaware that a family meeting on the other side of town would change his life forever.

Chapter Four

Abiel Wilcox wandered out to his garden. He spied a lone flower – a blue aster. He raised his eyebrows, then bent down to pick the flower. He returned to the house where his daughter-in-law, Hope, awaited with a mug of warm cider.

"Here, Father. You mustn't go out without your coat. There's a chill in the air."

Abiel smiled and took the mug, handing his daughter-in-law the bloom. "Fix this up nice. You got a piece of ribbon or something?"

"I do."

"Good."

"Why? Who's it for?"

"Never you mind," he said, sitting down at the table and taking a drink.

When the flower was done up and he'd finished his cider, he took his coat, donned his hat and grabbed the flower before leaving his small home. Hope had been right, the air had turned from simply chilly to darn right cold. He fastened the buttons on his coat and picked up his pace as he headed toward the Inn.

Martha Chesney stood in front of the Inn, sweeping the entryway. Under her apron, she wore a dark pink frock that set off her silver hair perfectly. Abiel stopped for a moment. Yes, he had a plan, but he had to admit to himself that cozying up to Martha Chesney would be a pleasure as she was mighty easy on the eyes. As he approached, she stopped, leaned on the broom and cast her gaze to Abiel.

"Good day, Sheriff. How be ye?"

Abiel nodded and removed his hat. "Fine, milady. Fine. How be yourself?"

She nodded.

"I picked this because it reminded me of you." He offered her the flower.

Martha cast doubting eyes on him. "Do tell." She brought the flower to her nose.

"No scent. But its beauty is equaled only by your own," Abiel said.

"Poppycock! Butter wouldn't melt in your mouth, Sheriff. What are you wantin'?"

"Please call me Abiel."

Martha held the flower up and narrowed her eyes.

"Sheriff is best. Don't know you much," she said.

"I'm aimin' to change that," he said. "We'll be taking our evening meal with you tonight. And as often as my purse allows," he said, making a sweeping bow before turning to exit.

"Thank you, Sheriff. Much obliged. I'll set places for you and your family. Seating at six."

He shot her a warm grin and was rewarded with a smile, which lit up her lovely face.

Abiel shoved his hat back on his head and trudged home. Recent rain made the way muddy in spots. He grinned to himself. His plans for a secure future for him, his daughter, and granddaughter took shape.

Life had been hard for Abiel and the girls since he lost his wife, Lavinia, to sickness, and Hope's husband was killed during a bank robbery. They'd scraped by on Abiel's salary. If he married Martha, they would be assured a roof over their heads and good meals.

He used all the funds he received from the sale of his house in Torrington, Connecticut to buy this house and feed his family. Now they lived off their garden and trades they made for meat and milk. Hope tutored some of the children and even adults who could not read. Abiel had squirreled away enough to pay for occasional meals at the Inn, since Martha charged them a pittance. He remembered her reason.

"Your women folk don't eat much. They can pay half."

He'd been mighty grateful as her cooking far surpassed that of either Hope or Violet. While Lavinnia had been a fine cook, she hadn't lived long enough to teach her daughter-in-law much. Abiel missed the companionship of a grown woman, too. He fancied Martha Chesney and hoped she'd grow to feel the same.

As Sheriff of Torrington, he'd received a good stipend and much kind generosity from the people of the town. He ate and drank free at the town saloon. And when he became widowed, he'd been invited to dine at every home that had an unwed female residing there.

But in Fitch's Eddy, where he received a pittance for keeping the peace, he struggled. At his age, there weren't many families that looked upon him as a likely suitor, and there weren't many females who would consider him a good prospect.

Marrying a woman who ran a boarding house and restaurant would be the perfect solution. And since he was a man, he would take over ownership of the establishment, thus securing his own future and that of his daughter-in-law, Hope. He'd already set a plan in motion to find Violet a good home with a man who could provide for her.

He didn't worry about Sam losing ownership of the Inn. The young man had plans to own a farm. He couldn't do that and run the Inn at the same time. Abiel would be happy to take that responsibility off his hands.

Of course, Abiel couldn't cook and wouldn't lower himself to make beds or do the laundry. Martha would be there to do all those things while he kept track of the finances and made decisions. He smiled at the idea of himself as an innkeeper. He'd decided the role would suit him perfectly. Now, he simply had to get Martha to agree.

But first he needed to get Violet situated before people guessed about her condition. Returning from his walk to the Inn, he settled himself in his favorite chair as Hope prepared tea.

"Violet?" he called. "Come in here."

"Yes, Grandpapa," she said, scurrying into the room. She slid onto the seat next to him. "What is it?"

"It's time we had a plan. Sam Chesney is looking for a wife. He plans to have his own farm. That would be perfect for you, dear. You could live there with him and no one would ever know that you were with child before you married him."

"But Sam is sweet on Becky Rhodes."

"I happen to know for a fact that she turned him down this morning."

"She did?" Violet asked, her blue eyes growing wide. "Why'd she do that?"

Abiel cleared his throat. If he told his granddaughter why Becky said "no," Violet would never agree to marry Sam. Although he didn't want her to become a farmhand either, it beat becoming the town pariah, shunned by all.

"I don't know," he lied. "Maybe she's not as sweet on Sam as you thought."

Violet shrugged. "He's sure a handsome one," she said.

"You like him?" Abiel asked, raising his eyebrows. This was going to be like catching fish in a barrel.

"He's always been polite to me. But he's in love with Becky."

"Not anymore. Now he's all yours for the taking," Abiel said.

Hope moved to her daughter's side. "He's right, dear. Sam Chesney would be a good choice for you. He's hard-working, from what I hear."

"But how can I get him to propose to me?" Violet asked.

"Hope, advise the child, and fetch my pipe," he said, then rose from his chair and headed for the door. "We're dining at the Inn tonight. You can work your charm on Mr. Chesney then."

With that comment, Abiel stuffed his pipe in his pocket and opened the door. Loathe to hear the conversation between the two women, he beat a hasty retreat to his garden.

The women sipped their tea, talked, then readied themselves for their trip to the Inn to dine with the Chesneys and any residents of the boarding house. Violet brushed her hair and put on one of her best dresses.

When it was time to walk down to the Inn, Abiel Wilcox, Hope, and Violet met at the front of the house and made the short journey together. Abiel's conscience pricked at the chicanery his family was about to embark on. But he justified it to himself as a man taking care of his only grandchild as best he could. Besides, Sam would be getting himself the prettiest woman in Fitch's Eddy for his bride, and perhaps a son to help him farm.

MARTHA GAVE HER RABBIT stew a final stir before climbing the stairs to change into a better dress. She had narrowed her eyes in a shrewd stare at Abiel Wilcox when he'd dropped in earlier. Martha suspected he wanted something. But she didn't know what. Surely a robust man like Abiel didn't want to tie the knot with a wizened old lady like herself, did he?

She examined her three best-looking dresses, then decided on something more simple. She'd save the best for the harvest festival. Wouldn't do no good to give Abiel ideas that she was sweet on him by donning her finest. She chuckled to herself at the idea that a woman could get a little thrill out of an innocent flirtation, even at her advanced age.

She selected her dark blue muslin with white lace collar and cuffs. While not her best dress, it was fine enough for the occasion. She untied her hair, combed it and fastened it again in a bun on the top of her head. She stuck a hairpin Caleb made for her from a pretty orange and gray stone in her hair, then added the finishing touch – a drop or two of vanilla water dabbed behind her ears.

Martha hiked up her dress and descended the stairs slowly. The delicious smell of her stew permeated the Inn. The vegetables blended nicely with the meat. Some folks like to cook up the vegetables separately. But she liked to throw them in the pot with the meat. She had turnips, rutabagas, and parsnips from the root cellar. It was time to use them up before they gathered a new crop this coming winter.

Her granddaughter, Lizzy, almost ran Martha down on her way to the kitchen.

"Aren't you supposed to be minding that chicken, roasting over the fire?" Since her family had grown, Martha had taken to making extra food for them. Caleb always had a mighty big appetite, and little Jem followed along in his father's footsteps.

"Yes, but it's time to feed Sunshine," the young girl said.

"That goat can wait. We need that chicken to be finished in time for the evening meal. Back you go, young lady."

"But Sunshine is hungry," Lizzy whined.

"Sunshine is always hungry. Let me take a look at the chicken," Martha said, brushing by the girl and stepping closer to the fire. She examined the fowl cooking over a spit.

"Hmm. Seems like it should be done soon. Finish the job and I'll give Sunshine a parsnip as a treat, and a cookie for you."

"Yes, Grandma," Lizzy said followed by a long sigh.

Martha peeled half a dozen onions and tossed them in the stew pot. A cool wind caught her attention. Abigail Chesney Tanner, her daughter-in-law, entered.

"Howdy, Abby. Gonna make pies for supper tonight?"

She nodded, then narrowed her eyes. "You're dressed mighty fancy today, Martha."

Embarrassment heated the older woman's face. "Just my old blue muslin."

"Hah! I don't believe that for a minute. That's your best muslin, isn't it?" Abby stared up and down the slim woman's form.

"Maybe it is and maybe it ain't."

"How many for supper tonight?" Abigail asked.

"Twelve, I reckon," Martha said.

"Twelve?" Abby raised her eyebrows.

Lizzy shot a sly look at her mother. "That Sheriff man is coming. Mr. Wilcox."

"Oh?" Again Abby's eyebrows shot up. "He is?"

Martha sensed heat in her cheeks and turned away from making bread dough. "Maybe"

"Maybe, Martha?" Abby put her hands on her hips.

"Yes, I guess he is. With his daughter-in-law and granddaughter," she mumbled, shooting a hostile look at Lizzy. "It's no account to me. Just happy to have the extra money," Martha lied.

"Well, then. I'd best be sure not to burn the pie!" Abby said, hiding a smile with her hand.

Lizzy laughed outright.

JUST BEFORE THE WILCOX family reached the Inn, Hope put her hand on Violet's arm. They stopped.

"You know what to do, right?" she asked her daughter.

Violet nodded.

"You sure?"

"Your future rests on this, young lady," Abiel said, his lips pulled down into a frown.

"I know," Violet said, her eyes flashing. "I gotta win him over."

"If you'd have listened to me about that no-account Zeb..."

"I know Grandpa! I know!" Violet put her hands over her ears. "He's not a no-account."

"Oh? Then where is he? Now that you're in a fix, he's gone. I'd like to fix his flint," Abiel said fisting his right hand.

"Don't let Sam Chesney know you got designs on him. Let him think you just cotton to him natural like," Hope said.

"All right!"

"Hush. They'll hear you," Hope said, fluffing out Violet's skirt.

"She do look mighty pretty in that frock, Hope," Abiel said.

"Purple is her best color. I don't see how any young man in his right mind could resist such a pretty girl," Hope gushed.

Abiel pursed his lips. At least she wasn't showing yet. Sam would never know. The Sheriff tried to push thoughts about what he had asked his granddaughter to do out of his head. He wished there was another way, but he had to guard her honor and the honor of the Wilcox name.

Violet pulled out a small bag from her pocket. "I hope he likes peppermints," she mumbled.

"Never met a man in his right mind who didn't," Abiel said, opening the door to the Inn.

The Wilcox family crossed the threshold.

"Well, well, how nice to see you folks," Martha said, scurrying out from the kitchen and taking off her apron.

"HOW MIGHTY NICE TO see you again, Mrs. Chesney. You're looking right fine," Abiel said.

An attractive blush stained her cheeks. "You clean up nice yourself, Sheriff," she said. "This way." Martha led the way to the dining room.

Abigail, Caleb, Lizzy, and Jem were already seated at a table near the kitchen. Sam poured cider for them and took his seat. Violet sashayed up to Sam and held out two peppermints.

"Do you like peppermint, Mr. Chesney?" she asked, peeking out from under her long black lashes.

Sam turned so fast, he almost spilled the contents of the pitcher. His gaze traveled her length and color suffused his cheeks. "I sure do, Miss Wilcox. I sure do. Thank you," he said as she placed the candies in his palm then curled his fingers over the gift.

Abiel watched her spin her web around Sam Chesney. His granddaughter dripped charm – a quality he hadn't paid much mind to before. He smiled to himself. Sam didn't stand a chance against Violet's powers of seduction.

Sam popped one in his mouth. "Did you make these yourself, Miss Wilcox?" he asked.

"I did, indeed."

"Mighty fine," Sam said. "Best I ever et."

"I made apple tarts, too, this afternoon. You're most welcome to stop by after supper and sample one," Violet made eye contact with Sam before lowering her gaze.

"Mighty obliged. Thank you."

Hope shot a knowing look at her father-in-law, who gave a slight nod in return.

Martha narrowed her gaze. "Don't dillydally, Sam. Get to pourin'. People are hungry and thirsty. We got to get this meal goin.'"

The Wilcox family took their seats. Sam finished filling the glasses and returned to his seat.

"Lizzy!" Martha called.

The young girl scurried into the kitchen. She carried out each bowl filled to the brim with steaming rabbit stew. When all were served, Lizzy brought out loaves of bread and sweet butter and set them on each table.

Sam shifted in his chair so he could see Violet. As he ate, he lifted his gaze from his fork to her face. He'd been told it wasn't polite to stare, but outside of Becky, he'd never seen such a beautiful girl. Candlelight reflected in the silky black of her hair. The graceful shape of her face, the gentle rosiness of her skin, along with the delicate blue of her eyes captivated him.

He rested his gaze on her slender neck and shoulders. Barely able to tear his eyes away from the gentle swell of her breasts showing above the lacy neckline of her frock, he blushed when his mother cleared her throat. She leaned over to whisper in his ear.

"It's not polite to stare. Even at a girl as pretty as Violet."

In a heartbeat Sam returned his attention to his food, but not before he spied a warm smile from Violet directed his way. Did Violet fancy him, or was she only being neighborly? Of course she fancied him. He'd soon be a farmer with forty acres. A woman would be lucky to marry a man with property. And that was just what he'd be, and looking for a wife, too. He smiled to himself. It seemed his life would be all set before long. Now, if he could only convince such a girl to consider him as a suitor, he'd have the luck he'd hoped for.

"I love apple tarts," Sam mumbled to himself, but loud enough for the Wilcox family to hear. Abiel chuckled, and Violet smiled.

MARTHA CAST A SHREWD glance at her grandson. She'd painted a lovely picture in her mind of his marrying Becky and living in town, maybe in back of the general store. She'd envisioned great-grandchildren nearby. But the way he'd looked at Violet shattered that dream. Obviously, her Sam had other ideas.

While she enjoyed a little flirting with Abiel Wilcox, she didn't trust him. She wondered if he'd been behind this sudden flowering of an attraction between his granddaughter and her grandson.

Martha didn't know Violet, but she had to admit to herself that the girl was the most handsome in the town. A quick vision in her mind of their offspring confirmed they would have the most beautiful children in all of Fitch's Eddy. Still, she'd always thought Becky would be his intended.

Smiling to herself, Martha admitted that she was a mere mortal – who was she to predict who Sam would love and marry? The young man had a mind of his own. And right now she figured his sights were being reset to fall on the lovely Violet Wilcox.

That would make Abiel Wilcox kin. She'd have a hard time shakin' him off if he kept up his attentions. Looked like Martha would have to paint a different picture for herself, along with the one she envisioned for Sam. Abiel nudged Violet, and she smiled.

"Come, Sam. Your grandmother is cutting the pie," she said, taking his arm and snuggling up close.

Martha knit her brows. Seemed like Abiel had pushed Violet off on Sam – again. Suspicion rose in Martha's mind. What was Abiel up to?

While Lizzie refreshed everyone's tea, Martha served the confection. Violet complimented the pie while Sam wolfed his piece down quickly.

Seemed like he was anxious to finish up tonight.

When the meal was over, Abiel and his family rose to leave.

"Mighty fine meal, Mrs. Chesney. Thank you."

"Thank you, Sheriff." Martha gave him a nod as she cleared off the table. Abiel stopped short of the door and nudged his granddaughter.

"Oh, Sam, Sam? Wait," she said, moving toward him.

He stopped clearing the table and handed the dishes to his little sister, Lizzy, who made a face.

Violet drew a deep breath as though screwing up her courage. "Will you be coming by for a tart tonight?" she asked.

"I will if it suits you."

"Come to the back door," she said in a low voice, then rushed to rejoin her family.

He nodded.

Martha frowned. Neither her grandson nor Violet had seemed aware of her presence, probably didn't know she'd overheard. It wasn't good for a young man to be out after dark alone with a young lady. People would talk – especially the Bloodgoode sisters.

Violet thanked Martha with a sly grin probably not intended to be viewed by her. But nothing escaped the older woman's eye.

"Abiel Wilcox's up to something," Martha muttered as she covered the pie and returned it to the kitchen. She didn't know what that crafty old man had up his sleeve, but she resolved to herself to find out. She simply could not shake the feeling that Sam was walking into a hornet's nest unprotected. But he was of age, so there was nothing she could do about it.

VIOLET GLANCED BACK and saw Sam standing by the window, watching her. Then she heard Martha sharply call out, "Sam!"

He gave a start then left the window.

Abiel grinned. "She's already got that young man taking the bait."

Hope frowned. "Be respectful, Father."

"I will, I will. But I marvel at Violet's ability to attract suitors."

"Maybe this time she's chosen the right young man," Hope said, tucking Violet's arm through hers.

When they arrived home, Abiel and Hope made themselves scarce. They huddled by the small fireplace in the back room while Violet took over the kitchen. The aroma of cinnamon and apple heating in the oven scented the small space. Within a short time she took them out. Five tarts rested proudly on the table, tempting anyone who came near. Violet leaned down to inhale their delicious scent. Confident about her baking, she smiled to herself. If Sam was as vulnerable to the appetite-pleasing charm of her tarts as Zeb had been, he would soon be hers.

She added a small log to the kitchen fireplace and sank down into a chair to wait for Sam. She stared at the flames licking the new piece of wood and thought about Zeb. With a queasy stomach, she tried to quell her qualms about the unfaithful act she was about to commit.

She had loved Zeb, trusted him completely and what good had it done her? Now when she was in the family way, he was nowhere to be found. Feelings of betrayal rose in her bosom. Zeb had deserted her, so she had every right to do whatever she could to secure a safe future for herself and her child.

Sam seemed a pleasant enough fellow. He was handsome in a rough-around-the-edges sort of way. Not as polished as Zeb, but still pleasing to her eye. He seemed nice and kind of taken with her. Maybe her grandfather was right that she could do worse than marry Sam.

She thought about his family. Chesneys were all right, but his Wolcott background gave him standing in the state. Although she didn't find being a farm wife appealing, if it didn't work out, they could take control of the Inn, as it was Sam's right to do as the male heir.

The idea of running the Inn appealed to Violet. Nice steady income, not too much work outside and always food on the table. It might be the ideal life for her and her child. It sure beat living on Abiel's wages and eating whatever they could grow or barter for.

As she waited for Sam, the fire heated the room and the idea of marrying him warmed her heart. A quiet tap on the door interrupted Violet's thoughts. She pushed to her feet, smoothed her skirt, and smiled as she opened the door.

Sam stood there, his dark hair brushed back from his forehead, his jacket free of dirt, sticks or weeds. His eyebrows drawn down over dark eyes, he offered a small smile.

"Still have those tarts?" he asked.

Violet closed her fingers around his lapel and pulled him inside. "Of course. Come in. It's cold outside. Warm up by the fire," she said, shutting the door behind him.

"Sure smells good in here," Sam said, taking off his hat and opening his coat. He wandered over to the fire. Violet took his hat and placed it on the sideboard.

"There they are. Take the biggest one," she said, lifting a plate down from a cabinet.

"This one looks mighty fine," Sam said.

Violet put it on the plate, added a fork, and handed it to Sam. He sat at the small table.

"Aren't you gonna have one, too?" Sam asked.

"I've already eaten my fill. But I'll sit with you anyway," she said, easing onto a chair next to him.

Sam took his first bite and closed his eyes. He opened them before speaking.

"My ma makes great apple pies, but nothing like this," he said.

Heat seeped into Violet's cheeks. Landing Sam Chesney was going to be like shooting fish in a barrel. She smiled a grin of pleasure at his compliment and a sly joy that he'd be so easy to hook.

When he finished eating, the house was quiet. He pushed to his feet, grabbed his hat, and mumbled his thanks. She followed him to the door. When he turned, she stepped closer bringing their lips only an inch apart. Sam closed the distance and rested his mouth on hers. Violet tilted her head toward him.

In an instant, he pulled away.

"I'm awful sorry, Miss Violet. I shouldn't a done that," he said.

She smiled, feeling like the cat who'd caught the canary. "That's all right, Sam. Just a nice cozy way of showing your appreciation."

Sam's gaze flitted from her delicate hands to her ample bosom, partially displayed, to her blue eyes, then her lips. She sensed his polite manners and his control slipping.

"Mighty obliged, Miss Violet. Mighty," he said, easing through the doorway and making a hasty retreat. A few steps down the walkway, he stopped and turned. She stood in the doorway, hugging the door and grinning. Violet narrowed her eyes and leaned slightly toward him.

"Goodnight, Sam," she said, her voice soft and sultry.

In the light of the moon, she swore she saw color stain his cheeks. He rushed up to the door and stole another kiss. "Goodnight, Miss Violet." He donned his hat quickly and made haste down the walkway to the road.

She watched him run down the path then laughed while closing the door.

Chapter Five

Guided by moonlight, Sam stumbled his way home. His belly was full of the best apple tarts ever, his lips still burned from the fire ignited by the lips of Miss Violet Wilcox. His heart swelled. It had taken him almost a year before Becky would let him kiss her. And then, just a peck. If he'd tried to make it longer, she'd push him away with a scolding expression.

"Sam Chesney! Mind your manners," she'd admonished him.

Chastened, Sam had walked home crestfallen. But not tonight. He was on fire, fire for Violet Wilcox. He'd be damned if she didn't hold a small flame for him, too. He didn't know what to do with the new feelings that knotted up his stomach. He needed help.

But who could he go to for advice? Not Benjamin. He'd give Sam more information than Sam could handle and all of it would be about Sam's sister, so he'd have to punch Benjamin. No, not him. He was a mite too old to run to his mother for advice, though she'd been his old reliable for all his youth. Even his grandmother had shared her wisdom with him on occasion. Although he respected these women in his life, this called for the guidance from a man and only a man. Caleb was the only one.

In that instance, he wondered if Caleb had felt like the same way about Sam's mother. The idea mortified him. That was the last thing he wanted to know anything about. But Caleb was the wisest man he knew, so Caleb it would be. Sam reminded himself to make sure to tell Caleb not to share anything personal-like about his mother.

Drunk with passion, Sam staggered up the walkway to the Inn. His grandmother and mother bustled about the kitchen, making preparations for meals for the next day. Lizzy and Jem had gone to bed in the room Caleb had built on his house for his son and stepdaughter.

"Coming in mighty late, young man," Martha Chesney said, casting a cool eye on her grandson.

"Goodnight, Grandma," Sam said, avoiding her stare and pushing through the door to his room. He shut it quickly, putting an end to conversation.

He undressed and slipped into bed. He knew he'd have to wait until the fire in his belly went out before he could sleep. Staring out the lone window, his gaze rested on the large autumn moon. He wondered if Violet knew anything about farming. Sure it would be a good thing to have a wife who knew as much about kissing as Violet did, but he'd need a wife who knew about the land, too.

Would she be content as a farmer's wife, or did she want to live in town with her father for the rest of her life? The young woman could cook, well, bake anyway. That would be helpful.

He shut his eyes and conjured up an image of the beautiful Violet greeting him at the door to their little farmhouse after he'd spent a long day in the fields, planting and harvesting. Would she be up with him, fixing breakfast before he went out to milk the cow, and feeding the chickens? The glorious image in his mind grew, filled in by the alluring blue of her eyes, the deep purple of her frock, and the brilliance of her smile. Lucky would be the man who could call her his wife.

He rolled over on his side. His eyelids grew heavy as the image of Violet faded slowly, giving his mind over to the sleep he needed to recharge his energy for work of the next day. But the picture had burned in his brain, and he'd not soon forget how lovely Violet looked wearing her apron and providing the warmth of home for Sam.

THE NEXT MORNING, SAM got caught up in the hustle and bustle of breakfast and preparing for a day of smithing. He welcomed the cooler days of autumn, which tempered the heat of the shop. During fall and spring, the fire from the blacksmith shop balanced out the chill in the air to make his days perfectly comfortable. Winter and summer were different.

There were days of bitter cold in the winter when the hot fires of the shop barely took the edge off. He'd add an extra shirt on those days. In the summer, the heat from the shop became unbearable more days than it didn't. After the day's work finished, Sam would run off to a nearby pond to cool off. He'd race his dog, Lucky, from the shop to the water and jump in. A good swimmer, Lucky followed his master.

Today was different. As Caleb turned to meet his wife at the Inn for his midday meal, Sam grabbed his sleeve. Caleb stopped and raised his eyebrows.

"What?"

"Can I talk to you about something?" Sam asked, pulling on his earlobe.

"Be quick about it. I'm hungry," Caleb said.

"It's about Violet."

"Violet? Violet who?"

"Violet Wilcox."

"What about her?"

"Do you think she'd make a good farm wife?" Sam blurted out.

Caleb laughed. "I don't know her, son."

"She's mighty pretty," Sam said.

"Does she know anything about farming? Do you?"

Sam frowned and pushed himself to his full height. "I know a lot about farming. I worked with my dad on our farm."

"So, you thinking of asking Violet Wilcox to marry you?"

"Sort of. Maybe."

"Do you even know her?"

Sam stuck his chin out. "Sure do. Even kissed her. Twice!"

Caleb's eyebrow shot up. "You've kissed her?"

"Twice!"

Caleb rubbed his chin. "I'd say that makes her almost spoken for."

Sam smiled, then made eye contact. "You're makin' fun."

Caleb burst out laughing. "Guess so. Just kissing a woman doesn't tell you anything."

"Oh?"

"Yep. Marrying is different. You gotta want the same life. Like with your mother..."

Sam clapped his hands over his ears. "Don't go tellin' me about my ma!"

Caleb pulled Sam's hands down. "Wasn't gonna say anything untoward. Just that your ma and I wanted the same kinda life. You know. Raisin' young'uns, being a family. Do you have any idea what Violet Wilcox wants?"

Sam frowned. "No."

"Well, then. You'd better start courtin' and tell her what you have in mind and see if she'd like the same kinda life."

Sam nodded. "You're right. Thanks, Caleb."

Caleb stopped. "Are you sure you want to do this, Sam?"

Rubbing the back of his neck before replying, Sam finally admitted, "Yep. Yep. I'm sure."

"Well, then, you have your answer. Just don't go steppin' out of bounds with her now. Take it easy."

"Oh, no. I won't do that," Sam said. But he wasn't so sure he'd be able to keep his word. She sure was beautiful and didn't seem to mind his admiring her or kissing her, either. Caleb pushed out the door and waited for Sam to join him. They headed to the Inn for their midday meal.

Sam helped his grandmother put the bowls of roasted vegetables on the table. Lizzy brought out two loaves of freshly baked bread.

"Jem, get the butter, will you?" Martha said to her youngest grand-child. "That's a good boy."

At the other end of the table from his mother and Caleb, Sam ate quietly.

"Cat got your tongue, boy?" Martha asked.

"Just thinkin', Grandma."

She nodded. "All right, then."

While he ate, he mulled over what Caleb had said. Yes, he'd better get to courtin' Violet Wilcox before some other man got the same idea. That cobbler's son had a business and could offer her a better life, maybe. But he was as plain as mud to look at. Sam resolved to call on Abiel Wilcox that evening before supper to get permission to court his granddaughter. Time was a wastin'. Once he made up his mind, he wolfed down the rest of his food and went back to work.

He was eager for the workday to be over so he could stake his claim on Violet Wilcox and get his dream started. He returned to the Inn to wash up. He even fetched a clean shirt and combed his hair before he set out for the Wilcox cottage.

AS HE STEPPED UP TO the front door, the pungent odor of burn-ing pipe tobacco met him. He wrinkled his nose. Smoking would be something Sam would not have in common with his father-in-law. Af-ter he married Violet, Sam hoped he could convince Abiel to leave his pipe at home when he came visiting.

Sam knocked. In a few seconds, the pretty Violet opened the door.

"Sam! What a surprise!"

"I'm here to speak to your grandfather, Miss Violet."

"He's in the living room by the fire. Please do come in," she said, stepping back to let Sam through the door.

Sam took off his hat and swallowed. He spotted the big man stuffed in a chair close to the fire. Abiel took his pipe from his mouth and gestured.

"Come in, young man. Come in." He pointed to a chair. "Rest your bones."

Sam warmed his hands near the flames before he sat down.

"Come to see me or my beautiful granddaughter?" Abiel asked.

"You, sir." Sam swallowed again.

"What's on your mind, son?" Abiel looked directly at Sam.

"Uh, well. I was thinkin'," Sam said, then stopped.

"Go on. Spit it out."

"I was thinking Violet would make a mighty fine wife and I'd like to be courtin' her."

"You intend to marry her?" Abiel asked, raising his eyebrows.

"Yes sir. Yes sir, I do." Sam crushed his hat in his fist then let go. "I do, sir."

"As long as your intentions are honorable, then I agree." Abiel smiled.

"Really?" Sam had not expected Abiel to agree so quickly.

"Of course. You're a fine young man. Everyone in town says so."

"They do?" Sam's eyebrows shot up. "Yes. You can start courtin' tonight. Hmm, perhaps we should set a wedding date," Abiel said.

Things were moving much too fast for Sam.

"Did you have any date in mind?" Abiel asked.

"Right after harvest? Then we could get to plantin'. I have a farm. Would she like to live on a farm?"

"You have a farm? Such a young man. You own land?" Abiel smiled.

"Not really. I'm a tenant farm to Mr. Fitch," Sam said. "I have a nice plot, about forty acres right near town."

"Oh. Tenant farmer?"

"Yes. I owe Mr. Fitch some of my crops. But once he gets his due, the rest are mine to sell," Sam explained.

"And you expect my Violet to work in the fields? Such a delicate young woman?" Abiel's tone grew cold.

"No sir, no sir," Sam said, shaking his head rapidly. "I don't."

"What do you expect her to do?"

"To cook. She's a mighty fine baker. Keep house, maybe milk a cow?"

"I'm sure she can do those things. You'll need a ranch hand, though, won't you?"

"Not right away. I'm takin' over the farm right at late harvest. So I'll have all the food from the harvest, and I have three chickens. I'm looking into getting' a cow or a goat."

"I think we can give you another chicken. How about your grandmother's goat?"

"Sunshine belongs to my sister."

"Oh. Well, we have some time before the wedding. I'll see what else we can contribute."

"So you agree to my courtin'?" Sam stood up.

"I do, son," Abiel said, offering his hand.

The two men shook hands.

"Will you be joining us for our evening meal?" Abiel asked.

"Much obliged, sir." Sam said. He was curious to see if Violet could cook in addition to baking.

"Violet!" Abiel called. "Set another place at the table," he commanded.

Violet gave a wan smile and scurried from the room to perform the task.

Abiel slung his arm around the shoulders of his future son-in-law and escorted him to the table.

Sam spied a bowl of steaming, roasted root vegetables, a small pot of stew, and a nicely browned loaf of bread. He took the seat Abiel offered. His mouth watered. Violet's mother filled a mug with cider and handed it to Sam.

"Welcome, Mr. Chesney," Hope said, with a warm smile.

"Thank you, ma'am." Grateful for the beverage, Sam took a long drink of cider to wet his parched throat.

Relief flooded his veins. He'd done it. Asked Abiel for permission to court and marry his granddaughter. He was one big step closer to living his dream. Violet shot him a shy smile as she doled out food onto a plate and handed it to him.

AS HE PREPARED TO ENJOY a repast with his new family, twinges of guilt shot through him. He'd always thought that Becky's family would be his someday. That he'd be sitting beside her at their table. While he barely knew Violet, he'd known Becky longer. He knew of her strength, her intelligence, and her quickness to laughter. He also knew her bad side. She was often quick to judge and let her temper get the best of her. But she'd always forgiven Sam for any infraction.

He hoped she'd forgive him for marrying Violet. He consoled himself with the memory of his proposing to her first and being quickly turned down. Shocked, he didn't feel the true sting of her rejection until later that day, when it hit him that he couldn't count on her love and support anymore.

Nervous with his new family, he hoped that would pass. He wondered if he'd ever be as comfortable with the Wilcox's as he was with the Rhodes' family. He'd eaten at the Rhodes' table many times. Their meals were sumptuous, unlike the Wilcox's table, which was spare in comparison.

Still, if he meant what he had said to Caleb, about being serious regarding marrying Violet, he'd better learn to enjoy what her family provided. Or at least put up with it. He wanted her to join him, wanted her to want the same kind of life he envisioned.

"Sam, why don't you and Violet take a short stroll, get some air," suggested Abiel after their meal was complete. "But not too far, now."

THE COOL NIGHT AIR cleared the confusion from Sam's brain. He'd been dead set on Becky Rhodes becoming his wife, but now here he was with lovely Violet Wilcox on his arm. And no chaperone anywhere to be seen.

"This way," Violet said, leading Sam behind a large rhododendron bush. They were concealed from view of any of the townsfolk. Violet slowed down and brushed up against Sam. He felt parts of her he oughtn't to be feeling.

Heat crept up his chest and into his cheeks. He fanned his face for a moment. How could he be so hot when it was a cool autumn night?

"Sam," Violet whispered. "Let's sit for a spell." She stopped by a large flat rock and plopped down, pulling him down next to her.

"Ain't you cold?" he asked.

"Actually, I am. Can you put your arm around me?" she replied.

He did as she asked and she snuggled up against him. Suddenly he understood all the instructions and cautions Caleb had given him.

She turned and stared at his mouth. The moonlight kissed her hair with silver. He'd never seen a woman as beautiful as Violet.

"Don't you want to kiss me, Sam?" she whispered softly.

It was like she could read his mind. He'd never wanted to kiss anyone as much as he wanted to kiss Violet Wilcox. He grabbed her, pulling her up against him, and covered her mouth with his. His kiss was hungry and demanding. And she complied.

Chapter Six

Momentarily coming to his senses, Sam let go and leaned back. He stared hard at Violet. Her lovely face, shadowed by the moonlight, tilted up. She blinked, then her half-closed eyes met his. She cupped his cheek and flashed him a smoldering half smile. Sliding her hand up into his hair, she murmured.

"Sweet Sam, don't be afraid."

"I'm not, I'm not," he stammered.

"It's just nature. Meant to be. You and me," she said, sliding her palm down the side of his neck.

Heat grew rapidly in his body. He tugged at the collar of his shirt, hoping to let it out and cool down, but it didn't happen.

Don't lose control Caleb's words echoed in his head.

A sudden swift movement caught Sam and Violet's attention. She screamed and yanked her foot up and under her skirt.

"A mouse! A mouse!" Her eyes wide, her luscious lips trembled, and her body shook. She leaped into Sam's lap and clung to his chest.

Sam saw the guilty party glance up for a second before scurrying away under the bushes. He wound his arms around Violet. Sobs emanated from her mouth as her body shook. She buried her face in his neck.

"It's all right. It's gone."

"You must protect me," she whispered.

"I will. I will. I'll protect you forever," he said.

She sat up straight, placing her arms around his neck, drawing him closer. With her breasts crushed against his chest, she lifted her mouth to accept his. Sam took her mouth with a savage desire he couldn't stop.

"Sam, Sam, I love you," she muttered.

His control broke, all thought left him except for the overwhelming will to satisfy both his and her desire. Violet offered no resistance but instead encouraged him. And he did what any man would in that situation.

After their intimacy, Violet pushed her skirt down and smoothed the cotton fabric. Sam ran his fingers through his hair. What had he done? Shame filled him. He'd gone over the line and done the one thing Caleb told him not to do. But he couldn't take it back now.

He wracked his brain, looking for a way out, a way to make it better. While Violet fussed with her hair, an idea grew in his brain. Shyly, with a hoarse voice, Sam reached for Violet. He took her arm and gently turned her to face him.

"Violet, I love you. Your grandfather already said I can court you. Will you marry me?"

She laughed. "Feeling guilty already?"

"No, no," Sam lied.

"Yes, you are. If I don't end up with child, we can simply admit we got carried away. I won't hold you to your proposal. Here, help me with my dress," she said, turning her back to him.

He laced up the back, tying and fastening whatever he could see in the dim light before he spoke.

"But I did the wrong thing. I wasn't a gentleman. I took advantage."

"No, you didn't," she said, patting his cheek.

He took her hand and pressed it to his lips. "You're special, Violet."

She primped one last time. "How do I look?"

Sam leaned back a tad and looked her over. "I'll be darned. You look like you just stepped out of your house, ready to go to the harvest festival."

She smiled. "Thanks. Let's get you cleaned up," she said, fussing with his hair and buttoning his shirt. "You're half naked."

Cool air on his skin reminded him of his state of undress. He rose to his feet and put his clothing back together. Once he was dressed, he faced her.

"You're beautiful."

She took his face in her hands and kissed him soundly. "I love you, Sam Chesney."

"Come be my wife. Live with me on my farm." He stroked her cheek.

She smiled but kept silent. "I must get home."

"I'll speak to your grandfather again tomorrow," he said. "We can plan a weddin'."

She took his arm and matched her stride to his. "We'll see."

After he deposited her at home, he made haste to return to the Inn. Guilt pricked at him temporarily.

"But I'll marry her and then it will be right. I'll stand up for what's right and no one will know what happened." He let out a breath and gave a brief nod.

No one would know except Sam and Violet. He had to keep this to himself, even as he was bursting to confess to Caleb, his mother, and Ben. No, he especially couldn't tell Ben. Although they were fast friends, Ben never could hold onto a juicy bit of gossip. Next to Sarah, Ben was Sam's best source of tales of the folks in Fitch's Eddy.

His mother? Abigail loved and accepted Sam always, but she'd be disappointed, maybe even ashamed of him. He couldn't handle that. If she hung her head and cast hurting eyes on him while mumbling, "Sam, how could you?" he'd die. No, he couldn't confide in her.

Caleb would be the only one to hear his confession. Thus would Sam withstand the calling him to task – especially after being warned. Yes, Sam was man enough to take the anger of Caleb. Hoping to arrive at the Inn after all had departed to their bed chambers, Sam slowed his pace. He knew he could barely keep his secret when alone but didn't trust himself if confronted by a friend or relative and questioned about the lateness of his return home.

When he reached the Inn, he stopped briefly to stare at the glass windows to see if he showed any signs of his earlier activity, but it was too dark to see.

The clock chimed midnight. He frowned at the thought of how tired he'd be when he'd drag himself out of bed to go to work early the next morning. He opened the Inn door slowly, careful not to awaken anyone. He tiptoed across the floor.

"A bit late to be returning from dinner at the Wilcox's' home, isn't it?" came a firm voice. "Did you take the long way, across the Lee farm?"

Sam jumped and whirled around. "Grandma! What are you doing up?"

Sitting in a rocking chair, arms folded firmly across her chest, she replied, "Waiting for you." She looked him over before continuing her inquisition. "What took you so long? I hope you weren't up to any mischief," she said.

"No," he lied. "Of course not. It's late. I won't be able to get up for work if I don't get to bed."

She made a face.

Quickly averting his eyes from her searching stare, Sam muttered." Goodnight, Grandma," He beat a hasty retreat to avoid the scrutiny of her sharp eye.

"Goodnight," she muttered, shaking her head.

Sam shut his door, ripped off his clothes and fell into bed and was fast asleep the moment his head hit the pillow.

ACROSS TOWN, VIOLET stepped across the threshold of her home quietly. The fire in the main room still burned. She saw her grandfather in his chair snoring, his chin resting on his chest. Trying as hard as she could to move without making a sound, she bumped into a chair hiding in the shadows.

"What? What? Who's that?" Abiel Wilcox started awake.

"'Tis me, Grandfather."

Abiel knocked his pipe against a wooden bowl and set it down on a small table. "Violet?"

"Yes," she said, casting her eyes to the floor. She shivered, trying to cast off the ugliness of her shady behavior with Sam.

Abiel pushed to his feet, brushed off some telltale tobacco bits from his vest and stretched his arms up before turning to face his granddaughter. "Well?"

"It's done, Grandfather. It's done."

Abiel approached her. He cupped her chin. "I'm sorry child, but it was the only way."

"He'll be round to see you soon, I reckon," she said softly.

He nodded. "What's done is done. We have to make the best of it. You might like farm life," he ventured.

With full, angry eyes, Violet shot him a glare, then stormed out to her room and slammed the door.

Once inside, she ignored her sleeping mother and threw herself on the bed, sobbing.

"Zeb. Zeb. Where are you?" she said into her pillow, muffling the sound as best she could.

Her mother awoke and turned on her side. She stroked her daughter's back.

"It's best this way, Violet."

"No, it isn't, Mother. It isn't."

"I'm sorry, dear. You have only Zeb to blame. He led you on. I know you believed his love was true. This is for the best. You'll have your own house and a man who loves you. That should be a comfort."

Violet wiped her face and pulled the covers over her. She knew her mother was right. Marrying Sam should be a comfort. He was a good man. She'd have to work hard, but together they could build a life for her child. Yes, it should be a great comfort. But it wasn't. It simply was no comfort at all."

She closed her eyes and tried to sleep. Still troubled by Zeb's desertion, she wondered where he was and why he didn't take her with him when he rode out. He'd disappeared during the night – rode off to parts unknown. He'd left a letter for her in their secret hiding place, the crook of an old oak tree.

In his letter he repeated his love for her and said he'd be back for her as soon as he could, but that he didn't foresee that happening for a year or more. He had to get himself set up in his new life before he could ask her to join him. At the time, it gave her hope. But when she discovered her pregnancy, all hopes were dashed. By his own words, he would not be back in time to make her an honest woman and avoid the shame and shunning she'd surely receive in Fitch's Eddy if she became an unwed mother.

She touched her belly. Now someone else would be raising Zeb's child –and he'd never know. Even if he did come back for her, she'd be married to Sam and living on a farm. She'd been so happy to find him. But now her dream had shattered, and all she had to look forward to were a long, painful delivery and a dreary life of hard work, drudgery on a farm –isolated from her family and few friends. And living with a man she didn't love.

Tears returned. She cried herself to sleep.

"SAM!" IT WAS CALEB'S voice in his ear. Sam rolled over and pulled the pillow over his head.

"Get up!" Caleb shouted, ripping the covers down.

Cold air did more to rouse Sam than Caleb's harsh tone. The young man shivered. Caleb threw pants and a shirt at him.

"Get dressed."

Sam pushed to his feet and rubbed the sleep from his eyes. A knock on the door gave him incentive to put on his pants. It was his little sister, Lizzie. She held a bowl of warm milk and bread.

"Breakfast? Your sister waits on you? You're a lucky dog," Caleb said, shaking his head.

Sam's dog, Lucky, who had been tossed off the foot of the bed barked at the sound of his name.

"Not you, Lucky," Sam muttered. "Thank you, Lizzie."

"Better hurry up, Sam," Lizzie said, her eyes flashing her annoyance.

Sam gulped down the milk. He buttoned his shirt quickly, grabbed the bread, combed his fingers through his hair, and headed for the door. "I'm ready, Caleb."

His stepfather gave him a sideways glance and frowned. Once they had cleared the Inn and arrived at the blacksmith shop, Caleb stopped, put his hands on his hips and faced Sam.

"Something tells me you done something you shouldn't have?" Caleb narrowed his eyes.

Sam squirmed under the scrutiny. He ignored the question.

"I best be getting to this pot for Ol' Mr. Fitch," he mumbled, picking up the piece he'd been working on. Caleb put his palm on the pot and pushed it back on the bench.

"I asked you a question, son," he said, his brows drawn together, his eyes darkening.

"A man's got a right to privacy," Sam said, sticking out his chin.

"That so?"

"Yessir."

Caleb rubbed his cheek. "I daresay that tells me the truth. If you hadn't done the deed, you'd be protesting to me with all your vigor how innocent you are. You ain't doin' that."

Shame at being so transparent flooded Sam. He sensed heat creep into his cheeks.

"And now I can see by your face you're guilty!" Caleb said, sinking into a chair.

"So? So what? I ain't done nothin' the lady didn't want," Sam said, turning his back on Caleb.

"That so?"

Still facing the window, Sam nodded.

"You'd better hope she isn't with child."

"It's all right. I asked her to marry me," Sam said.

"You did?"

"Yep. Not right not to offer to make her an honest woman."

"I guess," Caleb said. "You got plans?"

"I got it all worked out. Violet will fit in just fine." Sam turned back to face his stepfather and picked up the bowl.

"What about Becky?" Caleb asked, rubbing his chin.

"She turned me down. Turned me loose. I'm free to find a different wife."

"True, true. Still."

"Becky doesn't want to be a farmer's wife. Violet does."

Caleb closed his lips firmly and gave a quick nod.

"That's all," Sam said, picking up a utensil and beginning work on the pot.

"If you say," Caleb said, putting on his apron. "We best be gettin' to work."

"Yessir."

Caleb started the fire. "When you fixin' to ask Miss Violet's grandpa?"

"Dunno. I asked him about courtin' her, but we didn't set any weddin' dates."

"I wouldn't be waitin' too long. You never know. Get this settled."

"Right, right."

Sam decided he'd mosey on over to the Wilcox home right after dinner.

"I'll do it tonight."

"Fine." Caleb manned the bellows, and within no time there was the hottest fire any smithy could want.

AFTER DINNER, CALEB raised his eyebrows and stared at Sam.

"Well?"

"Well, what?" Martha asked, her sharp glance darted back and forth between Caleb and Sam.

"Nothin', Grandma. Thanks for dinner. I best be goin'."

"Goin' where?"

"Now, Martha, let the young man be," Caleb said, pushing away from the table.

"I'll help clean up, Ma," Abigail said.

"Fine."

Sam slipped out the door and set his feet in the direction of the Wilcox home. As his mind worked, he slowed his pace. Somehow he couldn't get up much enthusiasm for the task at hand. He recalled how he'd counted the minutes until Becky opened the store the day he decided to propose to her. He'd been all het up, his breath comin' quick, his heart thumpin' like a racehorse on the home stretch.

Now he kept a steady even pace as he plotted out what to say to Mr. Wilcox. His breathing was even and steady as was his heartbeat.

"Is this what it is to be a man?" he asked himself in hushed tones. "Doin' the right thing?"

He knew it was, but that didn't make it any easier. It wasn't that he didn't like Violet Wilcox. He did. She made his blood run hot and he could barely take his eyes off her beauty. But she didn't capture his heart like Becky did.

"I'll learn to love her. That's what Caleb said." Resigned to his fate, he plodded ahead. "It ain't like I'm going to the gallows." Yeah, but it also wasn't like a big holiday, neither. He finally arrived at their door.

He swallowed, then raised his fist to knock on the door. Mr. Wilcox answered.

"Why, Sam, how nice for you to come for a visit," Abiel Wilcox said, as he took Sam by the arm and ushered him inside.

Maybe this is a little like a turkey feels the day before Thanksgiving, Sam thought, as he stepped across the threshold.

"Sit down, son. How nice for you to pay us a visit," Abiel said, taking the comfortable chair by the fire.

"Yessir," Sam said, taking off his hat.

"Something on your mind?" Abiel prompted.

Sam twisted his hand in his hand. This was it. The moment of truth.

"Yessir. I know we talked about me makin' Violet my wife. I'm ready to talk about dates now. If you don't have any objections," Sam blurted.

Abiel raised his eyebrows. "Will it be soon?? Have your prospects changed, Sam?"

"Like I told you, I'm fixin' to take over one of Mr. Fitch's farms." Sam twisted his hat in his hands. "It's already got a nice little house. Potatoes and carrots planted. I got seeds for squash, and plenty more. It's got apple trees, too. We'll have a big harvest in the fall. My sister's gonna give me some chickens. So, we'll have plenty of food. Violet won't go hungry. I'll take care of her. Take care of her real good."

"You think so?" Abiel tamped down the tobacco in his pipe and lit a match.

"We'll get flour and butter from the Inn. My grandma always has some to spare."

"I see. And you think Violet'll be happy there?" Abiel puffed on the pipe, drawing in the flame from the match.

"Yessir. She said she wanted to be a farmer's wife."

"You won't work her too hard, will you?" Abiel cast a severe glance Sam's way.

"No sir. No sir. I'll take care of her."

"I see."

"I love her, Mr. Wilcox," Sam lied.

"You do? Pretty quick, I'd say."

"When love hits, you don't need years to see it. At least that's what my grandma always says. Said she knew she'd marry my grandpa same day she met him."

Abiel nodded. "I see."

"Do I got your permission, Mr. Wilcox?" Sam untwisted his hat then twisted it up the other way.

"If Violet agrees to settin' the date, you have my blessing."

"I do?" Sam's voice went up an octave.

"You do. See you do take good care of her, Samuel Chesney. She's the apple of my eye."

"I will, Mr. Wilcox. I will. I promise."

"You're a fine lad. I believe you. Now, run along. It's late." Abiel Wilcox stood, tapped his pipe on the brick of the fireplace and yawned. Sam took the hint and scooted ahead to the door.

Once outside, he let out a breath. He'd done it. Now all he had to do was make the official proposal to Violet. After what he'd just been through, that seemed easy. Sweat broke out on his forehead. Soon he'd be a married man. And maybe with a child on the way?

His dream seemed closer, maybe even within his grasp. After his father had died suddenly, Sam had given up counting on good things happening to him. It seemed too good to be true that he might actually get his wish – a farm of his own and a wife to help him. He stopped for a moment to look up at the sky.

"Papa, I've got me a farm. I'm gonna follow you."

He grinned, then resumed his brisk walk home to bed. He'd need a good night's rest to face Violet in the morning. No lollygagging now. He needed to spur things along Time was a-wastin'.

Chapter Seven

Early the next morning, Sam took the bright sunshine as a good omen. He finished his breakfast in three gulps and set out to Violet's house. With the sun on his shoulders, he walked quickly, easily making his way along the now familiar path.

After a firm, confident rap on the door, he shifted his weight, waiting to be let in. Finally, the door was opened.

"Sam?" Violet said. "Come in." She tugged on his arm, and he stepped across the threshold.

"Morning, Miss Violet." Sam looked around, surprised to see they were alone.

"Morning. Can I get you some cider?" she asked. "Do you want to sit by the fire?"

Without the sunshine on his back, his body shivered slightly. Was it from the cold or nerves?

"Yes, thank you. You're mighty kind," he said, taking a chair by the fire.

Violet rushed out and returned quickly with a mug of cider and sat next to him.

"Violet, I've come to see you on a matter of great urgency," Sam said, pushing to his feet.

"Yes?" Her brilliant turquoise eyes made contact with his.

"It's about what we discussed."

"Oh?" she raised her eyebrows.

"About being a farm wife. I've spoken to your grandfather about settin' a date..."

"You have?"

"Yes. And he said the decision is yours."

"What decision?"

Sam put down the cider and took off his hat. He twisted it as his mind searched for the right words. "About becoming a farm wife."

"Oh? Who's asking?"

Sam grinned. "Oh come on, Violet. You know it's me."

She blushed. "Yes, I do. But I want to hear you say it."

Sam took her hand in his. "Will you, Vi? Will you marry me and live on my farm?"

Her hand was soft and smooth. He stared at it, wondering if it was strong enough to do the work of a farm wife.

"Well?" he asked, joining his gaze with hers.

"I will, Sam. I will marry you."

Relief flooded his veins. Not that he had doubts, but one never knew the mind of a woman when it came to love. After all, Becky had turned him down.

"You will?"

"Yes. That's what I said." As she pushed to her feet, her eyes filled. She ducked her head but not before Sam saw.

"What's the matter? Are you gonna cry?" he asked, anxiety plain in his voice.

"Tears of joy," Violet said and rushed from the room.

Confused, Sam waited for Violet or her mother or grandfather to return. When they didn't, he let himself out of the house and walked slowly to the blacksmith shop.

When he arrived at the shop, he hung up his coat, then turned to Caleb, "I guess I'm officially engaged."

Caleb looked up. "That's good news, isn't it?"

"I guess so. Still, she didn't seem very happy about it," Sam said. His brow furrowed. He picked up his apron.

"Best get to workin'. Smithin' lets you forget women."

"Maybe you're right. I sure don't seem to know much about women," Sam said.

"What man does?" Caleb asked with a chuckle. "Here. We got a new project for Fitch. Makin' a smaller pot tipper." Caleb tossed a piece of paper to Sam.

"Did you do this?" he asked, turning the paper right side up.

"Yep."

"Not bad. For a smithy," Sam said with a sly smile.

"You better cotton up to me or I'll tell your grandmother what you've been up to with Miss Violet Wilcox," Caleb said, feigning a ferocious face.

"Oh, you wouldn't!" Sam's eyebrows rose.

"Don't push me. That's a darn good drawing."

"It is, it is," Sam said, a playful smile tugging at his lips. "You wouldn't really tell my grandma, would you?"

"Nope. But I might tell your Ma."

"All right, all right. I'm working," he said, setting out his tools for the new job. He trusted his stepfather but knew enough not to push him. He needed all the allies he could get.

VIOLET THREW HERSELF on the bed sobbing.

"Quiet, child! He'll hear you!" Abiel Wilcox said, approaching his granddaughter's bed.

"I don't care."

"If he finds out why you're sobbing your eyes out, he'll back out. We can't have that."

Violet pushed to a sitting position.

"He's not all that bad, is he?" her mother asked.

"No. But he's not Zeb," Violet muttered.

"Gosh darn it! That no-account Zeb! You still harbor feelings for that scoundrel? He's the one responsible for you having to marry Sam. If he'd done the honorable thing...well, if he was that kind of man he would have respected you in the first place. This is all his fault."

"Your grandfather is right. How can you still care for him after what he's done?" Hope asked her daughter.

"He didn't know. He didn't know about my condition. If he had, he'd be here right now, taking vows with me," Violet said, sticking her chin out a bit.

"Maybe so. But he ain't. And we have to take steps," Abiel said. "Sam's a good man. He's doing the right thing."

Violet sighed. "Maybe so. Still..."

Hope patted her daughter on the shoulder. "I know. It's a bitter pill to swallow. You'll have a good life with Sam. If the farm doesn't work out, you can move into the Inn with Sam and the baby. You won't have to worry about anything."

"And you'll have your reputation, too," Abiel said.

"Is that really so important? Isn't love more important?" Violet asked.

"Did you write to that weasel about your condition?"

She nodded. "I did. But I didn't know where to send it. I sent it to general delivery where he used to live."

"Pish tush! He'll never get it. Seems to me he hightailed it out of town pretty quick. Like he already knew he'd left you in trouble."

"I don't think so. He'll get the letter eventually."

"By then your baby will be in school," Abiel muttered.

Violet fished a hanky from her pocket and wiped her face. "I need fresh air. I'm going for a walk."

"I'll go with you," Hope said, picking her shawl up off a chair.

Peeking into the main room, Abiel spoke. "Seems Sam's gone."

"Good. He got the answer he wanted. Now I want me some peace," Violet said, wrapping a wool shawl around her shoulders. "Come, Mother."

The two ladies strolled down the lane toward town.

"Might as well stop at the general store and get us some of those buns they be selling."

Violet put her hand on her mother's forearm. "Not today. Best not to go into the general store today."

"Oh? Why?"

"Becky Rhodes is probably crying her eyes out."

"Oh?"

"She's sweet on Sam."

"You took her man?"

"I heard she turned him down."

"Well, then. She ain't got no reason to be upset. Let's go. Those buns are mighty tasty."

The women picked up the pace and entered the general store.

BECKY TIDIED UP THE counter after filling an order for the Fitch family. She folded the fabric around the rest of the bolt, replaced the rejected spools of thread, and swept up the crumbs from the baked goods she'd packed up.

The tinkle of the bell over the door drew her attention. The Bloodgoode sisters, Charity and Catherine, the biggest gossips around, entered. Becky tried to keep from making a face. She plainly did not like these vicious young women, who spread lies and evil stories about everyone else in town.

Becky had never been the target of their malicious whisperings, thank God! She didn't take credit for living a blameless life, instead acknowledging to herself that they didn't attack her because her family owned the general store, and thus they were dependent on the generosity of Becky's family.

The Bloodgoode sisters were always angling to get things for free or at a reduced rate.

"The poor family of Fitch's Eddy's pastor shouldn't have to pay," Charity had said many times.

"I'm sorry, Charity. We give you a lower price, but everybody has to pay something. We have to pay for things. And so do you."

"Pastor's money doesn't go far," Catherine mumbled.

"Why don't you take to doing some needlework and selling it. Or take in laundry?" Becky said, working to stifle a smile.

"Take in laundry? A pastor's daughters? Pish tush!" Charity blustered. "We'll take a length of that grosgrain ribbon. In blue."

"Well then. Be content to be proud and do without," Becky quipped, pulling down the ribbon and measuring out the required size.

A nasty gleam glowed in Charity's eyes. "Of course we're proud. No one has toyed with our affections just to leave us high and dry," she said, a mean grin pulled at her lips.

"What are you talking about?"

Her sister nudged her in the ribs. "Hush, Charity. I told you not to mention that," Catherine said, her voice as fake as her sympathetic demeanor.

Becky looked up. "What in heaven's name are you two talking about?"

The sisters looked at each other, giggled, then leaned in closer to Becky. "We don't like to gossip or anything," Catherine said.

"You don't?" Becky cocked an eyebrow.

"Of course not. But news is news. And we figured you'd want to know first.

An uneasy feeling stole up Becky's back. "No, no I don't."

"Oh yes, you do," Catherine continued, cutting off Becky's escape by grabbing her arm and holding it fast.

"Stop," Becky said, struggling under the young woman's iron grip.

"Sam Chesney asked Violet Wilcox to marry him and she said yes!" Charity blurted out, then covered her mouth with her hand.

Heat rushed to Becky's face. "It's not true," she muttered.

"Oh, I'm afraid it is," said Catherine.

Becky felt faint. She heard a ringing in her ears and her heartbeat jumped. She grabbed her shawl and headed for the back door.

"What about our ribbon?" asked Charity.

"Take it. Take it. It's a gift. Just leave. Leave now!" Becky said.

Blood drained from her face as fast as it had gathered there, leaving her lightheaded. She ran out the door and continued as fast as her legs could carry her, impervious to the cold winter, but not the cold ice stealing into her heart. She made a beeline for the small willow tree next to a pond nestled in a clearing in the woods. It was the secret meeting place she had shared with Sam.

They went there whenever they wanted to be alone together. Becky would slip away from her family with a fabrication of making a delivery or following up on an order.

While they couldn't have much time there before being missed, they made good use of their precious minutes of privacy. That's where Becky got her first kiss. Sam never stepped over the boundaries. But they'd snuggle together and talk about the future.

Becky had fessed up to wanting a Smithy for a husband. She voiced her approval of Sam's profession. Sam never challenged her dreams with his own, which were so different. She thought he shared her wishes. Devastated to discover he had something else in mind, she'd set her dreams in stone and put her foot down – turning down his marriage proposal flat.

She'd cried about it for days and days but never changed her mind. Her plans shattered, she'd gone through weeks like an automaton, mechanically tending to the store and minding her parents. Joy had gone out of her life. Without Sam, she had nothing to look forward to. Her heart ached because she'd been so sure he'd follow her lead. She'd been so proud of him, picking himself up after the tragic death of his father and learning the smithing trade.

Everything seemed to go her way, until it didn't. She still had not found her way. And now to hear this horrible news. It sealed her fate.

Her future with Sam had died with his proposal to Violet and her acceptance.

She plopped down by the edge of the pond and picked at the few blades of grass that were still green. What would she do now? She still loved Sam. Remembering all the times they'd laughed and kissed under that willow tree made her heart ache. She needed him. But now he belonged to another and what could she do? Nothing.

Becky shivered in the cold. Wrapping her shawl tighter, she walked briskly back to the store. If she didn't return quickly, her parents would worry.

ON HER WAY BACK, A rambunctious dog bounded through tall grass to assail her by jumping up, licking her face and swatting at her legs with his busy tail.

"Lucky! What are you doing here?" she asked, gently easing the dog down.

Her eyes scanned the horizon. If Lucky was there, could Sam be far behind? She sucked in air. Sam! He was the last person she wanted to see. Hugging her shawl even tighter, she walked briskly toward the store, with Lucky following closely behind.

"Lucky, shoo, boy. Go back to Sam. Go on, Lucky. Home, boy. Home!" she said, to no avail. The dog stuck to her like glue.

"Becky! Becky!" She recognized Sam's voice behind her and quickened her pace.

"Wait! Wait! Becky! Gol darn it! Slow down!" A rush of cold air behind her came right before a large hand grabbed her elbow and jerked her backward.

"What are you doin' out here so late?" Sam asked. His hand held her fast while his other held his rifle.

"Me? I might ask you what you're doin' proposin' to Violet Wilcox," Becky said, struggling to control her tears.

"Oh, gosh. You know about that?"

Becky's heart sank. She'd hoped that her confronting Sam would result in his denial. But no such luck.

Unable to keep her voice from shaking, she simply nodded.

"Boy. Things travel fast."

"So you did?"

"Yeah. I did."

Fury gripped her, and she slapped him with all the power she could muster.

"Ouch! Darn! What was that for?" he asked, rubbing his cheek.

"You very well know what that's for, Sam Chesney. I never want to see you or talk to you again," Becky said. Mustering all the dignity she could, she straightened her spine and marched through the tall grass back toward the store.

She didn't get but a few steps before Sam caught up with her. He grabbed her and whipped her around to face him.

"How dare you be mad!"

"You proposed to Violet," Becky said, raising her chin in defiance.

"I asked you first. You said 'no.' What did you expect me to do? Never get married? Never farm the land?"

"Yes!" She stomped her foot. Even though it sounded ridiculous, that was exactly what she'd expected. After all, he belonged to her, didn't he? He simply couldn't move ahead in life without her.

Sam laughed, But there was no mirth in his voice. "Do you know how silly that sounds?"

"I don't care. You were mine. We promised." She raised her gaze to his.

"We never promised nothing!"

"Yes, we did," she insisted.

Sam narrowed his eyes. "Don't you be lyin' to me, Miss Becky Rhodes. I ain't never promised nothin'!"

"Well, maybe not exactly promised..." she backed off.

"Aha! Now the truth. I ain't promised nothin.'"

"Well, no. Maybe not. But it was, it was...understood." Becky bit her lip as her mind searched for the right words.

"I thought so, until you said 'no,'" Sam's tone softened.

Unable to contain herself any longer, Becky burst into tears. "Oh, Sam! Why'd you do it? Why did you propose to her?"

"Because I need a wife to farm."

"Now it's too late. She's said 'yes.' You have to go through with it. It's too late." Becky's tears flooded down her cheeks. Her breath came in sobs.

Sam stepped closer to her. Gently, he took her in his arms and held her tight. His hand stroked her back, then her hair. "Now, now. Stop your bawlin', honey," he said.

She pushed away from him. "Don't call me 'honey.' You've ruined everything. Now you'll have your dream, but what about mine?"

"Yours?" Sam scratched his head.

"My dream of being your wife, of bearing your children, of you being the best smithy in Fitch's Eddy. Of us having our own house?" She withdrew a small hanky and mopped her face, but it was inadequate to the task.

"I didn't know you had a dream, too. You never said."

Becky took a shuddering breath. "Well, I did. But it's gone now. It's over."

"I'm sorry. You never said," Sam said.

Becky straightened her shoulders. "Doesn't matter now, does it? It's too late. You're set to marry Violet Wilcox. And me? I'll have to find someone new."

Sam drew his brows together. "Find someone new?"

"You don't think I want to be an old maid, do you?"

"I guess I never thought about it."

"All wrapped up in your own life. Well, I wish you well, Sam Chesney. I need to get back."

"Lucky and I will take you home." He grasped her hand.

She pushed him away. "No need. I don't need an escort. I can get home on my own."

"I'm sorry, Becky. Real sorry."

As she pulled her hand away, she saw regret in his eyes.

"So am I, Sam. So am I," she said, her voice low. She pushed ahead toward the store with slow, heavy steps. As she neared, she turned around to look. Sam Chesney stood stock still, with Lucky at his side, watching her. Yes, that was her Sam. Waiting to see she got home safely. But he wasn't her Sam anymore, was he?

And this might be the last time he would be there to watch over her. She sighed and turned back toward the store. As a winterish wind picked up, piercing her shawl, she quickened her pace. Trembling in the cold, she hopped up the steps and took refuge in the store.

She could escape the winter chills, but not the coldness surrounding her heart.

THANKFULLY, THE BLOODGOODE sisters had gone...and taken their length of ribbon with them. Becky's mother was behind the counter, measuring lengths of cloth.

"Where've you been, Becky?" her mother asked after cutting a good-sized piece of fabric.

"Just went for a walk. Needed some air," she said, slipping into the back room, past her mother before she faced any more questions. She didn't light the oil lamp, just lay on her bed in the dark and stared out the window at the full moon.

After a fashion, she scooted under the blanket and curled up. What had Sam done? She went over his words again and again. As she stared out the window, the truth came home to her. It wasn't Sam's doing, but rather her own. What had she done?

"I didn't think he'd find someone else," she muttered aloud to herself. "I thought he'd give up the idea eventually and propose again to me."

But he hadn't. And now she had no future outside of working at the store forever and being alone with no one to love her except her parents.

"It wasn't supposed to be like this," she said with a sigh. One yawn and she was fast asleep before she could shed one more tear of regret.

After rolling over, voices disturbed her.

"Tell her to come in to supper," her father said.

"No, no. Leave her be. Something happened today."

"What? What happened?"

"I don't know. But she was out in the cold for a long time," her mother said.

"All the more reason she should eat a hearty meal."

"I'll put a plate aside for her," replied her mother.

"You women. Can't get a straight answer," her father said.

Becky listened to his footsteps as he went to the back of the house for his meal. The door opened. She couldn't face her parents with the truth yet, so she bought time by pretending to be asleep. Her mother stole softly into the room. She pulled the blanket up over Becky's shoulders and kissed her temple.

"It's all right, child. Rest. It'll be all right," she whispered, before tiptoeing out and closing the door.

When she was alone, Becky sat up. Moonlight lit a small portion of the room. She pulled up the blanket. Her thoughts turned to Violet Wilcox. She didn't like the girl. Ever since they arrived, Becky had been suspicious of Violet. Something about the girl she didn't trust. Violet always seemed kind of flirty, always playing helpless, though she was far from fragile. Although she was small, Becky had seen her lift heavy parcels and carry big milk cans.

She wondered if Violet had any idea what being a farmer's wife entailed. She reckoned the pretty girl didn't have one notion of the true life of a farmer's wife. Yes, Sam Chesney was bound to marry Violet Wilcox, but would she stick? Would she agree to carry her share of the load when Sam got his farm under way? Becky doubted it.

She threw the blanket open and swung her legs over the side. What would Sam do if Violet proved to be unsuited to farm life? Becky smiled. Wouldn't it serve them both right for taking her place and giving it to another?

Fortified by revenge, Becky pushed to her feet. She fixed the pins in her hair and strode out of the room. Raised to chase mean thoughts from her mind, Becky couldn't help but look forward to the failure of Mrs. Samuel Chesney. And Becky would be there to see it happen, to watch it all fall apart. A twinge of guilt shot through her. What about Sam? Well, he'd have to figure it out, wouldn't he? She popped in to join her parents for dinner.

"You all right, child?" her father asked.

"Perfectly fine," she said, taking her seat.

But that wasn't true. For the part of Becky that still loved Sam feared for what would happen to him if Violet proved to be unfit.

Chapter Eight

A week later, Sam and Lucky tromped through the dried-out winter grass to return to the Inn. He had been hunting with Benjamin and bagged two ducks. When he looked toward the sunrise, he spotted a flash of turquoise. He recognized Becky's blue dress.

He stopped and swallowed. His mouth went dry. His eyes perused the area. But he'd headed for a big clearing to make walking easier and there was absolutely no place to hide. He noticed her lazy gait and the movement of her black cat following along behind her. He froze.

When Becky looked up, their gazes met. She stopped so quickly, her cat practically tripped over her. Sam raised his hand in an attempt to be friendly.

Becky pasted a fake smile on her face. "Why Sam Chesney. Fancy meeting you here."

"Nothing fancy about it. I come this way to meet Benjamin every week."

"Yes. So you do."

"Look, Becky..." he started.

"Keep your distance!" She said, raising her hand in a defensive gesture.

"All right, all right. No need to be afraid. I wouldn't hurt you," Sam said, backing up.

Becky turned her face away. "But you already have. Worse than if you'd beaten me," came rushing out of her mouth. She slapped her hand over her lips.

"Becky, honey, I'm sorry," Sam said, taking one more step closer.

"Stay back! I mean it!"

"Fine, it's fine," Sam said, retreating.

They stood in uneasy silence. Sam switched his gun to his other arm, and Becky dug her toe in the dirt. Sam wanted to hold her, run his fingers through her shiny red hair, but he stayed still.

"Why'd you do it?" she asked, looking up into his eyes. "Why'd you do it?" she whispered.

"You know why. 'Cause I need a wife to help run the farm."

Silence fell again. Although the sun rose, the air between them only grew colder.

"Why didn't you tell me?"

Frustration, anger at her rejection bubbled up inside him. "Gol durn it, Becky! I'm a grown man. I don't gotta tell you everything I'm gonna do. I don't gotta get your permission. I can propose to whoever I want. Don't need you to say it's all right. Darn you! Don't be bossin' me, Miss Rebecca Rhodes. You were pretty high and mighty. Still are, I guess." Sam frowned and turned away. "I best be gettin' back. Grandma will be waitin'."

Becky put her hands on her hips. "That's right, Mr. Chesney. Best be gettin' back lest your grandma give you a whipping for being late," she said with a smirk.

"Don't you go talkin' to me like that."

"Whatcha gonna do about it?" she said, lifting her chin.

"Might have to spank you."

"Samuel Chesney! You wouldn't dare!" She wrapped her shawl tighter.

He laughed. "Naw. But I had you fooled. You'd deserve it, too."

Becky sighed and looked away.

"Did I break your heart,, Becky?" Sam moved closer, putting his hand on her upper arm.

She nodded, but didn't face him.

"Yeah? Well you broke mine first."

"What's going on?" came a male voice.

Becky and Sam turned to see Josiah Quint making his way through the tall grass. "Hmm, those are mighty fine fowl you got there, Sam. Your grandma gonna cook them up today?"

"Probably."

"I'll be by for dinner, then. Miss Rhodes. Good morning to ya," Josiah said, taking off his hat.

Becky stole a sly look at Sam. "Why Mr. Quint. What good fortune to meet you here. I believe I need an escort to the store. You never know what riffraff you're liable to meet out here." She cozied up closer to Josiah.

"I'd be honored, missy," Josiah said, offering his arm.

"You can't go off with him," Sam cried.

"Oh, yes I can. I'm a free woman," she said, with a haughty toss of her hair as she clutched Josiah's arm and marched off, hips swaying and skirt swishing.

Sam stood silently, watching his friend escort the woman he loved. Lucky barked. Sam stood, stock still. The dog grabbed Sam's pantleg with a gentle tug.

Sam looked down. "You're right, boy. Yep. I've lost her. She's movin' on. My own fault, too. Still, we'll do better on a farm than poundin' metal all day. Right, boy?"

Lucky barked and leaped toward the Inn.

"Yep. We best be getting home."

Sam swung the ducks up over his shoulder again and trudged through the dry grass. He raised his collar against the harsh wind blowing along the field. Sam knew Becky was lost to him forever now. He'd have to make the best of his decisions and pray to God things would turn out right.

He was so lost in thought, he didn't see the Inn looming right in front of him until he was almost at the entrance. Relieved to be getting out of the cold, he opened the door.

"That you, Sam?" his grandmother called.

"Yep. Bagged two."

"Mighty fine. Gimme those. Breakfast is on the table," she said, taking the ducks.

Lucky swatted her legs with his wagging tail.

"Yes, and for you, too, Lucky. Go on, now. Git," Grandma said, smiling.

THE FOLLOWING SUNDAY

After church, Caleb, his wife, Abigail, and Sam loaded the wagon with pots, pans, and kitchen utensils.

"These are all extras," Grandma said, pointing to a pile of items too small to use for the crowd she served every day. "These are too small for me. Just right for Sam and his new wife."

Anxious to look over his new lodgings, Sam barely sat still in the back with the goods. Abigail sat next to her husband as he drove the oxen over the rough road to Sam's new farm. They pulled up to a small, ramshackle, rectangular house with clapboard siding. The roof, covered in wooden shingles, had a steep pitch to facilitate snow sliding off and a big chimney to vent smoke from the hearth. The few windows were small and equipped with shutters. A stone foundation kept the house above ground.

They crossed a little stoop by the front door and went inside. There was a large room built around a big hearth, used for cooking and heating. Three chairs rested against a wall. In the center of the room there was a long table used for both preparing food and eating it. In the back was a partial wall and a cloth curtain that separated the sleeping room from the kitchen/sitting room.

Sam grinned. "It's grand, isn't it?"

"I wouldn't use the word 'grand,' but it'll do," his mother said, placing a small pot on the table. "The hearth is a good size."

Caleb tapped on the walls and floor. "Pretty sound. Ought to keep you dry enough and stay warm when you get a good blaze going."

"That's just what I think," Sam said, giving a nod in Caleb's direction.

"Not much equipment here," Caleb said. "Good thing your grandmother has extra."

Abigail parted the curtain and stepped into the sleeping room.

"There's a bed here. Should be big enough. No blankets, though," she called out.

There were no little things, small touches to show that a family had lived there. The house was empty except for the basic furniture. Sam shivered. The lack of personal items, even just blankets and plates, made the house cold and forbidding.

They unloaded the wagon and made a mental list of the things the house lacked.

Caleb and Abigail joined Sam on his walk about the hilly property over rough patches where crops had been harvested. He checked the fields. With an eagle eye, he spotted a potato or two here and there, and a small patch of carrots still in the ground, and some loose onions. He stuffed the food in a sack and tossed it into the buckboard.

"Fine piece of property," Caleb said, rubbing his chin.

"Thank you. What do you think, Mother?"

Abigail stood beside Sam, her arm around his waist. "Yes, your father would have been proud for you to be farming this land," she said.

Her words warmed him, allaying some of his fears at undertaking such a big responsibility with only little Violet to help. Worry had eaten at his gut. Now it was too late to back out.

The warmth of the sun weakened as the day crept into night.

"We must be going. Abigail, your mother-in-law will be wondering where we are."

"Yes. Come, Sam. We'll come back another time with blankets and more supplies."

"When is the wedding?" Caleb asked as they stumbled over the frozen fields.

"Next week. Violet said she needed time to prepare," Sam said.

"You know how women are," Caleb said with a smile.

"Oh?" Abby lifted an eyebrow. "And how are we?"

"You want everything to be perfect on your wedding day, right?" Caleb asked, his brows drawn together as he helped his wife get in the wagon.

"Right," Abigail said with a nod. She handed the reins to Caleb.

WEDNESDAY, THE FOLLOWING week

"Here, wear this, Sam," his grandmother said, tossing his grandfather's Sunday suit at him.

"Where did you get this?"

"You grandfather married me in that suit," she said with pride.

"But it's so old!"

"Pish tush. Good suits never grow old. It will look excellent on you, and I think you're about the right size," she said, picking a piece of lint off the suit's lapel.

"Did Grandpa have the money to buy this suit just for your wedding?" Sam asked, sloughing the suit jacket over his shoulders.

"No. He did odd jobs and saved up to buy this wedding suit. Your father wore it when he married your mother. So it should bring you good luck and a happy marriage."

Although Sam doubted the suit would bring him happiness married to a woman he didn't love, he agreed to wear it anyway. He knew he didn't have anything else fine enough to wear to a wedding.

Grandma answered a knock on the door. It was Charles with an invitation to go to dinner at the Fitches' house. Sam told Charles he'd be there.

"Lizzie, don't set a place for me tonight," Sam said. He donned his jacket and the wool scarf his grandmother had knitted for him and trudged up the hill to the Fitches' grand residence.

In answer to his knock, Charles opened the door.

"Mr. Sam. You are expected," Charles said.

"Thank you." Sam stepped into the large dwelling. While the foyer was cool, he felt heat coming from the living room, which had a large fireplace. His sister, large with child, waddled up to him.

"Sam! Come in, come in," she said, pulling on his arm.

Elijah and Ann Fitch were sitting on comfortable chairs close to the fire. Sam took an empty seat.

"Sarah, you're looking mighty big," Sam said.

"Of course she's big. She's expecting," Ann said with a sniff.

"When is the baby coming?" Sam asked.

"Any day now," Elijah said. "Which is why we wanted you to come to dinner tonight. It's not safe for Sarah to make the trip to town for your wedding tomorrow. I'm sorry, son, but you can see she is in no position to travel."

Benjamin entered the room. "Sam!" he said, rushing over to shake his friend's hand.

"I invited him, Benjamin. I wanted to see my brother one more time before he becomes a married man, a husband with responsibilities," Sarah said, patting Sam's hand.

The aroma of roasting meat blended with that of baking bread made Sam's stomach growl.

"And to give you a wedding present," Elijah Fitch said.

"A wedding present?" Sam asked, his gaze jumping from Elijah to Benjamin to Sarah.

"Yes, Sam. We're giving you a goat," Elijah said.

"A goat?" Sam's eyes grew wide. He desperately needed a goat or cow, especially now that Violet had told him she was definitely expecting.

"Yes, Sunshine's sister, Midnight," Sarah said.

"That's mighty decent of you. We sure could use the milk," Sam said.

"You can fetch her after dinner," Sarah said.

Giselle, their cook, entered the room. "Dinner is ready, madame," she said.

Benjamin helped his unwieldy wife up off the sofa.

"When is the child due?" Sam asked.

"Any day now," Benjamin said.

"Goodness. Good thing. You look a mite uncomfortable, sister," Sam said, following the family into the dining room.

"A mite?" Sarah laughed, then grabbed her belly. "Ouch!"

"Let me," Ben said, propping her up with a sturdy arm behind her waist. When the family was seated, Elijah said grace

Sam popped up as soon as the prayer was over. The sideboard groaned with platter after platter of scrumptious food. There was roast beef, a pot of chicken stew, a medley of roasted potatoes, carrots, and onions. Two kinds of bread. Fresh butter and a tray of French pastries, Giselle's specialty.

Sam's mouth watered. He loaded his plate, not caring if he looked like a pig. Not that his grandmother wasn't a good cook, but not being wealthy, she had to stretch every morsel as far as it would go. She learned to use a few herbs to spice up her fare. Sam appreciated her efforts and ate heartily at her table. But the Fitches' feast sated him beyond belief.

"Sarah, your plate is almost empty," Sam said, eyeing her dish.

"No room left for my stomach," she said patting her belly.

Elijah brought up the lumber mill with Benjamin during the meal. They discussed the week's output, Josiah's ideas for increasing output, and plans for the coming week.

So focused was he on the delicious flavors and textures of the food, Sam barely listened.

"Who will be here to go for the doctor this week?" Elijah asked.

"Charles will," Ann Fitch said.

"He's often busy outside the house. I want someone here to sit with Sarah. Benjamin, you're the father. Be here. We don't want to take any chances," Elijah said.

"Yes, Father. I will." Benjamin shot a warm smile at his wife.

"Sam, have you not had dessert?" Elijah asked.

"I'm not sure I have room, sir," Sam said.

"Oh, you must try. At least one of those little Napolean's. They are my favorite."

Sam returned to the sideboard and added a mini éclair and Napolean to his plate.

"That's it! Eat hearty. Farm life and marriage will wear you out," Elijah said chuckling.

When they finished eating, Sarah walked Sam to the door.

"Good luck tomorrow," she whispered, giving him a hug as best she could.

"Seems to me that you're the one needing luck," he said.

Sarah's lower lip quivered for a second.

"Sarah? Are you all right?"

"Just a little nervous," she said.

"The girl who's afraid of nothing?" Sam asked, raising his eyebrows.

"You won't be here to hold my hand."

"Benjamin will," Sam said.

"No. Doctor says no men allowed," Benjamin said.

Sam cupped Sarah's cheek. "You'll be fine. Becky's dad is a good doctor. I'll come as soon as I can," Sam said.

"Thank you," she whispered.

"Come on, let's get Midnight," Benjamin said, opening the door and giving Sam a little push.

"Hey! Just a gol darn minute," Sam said.

"It's getting late. I got someplace to be. With my wife. When you get married, you'll understand. Let's go," Ben said with a salacious grin. The darkness covered Sam's red face as he and Benjamin ambled down to the bigger of the Fitches' barns. Midnight was a black goat. Sam spoke softly to the animal and petted her nose. Benjamin fastened a lead to the animal. She gave a few bleats before following Sam.

He waved goodbye to his brother-in-law and moseyed down the rutted road to the Inn.

"You're gonna get to see Sunshine again," Sam said, leading the goat out back to the small shelter where Sunshine lived. When the animals got close enough they gently butted heads and bleated greetings.

Sam smiled. "Guess Sunshine is happy to see you, Midnight."

When he went inside, all was quiet. Sam slipped soundlessly into his room, undressed and slid under the covers. He waited, lying still, until his body warmed the bed. Relieved his family had retired, he pushed thoughts about his wedding out of his mind.

Starting tomorrow, he'd be traveling into the great unknown. After half an hour of second-guessing himself, he resolved his worries to the Fates.

"What will be, will be," he said, then shut his eyes.

Chapter Nine

November

Sam awoke with the sun. It was his wedding day. His stomach felt queasy, his mouth dry, and his nerves frayed. He eyed the black suit on the chair across the room.

A rap on his door drew his attention.

"Sam, dear boy. Time to get up. You're getting married today," his grandmother said.

"Don't remind me," he muttered, pulling the covers down, then putting them back. The air was brisk.

The knock came again, then the door opened slowly. "You decent?"

"Yes, Grandma. Come in," he said, resignation in his voice. It was practically impossible to keep her out once she'd made up her mind to enter.

She walked through the door carrying a cup of hot tea. She placed it on the night table, then eased the black suit over a bit giving her space to sit down.

"Thanks," he said, picking up the hot mug. The liquid went down easy, waking and warming him at the same time.

"You ready, Sam?" The old woman cast a shrewd gaze on him.

"Ready as ever."

"You don't sound none too happy."

He shrugged. How happy could he be marrying a woman he didn't love? He had to keep reminding himself that the woman he did love refused him, refused to put aside her own dreams to give his a chance.

The more he thought about it, the firmer his resolve grew to marry Violet.

"Fitches gave me a goat last night," Sam said, taking another sip.

"I thought I heard a lot of noise from Sunshine last night."

"It's Midnight, her sister."

"Guess even goats remember their relatives," Martha said with a smile.

Sam leaned forward. "Grandma, did you love Grandpa best when you married him?"

She chuckled. "Didn't love him at all. Didn't really know him. He needed a wife, and I needed a husband."

"Really?" Sam's eyebrows shot up.

"Yep. It was right after my parents died in a fire. I was orphaned. My aunt knew John Chesney's family. John was older than the other Chesney children. Very shy and not good at talking to women. But he was a hard worker and made a good living. So my aunt arranged for him to marry me."

"Didn't you even know him?"

"Not really. We met a couple of times. He wasn't much for talkin'. But he picked a beautiful bouquet of wildflowers for me."

"Romantic?"

"Oh, very. He built that rocker for me."

Sam nodded.

"He was a kind and generous man. Easy to love. So we kind of grew into love, if you know what I mean."

"I get it."

"You will, too."

Sam stiffened. "What makes you think I don't love Violet?"

She waved her hand at him. "Oh, come on, Sam. You've been in love with Becky Rhodes since you were twelve."

"So? A person can learn to love someone new, right?"

"Of course."

"Did you come to love Grandpa?"

"With all my heart. He was a wonderful man."

"I see."

She smiled. "I'm sure you'll do just fine with Violet. She sure is pretty enough. And she knows how to bake, too."

"Yep. Yep." The conversation didn't alleviate the butterflies in his stomach. He rubbed the back of his neck, then pulled down the covers and swung his legs over the side. Lucky, his dog, barked and rose.

Martha stood. "I've got to get the bread in the oven." She paused at the door. "You goin' huntin'?"

"Yep."

She left the room. Relieved to leave his conversation with Martha, Sam finished the tea and threw on his clothes but left the black suit where it lay. He loaded his rifle.

"Come on, boy!" he called to his dog.

Heading for the kitchen, he called out to his grandmother. "Grandma, goin' shootin.'"

The twosome burst out the back door and ran toward the woods. Maybe he didn't know how to be a husband, but he sure knew how to shoot a rifle and bring home game. He'd worry about that marriage stuff later. He found the perfect spot near the pond and knelt down to wait with Lucky by his side.

AT THE END OF TOWN, the Wilcox home bustled with excitement.

"I think this should do it, Vi. Come, try it on," Hope said, holding her old wedding dress.

"Good thing you packed that away careful like," Abiel Wilcox said to his daughter-in-law. "Looks almost new."

"It'll have to do. I took in a few tucks. Violet is more slender than I was when I married," Hope said. "Come, Violet." She held out the dress.

Violet brushed two tears away from her cheeks. Her lower lip quivered. "Zeb," she whispered. "Where are you?"

"Come, come, Violet. We don't want to keep the reverend waiting!" Her grandfather snapped.

She wondered what the old man had to be so testy about. She was the one marrying a man she didn't love.

"Sam's a good man. He's kind. He's hard-working," she muttered aloud to herself as she hurried into the main room. Her mother thrust the dress over her head. Violet struggled to get her arms into the sleeves. Abiel stepped forward and gave the dress a tug.

"Gentle, Father! Gentle!" said Hope.

"Bah!" Abiel stepped back, grabbed his pipe and stormed out of the house.

"What's he got to be so upset about? I'm the one marrying a stranger," Violet said.

"Sam's not a stranger, dear. Not anymore," Hope said, smoothing the dress down at the waist.

"Doing...that...doesn't mean you know someone," Violet said.

"I know, dear. But we've got to be positive. Sam wants you for his wife. He'll treat you well. And he comes from a good family. His mother is a Wolcott!"

Violet hissed. "What do I care who she is?"

"She's going to be family. She may be of use to you some day." Hope slowly straightened the long sleeves.

The gown was white silk, not yellowed much as it had been locked away in a trunk. There was lace at the neckline and around the wrists of the long sleeves. Although simple in style it was elegant, and on Violet it reflected her beauty.

A gasp at the front door drew the ladies' attention. It was Abiel.

"My dear! You are a vision! An angel! Sam is a lucky man." Abiel smiled and took Violet's hand, lifting it to his lips.

"Grandpa, you are too sentimental." Still, she colored and warmed at his praise.

"Never was there a more beautiful bride," he said.

Hope shot him a sharp look.

"Except your mother, of course. And your grandmother, may she rest in peace."

Violet turned left, then right. "Mama, you fixed it beautifully."

Hope nodded. "Fits perfect now. Let's do up your hair."

Violet took a seat while Hope twisted and pinned her daughter's hair into a lovely chignon.

The women took heavy capes, Abiel donned his jacket, and they set off to the church. It was to be a small ceremony with a luncheon at the Inn afterward.

Abigail and Caleb would attend, with Lizzy, Jem, and Martha Chesney. Benjamin would represent the Fitch family. Josiah Quint was given time off to attend the midday wedding. Of course, Charity and Catherine Bloodgoode would be there.

Bright sun did little to warm the trio as they made their way to the church. Still, Violet took it as a good omen to have the sun bright and the sky a clear blue with no clouds. She and her mother huddled together against the wind as they walked.

"Ol' Bloodgoode better have a good fire going," Abiel muttered, raising his collar against the wind.

Violet's teeth chattered. Was it from the chill in the air or her nerves? Her mind turned to Becky Rhodes. Violet felt sorry for the girl. Already nineteen and Sam was her only prospect. She'd probably be an old maid now. She wondered if Becky would come to the wedding. Anyone who wished to attend would be welcome. Still, wouldn't it be too painful?

Sympathy for the sweet redhead rose in Violet's breast. She knew what it was like not to have the man you loved. Becky would share that dubious honor now, too. A rush of gratitude flooded Violet's heart. Whatever she was giving up, she acknowledged that Sam Chesney would devote his life to taking care of her and making the best life he could for her baby. She wondered what Zeb would think if he ever found out about the child. She blinked. Long gone to greener pastures, Zeb had probably started a new life and he'd never know about the one he left behind.

Hope strode over to her daughter. "You're a mess!" She tucked in the stray stands the wind had undone from her carefully created chignon. "Wake up, child. The ceremony will start as soon as Sam comes," Hope said, fussing.

"Good day to you," said the Reverend Bloodgoode. "Is the groom here?"

"I don't think so," piped up Abiel Wilcox.

"Let's get ready. I'm sure he'll be along shortly," the Reverend replied.

Violet abandoned her thoughts of Zeb and Becky and focused on the shuffling of people. Seemed as if everyone had a different idea of where she should stand. Violet went along with each change quietly. She'd been brought up to be compliant and used her training when it best benefitted her, like now.

The Bloodgoode sisters took prime seats in the front of the chapel. Charity leaned over to whisper to her sister, "I wonder what Becky Rhodes is doing now?"

"Not getting married, that's for sure!" The sisters giggled.

"Hush!" said Violet, drawing her eyebrows down.

Silence fell on the room as all eyes turned to the door. Sam Chesney, wearing a military suit, which didn't fit at all, stood in the doorway. His pale face wore a grim expression.

"Come in, come in, lad," the Reverend said, gesturing. "Smile. This is a wedding, not a funeral."

Violet wondered if those words were true.

AN HOUR EARLIER AT the Inn

"Come, come, Sam. Let me look at you," Martha Chesney said.

Sam squirmed, tugging this way at the suit jacket he wore, and that way at the pants. The pants were too big and the jacket too small.

"Grandma, this doesn't fit."

Martha narrowed her eyes. "Hmm. I have a needle and thread. Take off those pants and give them to me."

Sam did as he was told.

"The jacket fits, sort of. If you don't button it. You have wide shoulders," she said, almost as an accusation.

Sam stood in his bedroom in underdrawers, shirt, and jacket.

"Not dressed yet?" boomed a voice from the doorway.

Benjamin Fitch stood leaning against the frame, a smirk on his face. "It's your wedding day. Hop to it!"

"Grandma's making me wear my grandfather's suit. But it doesn't fit."

"Can she fix it?"

"She's doing it now." Sam ran his finger around the edge of his collar.

"Too tight?" Ben asked.

"Not really."

"Nervous?"

"How'd you guess?" Sam replied.

"Been there myself. But at least I married someone I knew." Benjamin entered the room.

"Shut up, Ben," Sam said.

Benjamin laughed. "Violet sure is pretty."

"Yes," Sam said. "And she's nice, a good woman."

Ben cocked an eyebrow. "Hmm. Haven't tried out the pudding before the meal?"

Sam punched his friend in the shoulder.

"Ow!"

"Shut up. Shut up!" Sam hollered.

"Hey, don't worry. It's going to be all right. Getting married is the right thing." Ben plopped down on a chair and rubbed his arm.

"I can't run a farm by myself."

"How is Caleb going to manage without you?"

"He's looking for an apprentice," Sam said, picking up his black tie. Martha rushed into the room. "Here you go. They ought to fit now. We've got to hurry. Can't be late to your own wedding. Benjamin? Help him with the tie," Martha said.

Ben raised his hand. "I don't know nothin' about ties. My mother ties mine."

"You men. So helpless. Put the pants on and I'll do the tie," Martha said.

When Sam had dressed completely, Martha stood back and took a long look.

"He looks pretty good," Benjamin said.

"That he does. Come on, let's go."

"What about mother and Caleb?" Sam asked, pulling his own jacket over the suit.

"They said they would meet us there."

Sam offered his arm to his grandmother to help guide her over the frozen, rutted road. "Let's go," he said, holding the door open for his mother and friend.

When they arrived, everyone had taken a seat. Sam swallowed. In spite of the cold, Sam sweated. When his gaze connected with Violet, he took in a breath. The beautiful gown set off Violet's dark hair and sky-blue eyes to great advantage. She looked stunning.

"Come right in, Sam, You stand here," the reverend said.

After receiving an encouraging look from his mother, Sam took his place. Abiel Wilcox walked his granddaughter down the short aisle and deposited her hand in Sam's. He smiled.

"You look beautiful," he whispered, closing his trembling fingers around hers.

She blushed a becoming pink.

The reverend cleared his throat.

"We are gathered here today to join this man and this woman in holy matrimony in the sight of God..."

Sam tried to focus on the reverend's words, but his mind wandered. As he stood on the precipice of a new life, he longed for the steadying influence of his late father. George Chesney had not been a man to act rashly or take unnecessary risks. An honest, hard-working man, he lost his life protecting his two daughters from certain death. George Chesney had died a hero. He lived forever in the mind and heart of his only son, Sam.

Now that he would follow in his father's footsteps, fear gripped him. Could he be the same amazing man his father was? Sam had doubts.

"Place the ring on her finger and repeat after me," the Reverend said.

A small nudge from Violet brought Sam back to the ceremony. After they took their vows, the reverend spoke.

"You may kiss the bride," he said.

Sam leaned over and joined his lips with Violet's. As he uncoupled, a creak and a rush of cold air grabbed his attention. He stood up and his gaze went to the back of the church. The door was open slightly, in the space stood Becky Rhodes. Sam's gaze met hers briefly – long enough to see tears spill over and run down her cheeks. Then, in a flash, as if he had imagined it, she was gone and the door slammed shut.

Chapter Ten

After a hearty meal of lamb, bread, potatoes, carrots, onions, cider, beer, and apple pie, Sam helped Violet into Benjamin's wagon. Ben had agreed to cart them and their goods to their new home. Riding in the back with Midnight the goat and their belongings, sat Sam, quiet and thoughtful. Tethered on the back was a horse that Caleb and Abigail had purchased for the couple. Lucky loped alongside.

The clickety clack of the wheels over the rough, rocky road interfered with conversation. When they arrived at the house, the sun painted the sky pink and gold. The air grew chilly.

"Start a fire, Violet," Sam said, picking up a valise holding his belongings. "Ben. Help me with this chest."

Benjamin and Sam carried in the chest with Violet's clothing and other items in it. Sam untethered his new horse and rubbed him down. He placed the animal in the small barn and pumped water into the trough.

"Sam!" Ben called out, pointing. A cloud of smoke escaped out one window.

Sam raced inside. Smoke billowed from the fireplace. Violet crouched in the corner.

"I'm sorry. I lit the fire like you said," she said, coughing.

Sam picked her up and carried her outside. Then he put out the fire and checked the chimney.

"There's something up there. Looks like a nest." He grabbed a broom and shoved the handle up. A mess of twigs and leaves fell into the fireplace. He cleaned out the old logs and added new ones on top of kindling. Then, he retrieved a short pine bough, lit it and held it up the chimney. When he felt a draft, he lit the new logs.

"That should work."

Violet and Benjamin stood in the doorway.

"Are you all right?" Sam asked Violet.

She nodded.

"Some wedding night!" Benjamin said, laughing.

He finished unloading and left, wishing his friend good luck.

"Something's been living in our chimney," Sam said, eyeing it with suspicion. Violet had pulled a chair close to the fire and sat bundled up in two shawls.

"I'm tired," Sam said, carrying a chair over next to his wife.

"Me, too. We can set up the house in the morning, can't we?"

"Yes," Sam said. He pulled off the tight suit jacket and draped it on the back of a chair. Violet threw a quilt on the bed.

Suddenly shy, Sam slipped off the fancy suit pants and hung them over the chair on top of the jacket. "I'll leave so you can get undressed," he said, heading for the door in his drawers and shirt.

"No, wait. We're married now. We need to get used to undressing in front of each other. I need help with the buttons," Violet said, turning her back to him.

Sam tried to steady his trembling fingers as he fiddled with each button. He dreaded being too rough and ripping the beautiful garment, now less beautiful as it had a layer of soot covering some places. Finally, he finished.

"Please help me pull it over my head," she said.

He did as she instructed, then gently laid the dress over another chair. Violet untied some of her undergarments then crept into bed. Sam whistled, and Lucky bounded over.

"You sleep on the floor tonight, Lucky. We'll fix you a bed in the morning." The dog nuzzled Sam's hand, gave one short bark, circled then lay down next to the bed.

The bed was cold. Violet cuddled up to Sam who drew her into his arms, then pulled the quilt up as far as it would go.

He stroked her hair and spoke softly. "I promise to do my best to take care of you and our child, Violet."

"I know you will, Sam."

Then he uttered a silent prayer, asking for the strength and wisdom to do what he'd promised. He blew out the candle next to the bed, then made love to his new wife, as was his duty, while trying hard to banish the image of Becky Rhodes from his mind.

THE WINTER DAYS FILLED up with cooking, hunting, and tasks to prepare for the baby. Sam and Violet spent December chopping wood for the winter, harvesting their few winter crops and filling the root cellar with carrots, onions, rutabagas, and parsnips they received from Martha and Sarah. With the few apples remaining in the cellar, Violet made her famous apple tarts.

Sam and Josiah built a small cradle from wood left over at the sawmill. Violet knitted clothes and blankets for the baby. She baked bread and Sam hunted fowl. When he was successful, they ate well, when he wasn't, they had vegetable soup and bread.

Lucky had become expert at rooting out rabbits, and trees were plentiful, providing abundant wood for blazing fires to ward off the dead cold of winter.

Their evenings were spent resting and reading. They read from Sam's book, "Gulliver's Travels," aloud to each other. As Violet grew bigger quickly, Sam took over more and more of her chores. She appeared content to sit by the fire and knit while Sam read.

"I'm sorry I can't do more, Sam," she lamented.

"It's all right, dear. We need to keep you safe and rested so we can have a well-baby," Sam said.

As comfortable positions became more and more difficult for Violet, Sam gave her backrubs and foot rubs.

"Do you miss your old life?" he asked her one evening after their meal.

"I don't miss Grandfather's smelly pipe, that's for sure," she said, making a face, then laughing.

Sam shared his dreams for the future with his wife. He found her a good listener. From time-to-time, Benjamin would ride down early in the morning to hunt with Sam. He would then share a meal with the couple before returning home. During those visits, Sam listened eagerly to news of the town and his family.

Some days, dawn came too quickly for the newlyweds. The early March sun rose a little earlier. Sam yawned. The cluck-cluck of chickens met his ears. It had been too cold in the coop for the birds, so he had brought the four chickens inside and kept them in a wooden crate.

Sam rose and put more logs on the fire. He tossed on his regular clothes and pumped water into the kettle. He hung it over the hearth, before going outside to chop more wood.

Violet watched him from the bed, as she was too big to rise without help.

"Don't worry. It's cold now, but this fire will have the place warm soon."

Sam helped Violet out of bed. She fetched clothes she had borrowed from her mother's pregnancy days from years ago. She dressed quickly then set about getting the morning meal set up. She pulled out a teapot and added tea.

"Thank goodness for your grandmother's generosity," Violet said, unwrapping two loaves of bread, a small pot of jam, vegetables, and a small pie.

Sam hauled the chickens out to the barn. The horse had started in on a bale of hay already. The chickens pecked around at some seeds left by the former farmer. Sam returned to the house and brought out some bread crusts for the birds. They had already foraged for worms, and small bugs that had survived the winter. Before returning to the house, Sam spied some tree trunks that needed splitting. He'd do a few so they could have a fire all day long.

The sun grew bright, and the clouds fluttered away. Sam stopped on his way back to the house to survey his land. Pride filled his chest. "A beautiful wife. A beautiful farm. What more can a man want?" A bark drew his attention. "Oh, yes." He nodded. "And a faithful dog. You're right, Lucky. We have to find new places to hunt." Sam returned to the house.

A mug of hot tea with bread and jam awaited him.

"Thank you, Violet."

"You're welcome."

Sam wolfed down the food, then pushed to his feet. "Lucky and I are going huntin'. . We need meat for supper, then I'll milk the goat. Do you know how to make cheese?"

"Yes," she replied.

"Good." He patted his wife's belly, picked up a second slice of bread and hurried out the door. As he tromped through the uneven land, he wondered exactly what Violet's talents were. Could she milk a goat? Make jam? At least she said she could make cheese and knit beautiful blankets and baby clothes. Heck, anyone could make cheese, getting the milk from the goat was the challenge. He scratched his head.

His boots crunched over the dried grass and weeds.

"Which way is water, Lucky?" he asked.

The pooch cocked his head, then sniffed the air. With one bark, he took off running to a copse of trees off to the left. Sam picked up his pace as he followed his dog. When he got to the trees, he hunched down and took cover. His father, George, had taught him to be patient when hunting.

"Sit quiet like, Sam. Wait till the birds get comfortable and think you ain't around no more. Then they'll come out. But if you're noisy or they see you, they'll hide forever. Patience."

Lucky huddled up close to Sam for warmth. Sam got comfortable and waited. All the while his mind went over all the things he'd need to do to get the farm up and running. Too soon to plant, but he needed to turn over the soil as soon as it thawed. Getting the soil ready for planting would be the biggest part of the farm, with harvesting coming in second.

He'd have to check out the fields and see what he wanted to plant where. He conjured up a picture of roast potatoes, onions, and carrots with goat cheese on the side. He smacked his lips in anticipation of the tasty meal.

The sound of wings flapping caught his attention. Sure enough, a couple of ducks flew to a tiny pond not far in front of them. Sam put his palm on Lucky to calm the dog. He picked up his rifle and got a duck in his site. Working to steady his hand, he gently squeezed the trigger.

The loud shot scared the ducks, who squawked, then took off, soaring to the east. One fell over. He got one! Sam grinned. There would be meat for dinner.

"Lucky, fetch!" he said.

The dog jumped to his feet and bounded over the shrubbery. Like lightning he raced to the pond and picked up the duck in his mouth before a fox could lay claim to Sam's kill. He returned to his master. Sam packed the duck in his satchel.

"One is enough, don't you think?" Sam asked the dog. He broke off a piece of bread he'd packed for the hunt and gave it to Lucky.

"Here, boy. Good job."

Together they ambled back toward the house. A scream alerted Sam. Lucky barked and took off with Sam close behind. When they rounded the bend, Sam saw Violet, cowering in a corner of the yard in front of the barn. Midnight, the goat, head lowered, faced Violet and bleated angrily at the woman. Frozen in fear, Violet hugged the wall. Maybe this wasn't going to be as easy as Sam had thought.

AT THE FITCH HOUSEHOLD, tension grew. Sarah had started labor, then stopped. Even Elijah Fitch put aside his business duties to pace outside her room.

"What is she waitin' for?" Elijah asked.

"Now, now, Elijah. It's not Sarah. It's the baby."

"He'd better get here soon. I ain't growin' any younger," the older man said. "Benjamin, control your wife. Tell her to go ahead and birth this baby."

Benjamin hid a smile behind his hand. "Pa, I can't do that."

"Lily-livered, that's what you are," the old man muttered under his breath.

"Didn't you hear the doc? He said the baby would come in his own sweet time and there wasn't nothin' we could do about it," Benjamin said, a tone of annoyance in his voice.

Benjamin stood outside the door to his bedroom. A soft moan wafted to his ears.

"Sarah?" he said. "Sarah?" he called louder.

When she didn't reply, he cracked the door open to peek in at her. She was half lying, half sitting up in bed, her knees pulled up and her head resting back on the headboard. Her eyes were closed.

"Sarah? Honey? Are you all right?" he crept slowly into the room.

"Is something happening?" his father's loud voice boomed. Sarah's eyes flew open in a flash, and she groaned.

"Father! Get out of here!"

"I thought, I thought," mumbled Elijah Fitch.

Ben gave his father's shoulder a shove. "Leave her be!" He pushed him from the room and slammed the door in his face. Then he perched gently on the edge of the bed and took her hand in both of his.

"Are you all right?"

She lifted her hand to cup his cheek. "I don't know. I've never done this before. But it hurts. Hurts bad."

Benjamin pushed to his feet. "I'll get the doc."

She placed her hand on his forearm. "No, no. Stay. It doesn't hurt bad all the time. It just comes and goes."

"You want me to stay with you?"

She nodded.

"Can I get you anything? Food? Cider?"

"Water. I'm mighty thirsty," she said before leaning back against the bed again.

Ben rushed out the door and flew down the steps.

"What is it? What is it?" his father asked. His mother rose when Ben reached the bottom of the stairs.

"She's thirsty. She wants water," he said.

"That's all?" Ann Fitch asked.

"Yes. Please get out of my way," Benjamin replied before turning toward the kitchen. He grabbed a pitcher, filled it from the pump, then picked up a mug and headed toward the stairs. When he reached her room, he took a deep breath and slowed down before entering.

"That was fast," Sarah said.

"Whatever you want. What did the doctor say?" Ben filled the mug then put the pitcher on the nightstand.

"He said he'd be back later. Around sundown. He said sometimes it takes a while to birth a baby. He said sometimes the baby takes his own sweet time."

"I think my father will keel over if this baby doesn't come soon. He's apoplectic." He handed the water to his wife.

Sarah laughed then took a drink.

"You'd think he was having this baby," Benjamin said, shaking his head.

"Good thing he was born a man because he'd never survive birthing a baby," Sarah said.

When she finished the water, she handed the mug to Ben. He pushed to his feet.

"Please don't go," she said, then doubled up with a labor pain. Benjamin's heart squeezed as he watched her face grow pale with pain. She reached out and he took her hand. She clutched it to her chest. He returned to his seat on the bed.

"Can't be nothing good to hurt so bad," he said.

"Doc Rhodes said pain was part of birthing," Sarah said.

Benjamin raised her hand to his lips. "My brave wife."

When she tightened her grip on his fingers, he raised his gaze to her face. Her jaw clenched, and tears ran down her cheeks as she swallowed a moan. Sweat beaded on her forehead.

"Hold me, Benjamin, hold me," she whispered in a parched, hoarse voice.

Ben didn't know how to hold her. Her giant belly served as a wall between them. He inched nearer to her on the bed. When he got close enough, Sarah threw her arms around his neck. She buried her face in his shoulder and sobbed, muffling the noise with his shirt. His eyes filled, but he blinked the tears back.

There was a knock on the door.

"Benjamin. Sarah. Is everything all right?" came his mother's voice shaking with worry.

"Yes, Mother." Ben said as his large hands rubbed and soothed Sarah's back.

He could tell the pain had subsided because Sarah let go of him and fell back against the pillows. She closed her eyes, her breaths came in short spurts.

He rose and refilled her mug. "Drink this," he said, holding it to her lips.

Sarah pushed her hair off her forehead and took the drink with shaking hands. Benjamin folded his over hers to steady the water. She drank and drank again. When she emptied the mug, he took it.

"More?"

"No, no. Thank you," she said, her voice sounding more like the woman he knew.

When Ben placed the mug back on the table, he turned and glanced out the window.

"Ah, the sun is going down," he said.

"Really?" Sarah asked, sitting up as best she could.

"Yes."

"Good," she fell back against the pillows again and groaned. She held her belly as tears coursed down her cheeks.

"That means the doctor will be here soon," Benjamin said.

Sarah nodded. "They come more often now. No time to rest between them," she said.

Benjamin held her for a moment and kissed her head. "I hope it won't be long now."

Sarah nodded. "I don't know how much more I can take."

"Hold on to me. When the pain comes, hug me, squeeze my hands, my arms."

"I'm too weak to do that. I will last. I will. Because our child is coming. And I want this baby so much."

"Me, too," he whispered.

The couple froze in each other's arms as best they could. Then there was another knock and the door opened.

"Ready, Sarah?" It was Doc Rhodes.

"Yes."

"Benjamin, I'm afraid you'll have to leave now. Could you please send in your mother and Giselle?"

Ben leaned over to brush his lips over Sarah's dry ones and stood up. "Of course, Doc. Sarah, take care." He wanted to tell her he loved her, but not with Doc there. Instead he squeezed her hand. She raised her gaze to his, and he felt certain she could read it in his eyes. He walked swiftly to the door, stopped for one last loving look at his wife, then went out and shut the door.

"Mother! Giselle! Doc Rhodes wants you!" Benjamin called, barely able to control the panic in his voice. He'd never seen Sarah in so much pain, so weak, so vulnerable. And there was nothing he could do to help her. Always strong, confident, certain, Sarah had never let anything get her down for long. Even their little squabbles didn't daunt her for long. But this was different. For the first time in his life, Benjamin was afraid of losing Sarah. He did not feel confident that she would survive the birthing, but he kept his fears to himself.

Ann Fitch strode to the door with Giselle running up behind her. She stopped to squeeze her son's arm. "She'll be all right. Don't worry."

Bemjamin wanted to believe her, but he wasn't so sure. He carried a chair from the dining room to the hallway right outside the bedroom door. Too nervous to sit, he paced. His father joined him and they walked the hallway together.

THE FIRST SCREAM CUT through Benjamin's flesh right to his bone. He shivered.

"What are they doing to her?" he asked his father.

"I don't know, son. Men aren't allowed in."

"You didn't sit by Mother when she had me?" Benjamin stopped moving.

"No. Doctor wouldn't let me."

"Did you want to?" He raised his eyebrows.

"Well..." his father hedged, then ambled down the hall. But Ben pursued him.

"Didn't you?"

Elijah looked down at his hands fiddling with his belt. "No."

"No?"

"No. Ann was distraught, screaming, crying, carrying on."

"And so? You didn't want to comfort her?"

"I did, but I couldn't stand her suffering. We don't talk about these things," Elijah said.

"Talk about caring for your wife?"

"Right." Elijah sank down on a chair.

"Why not? You married her. You love her, right?" Ben stopped next to his father's chair.

"Of course, of course. But I don't like to talk about that. Your mother knows. I take good care of her. Provide well. Built her a fancy house. Pay for servants. She doesn't have to do much, just run things and never get her hands dirty."

"But there's more to it," Ben continued.

"Yes. But must we discuss this?" His father shifted in his seat.

"Sarah and I love each other. I look forward to the end of the day so I can get home to her."

He was interrupted by a scream and then sobbing. Sweat broke out on Ben's forehead.

"It sounds like they are killing her," he said.

"I know. I had to sit outside and listen to your mother."

"Did it bother you?"

Elijah's head snapped up. He shot a sharp look at his son. "Of course it did! Blast it all. You think I have no feelings?"

"I didn't say that."

"Better not. Sit down. You're making me nervous," Elijah said.

Benjamin eased down into the chair next to his father. His dog, Patches, joined him, curling up on the floor for a snooze. "You've always taught me that a man takes care of his wife. But she's in there, suffering, and I'm out here doing nothing."

"Some things, some places a man can't be. This is one of them."

"Will she forgive me?" Ben asked.

"Yes, of course. She has your mother there to hold her hand."

"Sometimes being a man is hard," Ben muttered to himself.

Elijah laughed. "Being a man is always hard!"

An hour later, hunger gripped Benjamin's stomach. "Giselle left a cold supper for us. Come. Let's eat," Elijah said. "It's not over yet, but we need to be fortified."

Hating to leave the door, Ben couldn't ignore the growling of his stomach. He followed his father into the dining room. A platter of cold roasted lamb started his mouth watering. There was also a bowl of roasted squash and onions. Some fried potatoes and carrots occupied another bowl. There was a half-loaf of bread and sweet butter on the table.

The men filled their plates then took their places at the table. Ben kept one ear tuned to any noise coming from the upstairs bedroom. He slipped a small piece of meat to Patches, who wolfed it down quickly.

He ate quickly and returned to his chair by the bedroom.

"Seems like she's been birthing this baby for two days," Ben said, glancing at the grandfather clock in the hall. It chimed the hour. Time appeared to crawl by. There was little noise coming from the bedroom.

"You don't think she died, do you?" Ben asked his father, his voice dripping with worry.

"No, no, of course not. If she had, they'd have come out and told us. Try to be patient."

"Oh, yes, yes. You're right."

Benjamin alternated between pacing and collapsing in his chair, exhausted. Finally, the knob on the door turned and it opened enough for the doctor to stick his head out.

Benjamin jumped up. "Doctor Rhodes?"

The doctor smiled. "You have a beautiful baby girl, Benjamin."

"I do?"

"Yes."

"How's Sarah? Is she all right?"

"She's fine. Quite tired, but doing fine. She's a brave woman, your wife."

Ben beamed with the biggest smile in the world. "She is. That she is, Doctor Rhodes."

"A girl?" Elijah said. "Damnation! I told her we wanted a boy!"

"I'm afraid you can't order up which you want, boy or girl. You have to take what you get," said Dr. Rhodes, frowning at Elijah. "Please don't complain about the baby to Sarah. She's recovering and needs peace, quiet, and rest. No yelling, no complaints. Just nice and quiet, if you please," Dr. Rhodes said, rolling down his sleeves.

"Can I see Sarah?" Ben asked, putting his hand on the door.

"Yes. But just for a little while. She needs to sleep." The doctor opened the door. Ann Fitch and Giselle were cleaning up the tools and gathering the cloths, bedclothes and nightgown to be washed.

Ben crept in quietly. Sarah sat back, wearing a fresh nightgown, her face washed. She smiled at Benjamin. "Look at our daughter. Isn't she beautiful?" Sarah said as she held the baby to her breast.

Overcome by awe, Ben slid down on a chair next to the bed and stared.

"Do you want to hold her?"

"She's so little. I might drop her," Ben said.

Sarah laughed. "No you won't. Move closer."

Benjamin rested his rump on the edge of the bed.

"Make your arms like a cradle," Sarah said. He did as she asked, and she slipped the swaddled child gently into his arms.

"She's so little," he said, staring down.

The baby looked up, fascinated. She didn't cry, just stared. Then gave a sort of smile, though it wasn't really. But Benjamin considered it to be and smiled back.

"She smiled at me, Sarah."

"Maybe."

He looked up. "Are you all right?"

"I will be," she said, sinking back into several pillows.

"She's beautiful, like her mother," Benjamin said, staring at the tiny child. "What shall we call her?"

"We had boys names, but none for a girl. How about Susannah? That was my grandmother's name – on my mother's side."

Ben laughed. "My mother will love that. Having her granddaughter named after a Wolcott!"

"You agree?"

"It's a beautiful name, just like her."

The baby started to cry, throwing fear into Benjamin. He frowned. "What do I do?" he asked, his voice panicky.

"Give her to me. She's hungry. Why don't you bring the cradle in here, she can sleep beside me. Then I don't have to get up to feed her."

"Good idea," he said, handing the baby back to his wife.

Benjamin stood up slowly. "Thank you, Sarah. For making such a beautiful baby." He crept quietly out of the room and bounded down the hall.

"Father. Help me," Ben said.

"What?"

"Sarah wants the cradle."

Together the men carried the heavy, hand-carved wooden cradle down the hall and set it up next to the bed. Elijah got his first look at the baby. Although it was a girl, he couldn't help but smile at the pretty child.

"Sarah needs to sleep. The baby, too. You could probably use some rest, too," said Dr. Rhodes.

Ben kissed Sarah and stopped at the cradle for one last look at his daughter before he left to rest in the guest room. He vowed he'd never seen such a beautiful child.

"Pretty baby. Too bad it's not a boy," Elijah said.

Benjamin stopped. He grabbed his father by his jacket and pulled him up, nose-to-nose.

"I don't ever want to hear you say that again! That's my daughter you're talking about, and you will speak with respect when you refer to her!" Ben's face grew red as he hollered.

Elijah paled and drew back. "Sorry," he muttered.

"Don't ever do that again." Benjamin let his father go. Elijah teetered a bit before he regained his footing.

Ann Fitch stood against the wall in the hallway. "I guess Benjamin's now bigger than you, Elijah. You'll have to mind your manners around him." She hid a smile behind her hand.

"Bah!" Elijah said, scowling as he strode down the hall.

Chapter Eleven

News of the birth of Susannah Fitch traveled fast. Sam and Violet rode to the Rhodes' store to buy supplies. Becky waited on them.

"We need sugar, flour, rice, cider, molasses, and salt," Violet said, avoiding eye contact with Becky.

"We also need seeds," Sam said.

"What kind of seeds?" Becky asked, shooting a chilly look in his direction.

"Hmm, let's see. Carrots, squash, and corn. Some seed potatoes. And onion bulbs," Sam said.

"How many of each?" Becky asked, shifting her weight from foot to foot.

"How many? Hmm. I don't rightly know."

"How much land you plantin'?" she asked.

"Two acres for each," he said.

Sam watched as Becky measured out enough seed to meet his plans. He noted how efficient she was, how knowledgeable. She knew how much could be planted on an acre. Maybe she would've made a good farmer's wife. It was her decision to turn him down, he reminded himself.

"Your sister had her baby," Becky said, making eye contact with Sam.

"She did? What did she have? Boy or girl?"

"A girl. They named her Susannah. There's gonna be a big celebration in a couple of weeks."

"A girl? Bet Elijah Fitch is fit to be tied," Sam muttered.

"A celebration?" Violet asked.

"For her christening," Becky said. "Excuse me. I'll get your seeds."

"Can we go to the celebration, Sam?" Violet asked. "Please?"

"We'll see how the plantin' goes. We gotta plant potatoes and onions before the last frost. The rest soon after."

Violet frowned but didn't say more. Becky explained the contents of each satchel, then bundled everything together. She added up the amount. Sam jingled the coins in his pocket. Money was growing scarce. He hoped to be able to make it through planting and harvest season.

As Sam loaded up the cart, a familiar voice called his name.

"Sam! Sam Chesney!"

He looked up. It was his grandmother.

"So glad I caught you. Isn't it wonderful about Sarah's new baby? You're an uncle now. I hope you and Violet will come to the celebration."

"We'll see," he said, facing her. "You're looking good, Grandma."

She smiled. "I got some stuff for you." She put down two bags. "Everything in these is for you and Violet. It's hard to start up a farm. Gotta stretch your pennies," Martha said.

Sam loaded the bags in the wagon. Violet peeked in each. "Thank you, Martha," she said.

"Yeah. Thanks, Grandma. We can use all the help we can get."

"You're always welcome at my table. You're family." She put her hand in the pocket of her dress and drew out some coins. She took Sam's hand, placed the coins carefully in his palm, and closed his fingers over them.

Sam hugged Martha and loaded up the rest of the goods from Rhodes'. He helped Violet up, then climbed on himself. He whistled and flapped the reins and the ox picked his head up from snacking on some early spring grass and made his way toward the farm.

On the way home, Sam handed the coins to Violet. "Count it, will ya?"

She nodded and took the coins. "Why, there's five dollars' worth!" she said.

"Should be just enough to get us to summer harvest," Sam said, grinning. "Thank you, Grandma!"

Since the days were growing longer, it was still light when Sam and Violet returned to the farm. He unloaded the wagon. Violet helped carry the food inside.

"Let's see what Martha gave us," she said, poking her nose in one of the bags. She unloaded two small pies.

"Apple?" Sam asked, sniffing the air.

"I think so. Oh, look. A third one. A meat pie," Violet said. "And bread. Lots of bread."

"Guess we got supper," Sam said, taking the heavy bags of flour and sugar to the small shed out back they used as a pantry.

While Sam put away the supplies, Violet put more logs on the fire and heated water for tea. She wrapped her shawl tighter against the chill in the air.

"Let me fix that," Sam said. He went out back and brought in more wood. He piled two more logs on the fire, gave it several good pokes and fanned it. Flames jumped up as if on command.

Violet stood with her palms facing the fire.

"Cold?" Sam asked.

"A little."

Sam brought two mugs to the table. He divided the morning's tea leaves in each.

"Someday we won't have to use the leaves so many times," Sam said. "Someday we'll have leaves to burn."

"It's all right. I knew what it would be like," she said. She took a loaf of bread from the bag and a pot of butter from the small larder and put both on the table. Then she fetched plates and the meat pie.

When she reached for the steaming kettle, Sam put his hand on her shoulder. "I'll do that. Don't want you getting burned. It's heavy." He took down the kettle and filled the mugs.

"Do we have any of that fine goat cheese you made last week?" he asked.

"Yes, we do." She pulled the goat cheese from the larder.

They sat down at the table. Violet said grace. Sam looked at the food and smiled.

"This is a meal fit for a king," he said, licking his lips.

"Nothing like the table at the Fitches' house, though," Violet put in, tearing off a piece of bread.

"No. But I ain't as old as Fitch. When I am, I'll have the biggest farm in the county with lots of tenant farmers working my land. And I won't have to ride behind a stinkin' ox to sow seeds. And I'll have a French baker, too, just like Fitch."

Violet laughed.

Sam bristled. "Them dreams will be real someday."

"No, they won't."

"Why not?" Anger tinged his voice.

"Because you'll never be as mean or greedy as ol' Elijah Fitch. That's why," she said, taking a sip of tea.

Sam put down his fork and stared at his wife. Then he leaned over to kiss her.

"Darned if I didn't marry the right woman after all," Sam said, then resumed eating.

EVERY MORNING, SAM and Lucky got up with the sun. They went hunting. Most days they didn't get anything. Sometimes a careless rabbit would cross their path. When he returned home, Sam had a meager breakfast of bread, goat cheese, butter, and tea.

Violet took charge of milking the goat. The three hens and the rooster, the goat, and the ox foraged for food. They had returned the horse to Abigail and Caleb. Pickings were slimmer in winter months. But the weather was warming some and grass had already poked up in places.

Eggs from their three hens were saved for dinner, their midday meal, the biggest meal of the day. Sam had scoured the property and found a few potatoes, carrots, and the odd onion or two that had not been harvested by the last tenant. Violet added them to their meal.

Unused to cooking on the old stove, Violet occasionally burned food, but Sam ate it anyway. What choice did he have? He tried not to make her feel bad, but she cried anyway.

A late winter snow dusting, rain, or sleet kept him indoors. Bad weather put him behind in plowing and planting his fields. When he made this plan, twenty acres seemed like an easy task. But walking every inch of his land behind a stubborn ox pulling a plow took longer than he had planned.

He stopped to take a drink of cider and turned toward the house. He liked to keep an eye on Violet. He didn't know what pregnancy entailed, but he knew he needed to make sure she was safe. He saw her flit back and forth between planting a small garden by the house and hanging laundry. He spied a plate of food she'd left out on the front stoop.

To assuage feelings of hunger between mealtimes, she'd fix snacks of bread and butter or cheese. Sam grew uneasy as he saw the unattended dish. He reckoned they had bear, coyotes, foxes, and even raccoons living nearby and hungry enough to snatch her food.

A large dark figure moved into his line of vision. A bear! And it was going for Violet's plate. Too far away to do anything, he watched, frozen in place, hoping the bear would simply take the food and move on.

After she finished hanging the laundry, Violet turned back to the house. She stopped abruptly and screamed. Her scream interrupted the creature wolfing down the bread. Startled and afraid, the animal turned toward her, ready to defend himself. He growled loud enough for Sam to hear.

Energized by the threat to his wife, he took off running. Hollering, he gestured for her to get back in the house. But the bear had cut off her path. Trapped in a corner, she sank down to her knees. Black as night, huge, and menacing, the bear chomped on a piece of bread and drew near her. After it swallowed the last morsel, it roared again. She screamed, lowered her head, and covered her face with her hands.

Sam flew across the field, hollering, and waving his hands in an attempt to distract the bear. Lucky followed, going twice as fast as his master. When he caught up to the bear, he stood his ground and barked at the critter.

The bear turned its head toward Lucky first, then Sam. The bear picked up the remaining food from the plate and lumbered off quickly in the direction of the woods. Seeing the bear moving away from Violet, Sam ran into the house and got his rifle. Upon returning to the scene, he raised it and fired. But the bear had already reached the safety of the woods.

Sam waved his fist at the bear. "And don't come back!" He returned to his wife, who was still on her knees and trembling. He grasped her upper arms and lifted her slowly to her feet.

"Are you all right?"

She stared at him, nodding. When he drew closer, she threw herself into his arms and sobbed against his chest. He held her tight, stroking her hair and speaking softly. As soon as she had calmed some, he turned them around and guided her back inside the house.

He led her to a chair then opened a bottle of wine. He poured a small amount in a mug.

"Drink this," he said, handing it to her.

She took a sip and made a face.

"A little more," he said.

She did as she was told. Sam picked her up and sat in the chair, depositing her in his lap. She clung to him.

"There are dangerous animals living out here. It's not like in town."

"Bears," she moaned with a shiver.

"Yes, and coyotes, foxes, and even raccoons can decide your food is their food. You can't leave food outside like that."

"It's not my fault," she said bristling.

"No, of course not, honey. It's the big ol' bear's fault. Still. If you want something, best to eat it inside, where it's safe."

"All right," she said with a nod.

"Good. We'll have to protect the chickens, too." Sam rubbed his chin. "I'm gonna have to build a pen or something to keep the coyotes away. Lucky, can you stand guard on those chickens?"

Lucky wagged his tail. Violet smiled. "He's as brave as you are."

She curled up in his lap and rested her head against his shoulder. Sam drew her nearer. He took a deep breath, enjoying the lovely scent of her hair. As they sat there cuddled together. Sam got an idea that he could take a break from the plowing to make love to his wife.

"Guard the door, Lucky," Sam said, standing with Violet in his arms.

"Is it all right?" he asked, moving toward the bedroom.

She nodded, a pretty pink blush stole across her cheeks. He carried her into the bedroom and closed the door with his foot as Lucky curled up by the front door.

BACK IN FITCH'S EDDY, the town was abuzz with preparations for the christening of Susannah Wolcott Fitch.

Preparations at the Fitch mansion bubbled. At the dinner table, Ann Fitch fussed. "Everything must be just so. Elijah, you, and Benjamin have to help."

"Isn't that what we have servants for?" Elijah said, scooping up some delicious squash soup with his spoon.

"There's too much to do." She cut a potato into small pieces.

"She's only one small baby," Elijah said, tossing a critical stare at the baby in Sarah's arms. "Very small baby."

"She's not small. Doc Rhodes says she's a good size," Sarah piped up.

"All babies look small, Elijah." Ann sniffed.

"She's beautiful," Benjamin said, cooing at his daughter, who smiled at him.

"When is this event going to take place?" Elijah asked, turning to his wife.

"As soon as I can get everything together and I'm sure it won't be too cold."

"We're not taking Susannah out in the cold," Sarah said, her mouth compressing into a firm line.

"No, no, of course not," Ann said. She buttered a piece of bread.

"I would guess April," Ben said, cutting into the lamb on his plate.

"April? I have to live through this jabbering and fussing until April?" Elijah raised his eyebrows as he stabbed a carrot with his fork.

"It's only a month away. And I have so much to do!" Ann pushed away from the table in a tizzy.

"Why not make it July? It's sure to be warm enough then," Elijah called after his wife.

"Stop it, Father. Your teasing only makes her worse," Ben said, before putting a forkful of food in his mouth.

"Oh she loves to get as ruffled as a wet hen. Who cares if everything isn't perfect? It's for the townsfolk, not just us."

"Now, now, Elijah, be honest. You care," piped up Sarah, picking up a piece of buttered bread.

"Bosh!" Elijah stroked his chin. "Well, maybe a little. It should be perfect. It will be a Fitch christening."

"You get away with everything," Ben said, turning to his wife. "If I talked to him like that I'd get my ears boxed." Ben used his fork to stab the meat he'd cut and put it in his mouth.

"Not anymore, you're too big," Elijah said with a twinkle in his eye.

"Nevertheless," Benjamin said.

"I'm lucky, that's all," Sarah quipped, putting the bread in her mouth.

"She's like my own daughter," Elijah said, training a warm smile on her. "Besides, she's not afraid to speak up to me." He took a last bite of food, then wiped his mouth with a napkin.

Giselle cleared the dishes from the table, and then the food platters. She brought out several plates of French pastries for dessert. There were mini eclairs, brownies, milles feuilles, and small cream puffs.

Ann rejoined the family. Charles, their butler, interrupted the meal.

"Excuse me, sir. This just came. I thought it might be urgent.

"Thank you, Charles," Elijah said, ripping open the envelope. "Well, well, the cabinet maker, Micah Edwards and his family will be arriving by the first of June. Benjamin, is their house ready?"

"No. Digby and Jedidiah Whitfield have been working, but rain and snow have slowed them down."

"Odds Bodkins!" Elijah slammed his palm down on the table. The baby started to cried.

"Elijah!" Sarah barked, cradling her child, and whispering to her.

"It has to be finished! They will be here soon! They can't sleep in the street!" Elijah pushed up from his chair, barking orders at Benjamin who followed him around like a lost puppy.

The men pushed out the back door and strode over the muddy earth in the direction of the office building at the north end of the Fitch property. Ann Fitch returned to the table.

"I'm going to feed Susannah," Sarah said.

"Fine and when she goes down for a nap, will you please join me? We need to finish the plans for the Christening. I don't want to leave anything until the last minute."

"Of course."

The ladies pushed away from the table and went in opposite directions. Sarah sought the peace and quiet of her bedroom. She positioned herself on the big rocking chair and put the baby to her breast. She shook her head, convinced that most families held christenings without all this fuss and bother.

But, she had to remind herself, now she was a Fitch. And they did things differently. She stroked her baby's head as she wondered if Susannah would even be awake for the event. As she thought about Susannah being at all close to Reverend Bloodgoode, a frown curled the corners of her mouth down. She detested him and didn't want him touching her child. But he was the only clergy for many, many miles, so she'd have to put up with him.

When the child finished feeding and fell asleep, she put her down, then crawled into her own bed and was instantly asleep.

MARCH

Walking behind the plow with Ol' Amos the ox, Sam spotted a wagon pulling up beside his house. He shielded his eyes from the early morning sun and spied Hope and Abiel Wilcox arriving. He didn't have time to stop work and visit. Why didn't they come in the evening, after work was done? He wiped his brow with his sleeve and continued on. With snow and rain, he had fallen behind in his planting, so he didn't have time to waste jawin' with Violet's family.

After he plowed a dozen rows, he'd plant. He thought he'd remembered that all the fields had full sun, but once he started planting, he realized that the trees that were bare in the winter wouldn't be during the warmest time of the year. There were plenty of trees to provide some shade across his field. He needed to find a crop that would do well in the shade, for he was plumb certain that potatoes, onions, corn, and carrots needed plenty of sun to grow.

Times like these he needed his father's wisdom and experience. Sam scratched his head, as if that would put in memories of farming with his dad in his brain. He needed all the tricks his father used and the knowledge of what to plant where and when to harvest. He'd hoped he'd remember when the time came and do things right, but he wasn't confident about it.

He swung the pouch containing seeds over his shoulder and marched along each row, planting. Then he'd go back and use his long hoe to cover the seeds with soil. Sam looked up at the sound of wagon wheels bumping along the rutted road. Hope Wilcox and Abiel Wilcox approached in a wagon with a horse tethered at the rear. Sam faced the house. Violet stood on the steps, calling to and waving at first at her relatives, then at Sam.

At that moment, it crossed his mind that perhaps Hope had brought one of her berry or apple pies. A low rumble ambled through his belly. Hope was an excellent cook and baker.

"All right, Amos. Time to catch a rest," Sam said, leading the ox to the water trough in the shade. He stuck his head under the pump and washed himself down. He used the rag draped over the pump as a towel and did his best to appear presentable. But plowin' and plantin' weren't no pretty pastime like quilting or reading, so he settled himself on some basic cleanliness and nothing else. Figuring that Sam would be finding refreshment inside, Lucky picked himself up off his shady soft napping mound of leaves and pine needles to join his master inside.

"Howdy, Mrs. Wilcox, Mr. Wilcox." Sam said, combing his hair back from his forehead with his fingers.

Abiel Wilcox stepped forward and offered his hand. "Hope and Abiel to you, son."

"I'm sorry to bother you. You working so hard and all. But I had a hankering to see my daughter. Grandpa will tell you. I been moping about all week on account of missing my Violet."

"Pleasure to have you," Sam said. His gaze searched the room until it lit on two satchels. His mouth watered at the idea of something special to eat. He walked over to the table. "Whatcha got there, Hope?"

"Nothing but your favorite pies, Sam Chesney! Apple and berry."

As if he'd just won at a hand of poker, Sam's face lit up. "Pies? Really? For me?"

"And Violet, too, of course," Hope said, with a slight admonishment in her tone.

"Of course, of course."

Hope Wilcox took her daughter's hands in hers. "Why, look at your hands! They're all brown and rough." She raised the work-worn palms to her lips. "My poor girl."

"She's a farmer's wife now. Comes with the territory," Sam said.

"Let's cut up those pies," Abiel said.

"I'll do it. You work hard enough, Vy," Hope said, bustling over to the table.

Sam ate his two generous slices of pie in silence, savoring each bite and almost listening to the ladies spreading the town gossip. When he heard words about the Fitches' christening celebration, his ears pricked up.

"Yes, your sister-in-law and her mother are fixing to throw a right royal party for that babe," Hope said. "You're a member of the Fitch family now, too, Violet. Remember that."

"No she ain't. I ain't either. We're Chesneys and Wolcotts, but not Fitches," Sam said.

"You're kin to the Fitch clan, then," Hope insisted with a sniff.

"Mebbe," Sam muttered between bites of the scrumptious pastries.

"I want to go. Can I, Sam?"

"We'll see how you're feeling," Sam said, wondering how long it would take Ol' Amos to make the trip.

"You can't go parading around in your condition. You're getting mighty big with child, Violet," Abiel Wilcox said.

"So what? I'm a married woman. No shame in that," she replied, jutting her chin out a bit.

"That's right. She should be there. She has every right to be there. And the company would be good for her. And the food, too," Hope said, with a disdainful glance around the kitchen.

"We eat good. Lucky and I go out hunting every morning. And most days we come home with fresh meat," Sam said.

"That true?" Abiel asked, narrowing his eyes.

"Yes, Grandpa. Sam is a right good shot. A prime hunter."

"Glad to hear it, child. Glad to hear it. You're eatin' for two now," Abiel said with a chuckle.

"When you come to town, you can stay with us," Hope said. "Right, Grandpa?"

"Yes, yes, of course. We have just enough room for them. And will for the baby, too, when it comes."

"So can I go, Sam? Please?"

Her face, browned by the sun, had not lost any of its beauty. The idea of the party perked her up. Her eyes got their luster back. So what if she looked like she was expecting? She was a married woman now and that would be natural. He didn't care. But taking a day or two away from plowing worried him.

"It's only a day or two. We'll be back. You and Amos will probably have more energy after a rest," Violet said, reading his mind.

"All right. You convinced me. We'll go. Lucky, too?" Sam asked, bending over to scratch the pooch behind the ears.

"Lucky, too, if he must," Abiel said, but he made a face.

"Lucky's our protector. He chased a fox away from the chickens," Violet said.

Abiel reached into the satchel and ripped off a piece of bread. "Then the hound deserves a reward," he said, tossing the bread to the dog who caught it on the fly.

Maybe Violet was right. Maybe he could work twice as fast after resting for a day. Anyway, he'd agreed so now he'd have to live with his decision. After all, wasn't Violet entitled to some fun and a chance to do something she wanted to do for a change? Their lives were taken up with work most of the daylight hours. He longed to see his family, too. And his friend, Benjamin. Besides, if the Fitches were hosting, the food would be excellent. That alone would be worth the trip.

They unloaded the vittles from Hope and Abiel's wagon. Gratitude flooded Sam's heart. They were getting a bit low on a few things, like flour and sugar. Hope and Violet made the evening meal. Abiel lit his pipe, and Sam and Lucky shared space on a rug on the floor.

"Why don't we take Violet home with us? She should visit the doctor. Then she'd be in town for the celebration," Hope said.

"We'll leave you a horse, so you can join us," Abiel said.

"Would you mind, Sam? It's only a week until the celebration," Violet said.

Truth was he did mind and he didn't mind. He'd be relieved of worrying about her safety. But he'd be missing a week of her cooking and tending to the animals. Besides, there were her wifely duties, too. Still, she worked hard and deserved to be taken care of and live easy for a bit.

"No, it's all right with me. Violet works hard. She deserves a rest. Specially on account of her being with child and all," Sam said.

"Bless you, Sam Chesney!" Hope said, giving him a hug. She hurried off to pack up a few things for Violet, which Abiel loaded in the wagon.

When they got up to leave, Sam helped his wife into their wagon and waved goodbye with Lucky at his side.

When they were beyond waving distance, he turned and cast a concerned gaze at the acres left to be plowed and planted. Shading his eyes with his hand, he frowned. Could he and Amos do it? He prayed they could because success was his only option. He planned to work night and day until the celebration. But could he do that with so many extra chores now on his plate?

"My father would dig in. He'd say stop complaining. You have acres to plow. Get to it," Sam said aloud to Lucky, who barked once.

"And how am I going to get you to town, my friend?" Sam scratched his chin. Lucky would have to run alongside or maybe Sam could rig up some way to keep the dog across the saddle with him. He'd figure it out. For now he was glad to have Lucky's companionship for he was already feeling the chill of loneliness without his wife.

Chapter Twelve

A*pril*
Violet tried not to show how happy she was to be home. Though in reality, this wasn't her home anymore, it would always be home to her. She looked forward to sleeping in her own bed and having her mother to do the chores.

She understood the bargain she'd made with Sam when she married him. But the reality of working hard and being pregnant left her exhausted at night. No longer the fun girl who enjoyed a moonlight stroll or a bath in the river with her lover, Violet now took the role of married woman and helpmate.

She retired early and slept in. When she awoke, her mother offered her fresh cinnamon biscuits and eggs. This was the life! She accompanied her mother to the general store.

"Becky, is your father seeing people this morning?" Hope asked, gathering foodstuffs and ribbon.

"I think so. Let me ask him when he can see you."

"Not me. Violet," Hope said.

Becky's glance scooted down the young woman's form and her eyes widened.

"Oh, I see. Yes. I'll tell him you're here."

Violet leaned over to whisper in her mother's ear, "I hope she's not upset."

Hope raised her chin. "I believe she had a chance to marry him and turned up her nose. Serves her right."

"Can I have a peppermint stick?" Violet asked.

"Of course, dear. Get a licorice one for Grandpa," Hope said.

Becky returned quickly. "He can see her now."

"Fine. I'll finish my shopping while he examines her."

Becky nodded. Her face paler than usual, the young woman set about filling Hope's order. But the older woman could tell Becky was uncomfortable. Hope thought about saying something but decided against it. When she finished her order, she went around back to collect her daughter.

The exam was finished and Dr. Rhodes was talking to Violet when Hope entered the room.

"Now, missy, I know this baby has been growing inside you a mite longer than you've been married."

Violet looked down at her hands. "Yes," she mumbled so low it was almost unintelligible.

"Never you mind. What's important is that we are ready for delivery. Be prepared. Can you give me an approximate date when you think this event...occurred?"

Violet cast her gaze to her hands.

"I can." And she did.

"Well, then. Taking that into account and my examination of you, I expect you to be delivering in about six or seven weeks. Keep track. I'll stop out and see you about then."

"Thank you, doctor," Violet said.

"You won't tell anyone, Doctor?" Hope asked, wringing her hands.

"Nobody's business, Mrs. Wilcox. Nobody's business."

Hope and Violet stopped in the store to buy some spice sticks.

"We have a new flavor, clove."

"Cloves are mighty strong," Hope said, shaking her head.

"I might try it," Violet said.

Becky eyed her coolly. "Why don't you smell it first?"

"All right."

Becky unwrapped a stick and held it out. Violet leaned over and took a good whiff. She coughed. "It's a might strong, but I like it. I'll take it."

Becky handed the clove stick to the young woman and the honey stick to her mother. Violet took a lick. "Hmm. This is mighty spicy but good. Thank you, Becky," she said.

Becky gave a nod. Her gaze swept over Violet and took in the obvious bulge of a growing child. Violet noticed the redhead's face color slowly and her eyes water. Guilt grabbed Violet's gut. If it hadn't been for her and the trick she played on Sam, Becky might be the married one expecting Sam's child. She eased her bulk behind the counter and dabbed Becky's face with her hanky.

"I'm so sorry, Becky. So sorry," Violet said. Although Becky didn't know it, Violet understood the pain of a broken heart and the longing to be with that one special man.

"Sorry? For what? I had my chance with Sam Chesney. He proposed to me first, you know. Yes, he did. And I turned him down. So don't go feelin' sorry for me, missy." Becky swiped at Violet's hand and pushed by her to enter the back room.

Hope tugged on Violet's sleeve. "Come on. Time to get supper ready."

The women returned to the Abiel Wilcox home. Violet knitted a pair of booties for the baby while Hope got the meal ready. Abiel Wilcox lit his pipe and sat back in his rocker.

"Mighty nice to have you home, Violet. Mighty nice."

"Miss me, Grampa?"

He nodded as he pressed a lit match to his tobacco.

"I miss you, too. It's hard being a farmer's wife."

"I don't doubt it."

They sat sharing the room in easy silence until supper was on the table. Violet ate, then climbed in bed. She closed her eyes and dreamed that Zeb showed up at the christening. Tossing and turning, she started awake, still sleepy with her dream. Reality hit her. Zeb was probably a thousand miles away and wishing for him to come back was a waste of time. She laid back down, closed her eyes and returned to a more peaceful sleep.

SAM GOT THE ANIMALS settled in for the night, then poked around in the kitchen, looking for something to eat. He didn't much like having to make his own meals, tend the little garden, or make sure the animals had water. Those were Violet's jobs.

And he had to do them after putting in a full day from sun up to sun down plowing and planting. He'd worked extra hard, walking faster and urging Ol' Amos to speed up. The ox gave a snort or two but otherwise tried to oblige his master. Plowing, planting, plowing, planting, rustling up some leftover stew and brew for sustenance at night made his days long and arduous.

Still a young man, he yearned for some fun. When he'd been an apprentice blacksmith, he had time at night for fun. He'd get together with Benjamin or Josiah or both, drink some beer, throw darts, or play cards.

Now his life was work, eat, sleep, only to get up and start all over again. He missed his friends and the fun of being young and carefree. With a child coming, Sam saw that his days of fun would be permanently behind him. He had to be responsible, harvest and sell his vegetables and make enough money to take care of his offspring.

The burden of being a father weighed heavily on Sam. His father seemed to be such a natural at fathering. Sam recalled days spent working alongside his father and nights spent around a fire, his dad telling stories, and them eating sugar candies.

Sure at nineteen he was old enough to be a father, still he didn't feel it. He heated a mug of cider and stood in the doorway of the small house looking out over the field. By gum, he wouldn't have all the fields plowed come April. But he'd do his darndest to have them all planted by halfway through that month.

He bit his lip. Lucky joined him.

"Golly, Lucky. We're late planting. Do you think our crops will be smaller?"

The dog turned soulful eyes on his master and thumped his tail once, slowly.

"Yeah. Right. I don't think so, either. If we can harvest three quarters of our land, we'll have enough to make it through the winter and put some away, too." Sam knew that was a big "if." They had yet to make it through the rainy season. How much of their planted seeds would wash away in a heavy spring storm? He shuddered to think.

"We'll have to trust in God to be behind us, Lucky," Sam said, reaching down to scratch the dog behind the ears before turning to go into the house.

The small space was quiet. Too quiet for Sam's liking. Violet wasn't there to be banging about in the kitchen, jabbering away about the christening, the difficulty in peeling potatoes, and her hopes she wouldn't burn the stew this time.

He'd grown accustomed to her presence. Somehow, having Violet there made it not just a house, but a home. Sam uncovered leftovers and set them to warm up over the fire. He'd be there two more days with only Lucky for company. He frowned as he thought about how he'd make meals. What would he eat? The bread would be gone, and he'd never baked bread before. This was no time to try to figure it out.

He did have root vegetables in the larder, and he and Lucky could attempt to bag a duck. That would suffice. Oh, and the leftover pies. He smiled at Hope's generosity. She'd made the larger sized pies so there would be plenty.

"Not so bad, my friend," he said to the dog. "We'll get by. Might go into town a bit early. Maybe in time for dinner. What you say?" He glanced at the dog, who barked.

At sunset, Sam crawled into bed alone. The bed that had always appeared to be too small for Sam and his wife, now seemed too big. He ran his palm over the sheet next to him. He missed Violet. Snuggling together with her made their thin quilts enough protection against cold nights. Her soft warmth pleased him. Lucky seized the opportunity and jumped on the bed.

"Just this once, boy, just this once," said a sleepy Sam.

The dog curled up next to him, bringing warmth and companionship. The two slept peacefully through the night until daybreak.

AT SUNRISE, SAM FINISHED the row he'd begun plowing the day before, then took care of the animals. He petted Midnight's head. She liked him better than Violet. When his chores were done, he saddled up the horse, fed himself and Lucky and set out for Fitch's Eddy.

It wasn't a long trip. The town was roughly eight miles away. He figured it would take about an hour on horseback with Lucky running alongside to traverse the rough road. If Lucky slowed, He'd simply drape his buddy across the saddle and continue on. Sam took care with the horse to make sure he didn't stumble and fall. If the creature broke a leg or even got a serious injury, that would be the end of him. So Sam slowed the journey down.

He figured he'd be at the Abiel Wilcox house by breakfast time.

"Just in time for some of those cinnamon buns, boy," Sam said to Lucky.

His stomach growled, and his mouth watered at the thought of that delicacy. He'd been without decent cooking long enough and craved the meals his wife and her family would prepare. He had a hankering for his wife that a man got when they'd been separated. But he doubted he'd be able to sate that appetite under someone else's roof.

Setting easy in the saddle, Sam, the horse, and Lucky picked their way through ruts, rocks, and tree roots that dotted the road to town.

He took time to look around and enjoy watching the sun wake up the world with light and beautiful colors. The sky couldn't have been a clearer blue. He smiled at the idea that the christening of his sister's child would happen on a clear, lovely day.

Of course, he wouldn't have a big christening like the Fitches when his child was born. He hoped his Grandmother would have a gathering at the Inn for the christening. Suddenly he wondered if he'd be the father of a son or daughter?

"Don't matter none to me, Lucky, if the baby's a boy or girl," Sam said to his companion. His thoughts turned to his ability to be a good father. "All I gotta do is do like my father did, boy," Sam said to the dog. "And I'll be the best father this little Chesney ever had."

Pleased with himself for figuring out parenting so neatly, he chuckled. "Ain't nothin' to it. I'll take care of that little one the moment he...or she comes into the world."

They rode on in peaceful silence, enjoying the rough countryside, the tall elms and oaks providing necessary shade on a warm spring day. The rising sun provided enough warmth for the small pack to be fairly comfortable on their journey. The air, still nippy, had not succumbed to spring and turned warm and sweet with the scent of honeysuckle yet.

A little over an hour, they rounded the bend and rode into Fitch's Eddy. Lucky still maintained his stride, but Sam figured he could use a long drink of water. He had acquired a mighty thirst as well. When they got to the Wilcox home, Sam dismounted and brought the horse and dog to the pump. He pumped vigorously, filling a bucket. He put it between the dog and horse and returned to the pump to get fresh water for himself.

Before he could knock on the door, Violet opened. "Sam!" she said, grinning.

She ran out and was in his arms in a flash. Her mother and grandfather interrupted Sam's hungry kiss.

"Sam, my boy, come in, come in," Abiel Wilcox said.

"Breakfast is almost ready," Hope said, wiping her hands on her apron.

Breakfast! The word was a melody to his ears. Violet linked her arm with his and eased him toward the door. Lucky barked, jumped up to lick Violet in the face, then trotted along behind his master. Warmth from the house carried the aroma of cinnamon, sugar, and bacon to Sam's grateful nose.

"Come on, boy, let's eat," he said to the dog, stepping across the threshold. Lucky followed, then curled up on a rug near the fireplace.

WHEN THEY FINISHED breakfast, there was a knock on the door.

"Sam! Sam!" came a young voice. Abiel opened to find little Jem Tanner, Sam's young half-brother. The lad rushed into the house and over to Sam.

"Papa told me to come get you. It's time. Time for Susannah's christening!"

The little boy tugged on Sam's sleeve. "Come on. Come on!"

"Hold it, Jem. I'm coming," Sam said, looking around. "We're all coming."

"The wagons are here. They have sweet rolls and candy!" Jem's eyes grew wide.

Sam shrugged his jacket on. "Come on, Violet, Hope, Abiel. Let's go."

Jem hopped up and down while waiting for the family to be ready. Once all had coats on, they embarked. The walk to the church was about a quarter of a mile. Full of small child energy, Jem ran ahead.

"I'll tell them you're coming," he said.

Sam looked around. Some trees were already showing green leaves. Spring beckoned, reminding Sam that he was behind on planting. He frowned.

"The world will soon bloom again," Violet said. She took Sam's hand to steady herself over the rough, rocky road. As they drew near, they saw the crowd forming. People made their way down the road toward the church.

Sam spied his mother and stepfather ahead. Behind them was Josiah Quint, Sam's first friend in Fitch's Eddy. Benjamin stood by the wagons conferring with his parents. Even craning his neck, Sam couldn't find Sarah.

"Looking for your sister? She must be inside," Hope said, patting his arm.

"Right," Sam said.

He helped Violet trudge up the road as it rose in a slight hill. They stopped several times for her to catch her breath.

"I'm getting so big I can't even walk. Maybe I'm gonna give birth to a giant," she said, her eyebrows knitted.

Sam squeezed her hand. "It only feels like that. You don't look that big," Sam lied. "It'll be all right, honey," he whispered, griping her upper arm and lifting slightly.

Suddenly she stopped. Her face paled. "There are those hateful sisters, Charity and Catherine Bloodgoode."

"Don't worry about them," Hope said, coming up behind her daughter. "They're just jealous, mean-spirited women. They'll never have a good husband like Sam." She sniffed.

As they approached the church, Sam noticed the Bloodgoode sisters staring at Violet's belly with wide eyes. As they were about to say something, Sam caught their eye and shot them a stern look. They backed up a step or two. Catherine clapped her hand over her mouth.

Violet raised her head high and flounced by them as best she could. Sam stared at them while pressing his finger to his lips. Obviously flustered, they stood silently as the Wilcox women passed.

Inside, they took seats in the front. Sam rushed up to the altar to greet his sister. She stood, cradling the beautiful child with soft brown hair and bright eyes, dressed in an elaborate white satin gown.

"Sarah! You did it!" Sam said, attempting to hug her but finding himself blocked by the infant.

She trained a bright, loving smile on him. "Meet Susannah. Isn't she beautiful?"

He turned to gaze at the baby in his sister's arms. "She looks just like you."

"Thank you. Benjamin says the same thing."

"Where is he?"

"Out behind the church, setting up the food," Ann said, taking Susannah from her mother and rocking her.

Sam stopped at the pew where his wife was. "I'll be right back. Have to congratulate Ben."

He snaked his way through the crowd filling the church and ran behind the building. Makeshift tables had been set up, with boards supported by sawhorses. Benjamin picked up platters from the wagons and set them on the tables.

Sam ran up to him.

"Congratulations, old boy! You did it!"

"Sarah did it. I just paced outside the door."

"You've a beautiful daughter, Ben."

"Thank you, Sam. I saw Violet. I wish the same for you. Come, give me a hand."

The men unloaded the food with help from Fitch's servants.

When the task was finished, they stopped for a mug of cider before returning inside for the ceremony.

THE CHRISTENING WAS scheduled for eleven o'clock.

"I'm surprised your father agreed to such a lavish celebration," Sam said.

Benjamin laughed. "Let me tell you the story," he said, then recounted the conversation from two days earlier to his friend.

"But Elijah, it's your grandchild! Everyone will think you're mean if you don't offer food and drink," my mother said.

"What do I care what people think?" my father grumbled.

"Papa, please. Do it for me. For Benjamin," Sarah had pleaded.

"Poppycock!" Elijah said, striking a match and attempting to relight his pipe.

"Do it for Susannah," I said handing the crying infant to my father.

The moment the baby made eye contact with the old man, she stopped crying. His gaze met hers and he smiled.

"Then he asked her if she wanted him to give everyone dinner, and the baby made a squeaking noise and smiled. My dad laughed, and that's the end of the story. She's already got him wrapped around her little finger!" Ben said.

Benjamin and Sam laughed together, slapping each other on the back.

"Benjamin! Sam! The ceremony is about to begin," called Ann Fitch before she scurried back inside the church.

Ben ran ahead of Sam as he was to join his wife at the altar. Sam had a secure seat in front. He walked softly so as not to disturb the proceedings. The church was jammed to the hilt. There was a wall of people, four deep in some places, pouring out from the doors of the church.

Sam looked for a small space he could squirm through to get back to his seat. He bumped up against a young woman who turned and frowned at him. It was Becky!

Her eyes widened. "Sam..." she said, her voice unsteady.

"Miss Becky," he replied, tipping his hat. "You're looking mighty fine," he said.

"Shh!" said someone standing nearby.

She gave him a slight curtsy and inched to the left so he could scoot by. As he passed her, a feeling overwhelmed him. He stared into her eyes, and snaked his arm around her waist, pulling her up tight against him. She gasped. In a flash she pushed on his chest and he released her.

He sensed his face turning red. He muttered, "Sorry," in the softest whisper.

She gave a curt nod and put as much space between them as she could in the tight quarters. Sam's mood soured, and he pushed his way through the crowd. When he got to his seat, Violet whispered, "Where were you?"

"Stuck in the crowd," he said.

Although his eyes watched the ceremony, his mind was elsewhere. Seeing Becky again after such a long time and so much that had happened jarred his nerves. He couldn't believe the moment he pressed her up against him, his heart rate took off. He sensed his pulse racing and sweat breaking out on his forehead. Could it be he still had feelings for her?

He did. Strong feelings. Ashamed to admit to himself he was as much in love with Becky now as he was before he married Violet. At once the truth crashed down on him. He'd been more in love with his stupid dream than he had with either Violet or Becky. While the dream had appeared to be perfect when he pictured Becky as his wife, it had become rough around the edges with Violet as his wife.

Her pregnancy made her uncomfortable and she grumbled about it often. Her size prevented her from doing some of her chores, which landed on Sam. The idyllic he had envisioned had become a prison of non-stop work, hard labor in the fields, then tending the animals, and helping with meals.

The dream he chased after had been his all along. If only he'd stayed on with Caleb, saving up to open his own blacksmith shop one day, maybe in another town. And he'd have had Becky by his side. He stared at his hands, roughened from plowing, planting, and chopping wood.

He wouldn't be in this fix if he'd listened to Becky and made her dream his, too.

Now he had a child coming and he didn't have the first notion of how they were going to do the harvesting with a baby to tend to. The wisdom of his late father rang in his ears.

"One task at a time, son." He would follow his father's advice. Still, it seemed he'd messed up his life, lost the one woman who truly loved him. and there'd be no going back.

HAPPY TO SEE HER GRANDSON, but preferring to eat sitting down, Martha Chesney took her plate of food inside the church. A few other older citizens had seized on the same idea. Abiel Wilcox wandered in. He took a seat near Martha.

She eyed him with an unfriendly glare.

"Why, Mrs. Chesney, you are looking lovely today. I must say I admire that hat immensely."

"Butter don't melt in your mouth, do it? You're a mighty fancy talker. What's on your mind, Mr. Abiel Wilcox?" She narrowed her eyes as she gazed at him.

"Why nothing, Mrs. Chesney. Nothing. Can't a man admire an attractive woman?" he said.

"Poppycock. You always got too many compliments, too much flattery rolling off your tongue for the likes of me. What do you really want?"

"Why...nothing. Really."

"You know I'm pretty good at arithmetic, you know. Being an innkeeper and all. And something about your granddaughter, Violet, just don't add up."

"I don't know what you mean," he said, his tone indignant.

"Yes, you do. Stop pretending. I figured it out. She's a mite too big to be only five months along. Looks more like she's ready to give birth any day now." She cut a carrot in two with her fork.

"Why Mrs. Chesney, you insult my daughter, my granddaughter, and me!" he rose to his full height, and put his plate down on the pew.

"I ain't plannin' on telling nobody. I don't want to bring any hardship down on Miss Violet, but you've pulled a fast one on my grandson and I don't cotton to that. You'd better plan to help him out – since he's saved your bacon."

"I don't know what you mean," he insisted, but avoided her stare.

"Yes, you do. And you owe him the truth, too," she said, her eyes boring into his.

"What? I will not!"

"All right, then. I will. I give you one month to fess up to Sam, or I'll expose your lie to him myself."

"You wouldn't!"

"Oh, yes, I would. Sam's a good boy. An honest, hard-working boy. And you and your clan dun takin' advantage of him. He's got a right to know the truth. Mebbe he wants to keep things as they are and mebbe he don't. But it'll be his choice."

Abiel Wilcox turned beet red and hurried out of the building. Martha put the last piece of stew meat in her mouth and watched him leave.

"Martha, what did you say to Mr. Abiel Wilcox to make him leave so fast?" Abigail asked, sitting down next to her mother-in-law.

"Nothin'. Just a little truth talk. That's all."

Abigail dug into her stew, Martha tore off a piece of bread, and the two women ate in silence.

Chapter Thirteen

M id-April

Becky knew Violet was pregnant. She didn't expect her and Sam to be at the christening.

"Foolish girl," she spat out to herself. Of course, the baby was Sam's niece. He had to be there. She didn't want to see him. Startled when he came up behind her, she let out a gasp. Their gazes met. Shocked, Becky could swear she saw the same heat in Sam's eyes when he looked at her that she had always seen there. They had heat, glorious, fresh, wholesome heat.

When she thought she might run into him at the ceremony, she'd expected to see nothing in his eyes for her. He was married and about to become a father with another woman. What could he possibly feel for her? But she'd been wrong.

The expression on his face when they laid eyes on each other told her he'd read the truth in her eyes. She'd never stopped loving Sam, expected she never would. Had she known he would be right there up close, she'd have guarded her expression. But he'd taken her by surprise and so the truth showed in her eyes and on her face. And he saw it. She knew he saw it.

Ashamed, mortified to have Sam Chesney know she still loved him, she tried to avoid him the rest of the time. In fact, she'd implored her mother to leave early.

"Are you serious? Leave all this food? Not on your life. Do you see there? Those are French eclairs. Never had one myself, mind you. But I plan to have one today. What's your hurry? There's going to be music, too. I see Alexander Austin and Zacaria Lee brought their fiddles. This is a celebration. A new babe is born. Do you think I can talk your father into just one polka?"

Becky didn't hear half of what her mother was saying. Once she realized Mrs. Rhodes had no plans to leave soon, Becky looked for a way to avoid Sam. She stood by a tree as her gaze searched the crowd for him. If she could see where he was, she could move away.

"Avoiding me, are you?" came a masculine voice behind her. She jumped. Too late to run away. Trapped, she searched her mind for what to say.

"No, no, Mr. Chesney." Becky fussed with the pleats in her skirt as she looked for a way to escape.

"Mr. Chesney? Really?" Sam cocked an eyebrow.

"Yes," she said, digging a toe of her boot in the dirt.

"How are you? Are you all right?"

Anger rose in Becky's chest. "Of course, I'm all right. What did you think? Did you think? Did you think because you got married that I'd taken to my bed or died or something?"

"No, no. I didn't. I'm glad you're all right. I miss you," Sam said, then cast his gaze to his foot. "Sorry. I didn't mean to say that."

"But you did, didn't you?" Tears rose in Becky's throat. "Why did you do it, Sam? Why did you tear our hearts out?" she asked in a forceful whisper.

He took her hand and raised it to his lips. She yanked it away immediately.

"Don't. Don't," she said, her courage and control slipping.

"Becky, I..." When he raised his gaze to hers, she saw his pain. It tore through her and matched her own.

She pushed away from him, covered her mouth with her hand and skittered away, weaving through the crowd. She bumped into her mother.

"I'm going home," she said firmly.

"Why? What's wrong? You sick?" her mother asked, casting a concerned look her way.

"Just an upset stomach. I'll be fine. Bye," Becky kissed her mother's cheek then hurried away. She took the back road, the one where she and Sam used to meet secretly. Filled with memories the deserted path did nothing to quiet her nerves. With tears she could no longer contain streaming down her cheeks, she moved faster and faster, seeking the sanctuary of the store.

Finally, she was inside. She shut and bolted the door behind her. She rushed into the back room where there was a bed, threw herself down and sobbed.

Within two minutes she had regained her composure. She rinsed and dried her face, then went out to the store. She unlocked the door, sat on a stool behind the counter and awaited the arrival of the next customer.

SAM TOOK SEVERAL DEEP breaths in an attempt to regain his composure after his encounter with Becky. Hope Wilcox approached him.

"Hi, Sam. We were wondering if you'd give permission for Violet to stay with us for a while. Just until she delivers the baby. Your home is a little remote. When she goes into labor, she'd be far from the doctor. Here she would be close by. Doctor Rhodes said it wouldn't be long. Just a few weeks."

"If that's what Violet wants, it's fine."

"Oh, good. She wouldn't be much use to you these last few weeks anyway."

Sam tried to smile. Now he'd return alone to deal with plowing, planting, the animals and providing meals, but Hope was correct that Violet wouldn't be much use. And she'd require tending to also.

"I'll come by once a week with food for you. Heaven knows you probably don't know a thing about cooking."

"I'd be mighty obliged."

"Good. It's settled then."

Violet joined them.

"He's agreed, dear. Let me go get Father," Hope said, then faced Sam. "Abiel will drive you back to your house tonight." She left her daughter alone with her husband.

"Are you sure it's all right if I stay with Mother and Grandfather?" Violet's eyebrows knitted.

"Yes. She's right. It would take me a long time to get the doctor when your time comes."

She nodded. "I like living with you, it's just..."

He patted her hand. "I understand. It's all right, Vi. Don't worry."

Maybe this time alone would allow him to get Becky out of his system, though he doubted it. He hated to admit it, even to himself, but he and Violet were not truly suited to each other. Not like Sam and Becky. He told himself they'd only had six months together. Maybe after a year or two, they'd be more compatible. It wasn't that he didn't like Violet, he simply felt more comfortable with Becky, who shared his views on almost everything.

He looked up at the sky. Sundown wouldn't be for another couple of hours, but he might as well get home sooner rather than later. He turned his collar up against a stiff wind that had arrived. Abiel Wilcox's voice interrupted his thoughts.

"Ready, Sam?"

"I'll say goodbye to Sarah and Benjamin, then we can go," Sam said. He approached his sister who was fussing over the baby.

"I'm leaving, Sarah."

"Where's Violet?"

"She's going to stay here until she delivers," he said.

Sarah handed the baby to her mother-in-law and hugged her brother. Abigail joined them, then Caleb.

"Where's Violet?" Sam's mother asked.

"She's staying here until she delivers," Sam repeated. "You all keep asking me the same questions."

"We love you, dear boy," Abby said.

"I'm not a boy, Mother. I'm going to be a father, too, in a few weeks."

"True."

"Abigail, give Sam the respect he's due. He's got his own place now. He's a full gown man," Caleb said, clapping his stepson on the back.

Sam smiled. Though he wasn't Sam's biological father, Caleb always stuck up for Sam.

He bent to kiss the baby's head. "She sure looks a whole lot like you, Sarah."

He shook Benjamin's hand. His mother hugged him and farewells were said. Before he left, his grandmother took his arm and pulled him aside.

She looked nervous. "Sam, I want to ask you something."

He raised his eyebrows, "Yes, Grandma. What is it?"

Her eyes darted around.

"No one can hear us. What is it?" Sam tamped down his impatience.

"I...I...are you sure?"

"Sure of what?"

She made eye contact, then looked away. "Nothing, dear. Nothing." She patted his arm and graced him with a warm smile.

"Be well, Grandma," Sam said, hugging her. He looked for Abiel and waved.

"Ready?" his father-in-law asked.

"Yes," he said, then followed Abiel to the wagon.

Once he arrived home, he unloaded the food Hope had prepared and then pumped water for the animals, then fixed himself a mug of cider. He took a walk to the western most field on his property and watched the sun set. Shrubs were budding. New, light green leaves were peeking out of the branches of some trees.

He parceled out some of the chicken, potato and squash casserole for his supper. Glad he'd eaten to excess at the ceremony, for he now had little appetite. The house seemed empty without Violet's chatter and bustling about. He regretted agreeing to her staying in Fitch's Eddy. What could he do? With Hope pressing him, and the logic of her remaining there, he had no choice.

It was the baby's fault. For a moment the prospective father harbored resentment toward the unborn child who already interfered with Sam's farming plans.

Sam wiped his mouth and sat back, washing the food down with some beer. He recalled how beautiful little Susannah Fitch was. Surely babies were inconvenient, but she touched his heart. Maybe, despite the inconvenience, he'd be glad to have a small child part of his growing family? He hoped so, for it was too late to change his mind.

MAY

Sam had worked hard while Violet was away. He'd plowed and planted the last of the fields, finishing about the time the baby was due to arrive. Word reached him just before Violet delivered. Abiel fetched him in the wagon. By the time they got to the Wilcox home, the baby had arrived.

It was a beautiful baby boy.

"I want to name him Zachary," Violet said.

While Sam thought that was a strange choice, he agreed. "And George, after my father, for his middle name?"

"Fine. Zachary George Chesney," she said.

They spent two weeks at the Wilcox's home. Sam showed off his child to all his family and everyone in town. Elijah Fitch expressed some jealousy that Sam had had a son. While Elijah loved his granddaughter, he did regret she wasn't a boy.

Sam journeyed home often on horseback to pump water for the animals, but then returned to town. Although the planting was done, he had to be there to take care of the animals. He'd grown accustomed to living in his own home, small as it was.

Violet seemed happy in her family's house. Hope ran herself ragged taking care of them and the new baby. Even Abiel pitched in by chopping firewood

"I'm going home at the end of the week and plan to take my wife and son with me," Sam announced. "Violet?"

"All right," she said, but her expression was stiff and unyielding. "I have to go to the store before we leave."

Sam nodded. He wondered how it would be to live with a reluctant wife. He noticed she tucked a paper in her pocket before taking her leave. Though he wondered what it was, she bustled about gathering her things, giving him no chance to ask, and it was soon forgotten. He carted Violet's and Zachary's things to the wagon. Abiel and Violet holding the baby sat in front and Sam rode in back.

Spring had blossomed. Bright sunshine kissed the days, and the air grew warmer. Sam walked through his fields, looking for signs of sprouts. He prayed his seeds were taking root and that he would soon have vegetables a-plenty to sell and pay his farm debt, with some left to save. He remembered his father's guidance about having patience.

"Growing food in soil takes time, son," George Chesney had said when Sam insisted the carrots were ready and pulled up a few to find vegetables measuring only an inch.

In the meantime, he helped out at home, took the animals to graze on the new, fresh grass, milked the goat, and rocked the baby in the fine new rocker his sister had sent as a birthing gift. With cooking, washing, and sewing clothes for the baby, Violet's day filled up fast. Sam missed the days when they would sit by the barn and watch the sunset together.

After Zachary's birth, Violet grew distant. Of course, she had many more duties than before, but it wasn't simply that she was tired, she had turned cold. Gone were the little gestures of affection he'd come to look forward to. At night, she'd roll over and fall asleep or pretend to be asleep to avoid making love.

Sam didn't know what to do. He'd ask her what was wrong, and she simply shook her head and said "Nothing." But he didn't believe her. After pleading with her to tell him, he'd lose his temper and yell. Violet would take the baby and sink to the floor in a corner of the house and cry.

At his wits end, he decided to speak to Caleb. Before he could broach the subject of a trip to Fitch's Eddy, she spoke up.

"I want to go home. Visit my mother and grandfather." She sniffed.

"Fine idea. I need some things in town, too."

"Tomorrow. I want to go tomorrow."

"All right. But we'll have to take Amos. He's mighty slow."

"I don't care. Tomorrow it is," she'd said, then stomped off to the cradle to feed Zachary.

That night he prayed his stepfather would have the answer. Had his mother acted like that when Jem was born? He didn't see a change in how she reacted to Caleb. Maybe this was not typical behavior after a woman gave birth? He hoped to ask Benjamin as well. Between the two men, they should be able to share some wisdom with Sam.

AFTER THE LONG RIDE with Amos pulling their small wagon, Violet, Sam, and Zachary arrived in Fitch's Eddy. Hope was thrilled to see them. She donned her apron as soon as she saw them.

"Zachary is a darling!" Hope cooed over the child.

"Handsome young'un," Abiel said.

Violet lit up, her smile returning larger than before. Her pride in the child warmed Sam's heart. After getting his wife and son settled in, Sam headed for the blacksmith shop. The heat from the fire hit him like a hot tornado.

"I forgot how hot it gets in here," Sam said, stepping back.

"Howdy!" Caleb put his work down, took off the leather glove and shook Sam's hand. Then he patted the younger man on the back. "How are you doing? How's fatherhood?"

"I'm all right. Zachary is a good baby. Can you take a break for a few minutes? I need to talk to you."

Caleb's eyebrows drew together. "Sure, son. Give me a minute." Caleb put the piece he was working on down, took off his other glove and his apron. "Let's go outside. It's hot in here."

They sat on a bench behind the shop they used for a retreat when the heat threatened to overwhelm them. "Is there a problem?" Caleb frowned.

"Not with the baby. He's just fine. But it's... It's Violet."

"She sick or something?"

"No. She's not the same woman she was before the baby."

"Oh. That. Right. It takes their bodies some time to recover."

"How much time?" Sam asked, hope in his voice.

"Dunno. Depends on the woman, I guess."

"Oh, you mean before she... uh... she wants to..."

"Yeah, yeah," Caleb said quickly.

"Weeks? Months?" Sam asked.

"Depends on the woman. I'm not going to get more specific here because I'd be talking about your mother."

"Oh, right. Yes, then. But I mean. She's not nice to me anymore."

"Nice you mean...uh...at night?" Caleb shifted in his seat.

"No. Anytime. She doesn't smile at me. Or want to sit by me. We used to watch the sunset together every night. But no more. She avoids me. I don't know what to do."

"Wish I could help you. That didn't happen to me. But as I said. Every woman is different. Give her more time. I've got to get back to work," Caleb said, wiping sweat from his brow with his sleeve.

"Sure. Yes. All right. Thanks for the time and the advice," Sam said.

He left Caleb at the smithy shop and headed toward the general store. Despite what had happened at the christening, he wanted to see Becky. He needed a couple of nails – his excuse for going to the store.

He almost bumped into Violet coming out of the store. Again she carried a paper. At first glance it looked like an envelope. When she looked up and saw it was Sam, she stuffed the paper in her pocket. He raised his eyebrows, but before he could ask her about it, she spoke.

"I have to get back. Zachary's feeding time," she said, scurrying away.

Curiosity arose in Sam. He pushed through the door to the store and directed his gaze to the counter. Becky was there measuring fabric and cutting it for Mrs. Austin, the mother of William and Matthew.

"Be right with you, Sam," she said, wielding the scissors.

"How are those boys of yours, Mrs. Austin?"

"Full of the devil, I declare."

"Still visiting Sunshine?" Sam asked.

"Your grandmother traded one of Sunshine's babies to us for a ham. The boys be visiting her until she's old enough to come live with us. I declare they love those goats! I don't see the attraction," Mrs. Austin said. She paid for the material and placed it carefully in her sack.

"Good day to you, Mr. Chesney. And congratulations on your new son," Mrs. Austin said.

Sam tipped his hat, then took it off. "Thank you, Mrs. Austin. Glad to know the boys will be taking care of Sunshine's offspring."

Sam and Becky stood in silence until Mrs. Austin left the store.

"What do you want, Sam?" Becky asked, a note of annoyance in her voice.

"Nails. I need three. No, four. This size," he said, drawing out one from his pocket.

Becky picked up the nail and turned to face the stack of boxes against the back wall of the store. After finding the right box, she plucked out four nails.

"Here you go. That'll be two cents, please."

Sam reached into his pocket and pulled out the coins. He plunked them down on the counter. When Becky reached for them, he trapped her hand there by placing his over hers. She looked up.

"What?"

"Can't we be friends?" he asked, gently.

"No," she replied, pulling her hand out from under his.

"Why not?"

"You know why," Becky said, her voice trembling.

"I still care about you, Becky. I always will," he said.

"Then that's your cross to bear."

Sam sighed, put the nails in his pocket and turned toward the door.

"Wait," she said, grabbing his sleeve.

"What?"

"I think you ought to know that Violet has picked up two letters here in the past month."

"What?"

"You heard me. Two letters," Becky repeated.

"Do you know who they're from?" he asked.

She shook her head. "No, I don't. No return address. Just wondered if you knew. Guess you didn't."

"No, I didn't."

"Figured you being her husband had a right to know," She made eye contact.

"I do have a right to know. Might be something totally innocent," he said.

"Might be," she replied.

"Maybe a surprise she's planning for me?" Sam asked, grasping at straws.

"Might be," Becky said, then hesitated. "I hope it is."

"So do I." Sam turned toward the door. "Thank you for telling me."

"Figured you had a right to know," she repeated.

He walked slowly to the door. Before he opened it, he turned to face her. "We both know it isn't a surprise for me, don't we?" he asked her, a small shred of hope still echoing in his voice.

Becky shrugged. "Don't know. Don't wanna guess. Have a good day, Sam."

He gave a wan smile before he pushed open the door.

Chapter Fourteen

D
r. Rhodes, carrying his black bag, entered the store.

"Was that Sam Chesney I saw leaving?" he asked.

Becky looked up from sorting a new shipment of thread. "Yes."

"And?"

"And what?"

"Did you tell him?" The doctor plopped his rump on a stool behind the counter.

"I did." Becky wound ribbon around a piece of cardboard and fastened it with a pin, then placed it on the shelf.

"Do you think that was wise?" The doctor cocked an eyebrow.

Becky raised her chin. "He has a right to know," she insisted.

"But that isn't your business, is it?" her father pressed on.

"No. Maybe not. But since I'm workin' here, the post is my business."

"But not who gets mail and who doesn't and who it's from and what it's about."

"I don't know who it's from or what it's about. So I couldn't tell him."

"But you would if you could have?" her father asked.

"Probably. All right. Yes, I would," she admitted, unwrapping a second package of thread.

"Why? It doesn't concern you. Sam Chesney no longer concerns you. And his wife shouldn't either." Dr. Rhodes helped himself to a licorice stick.

"He has a right to know."

"That's his business." He unwrapped the stick and took a lick.

"But she's his wife. And she didn't tell him about the letters. He has a right to know 'cause she's his wife."

"Instead of you," the doctor said, his tone mellow.

"I don't know what you mean," Becky lied, dropping a spool of yellow thread on the floor.

"You know darn well, Rebecca, what I mean. You weren't perhaps trying to ruin her in her husband's eyes, were you?" The Doctor put the candy stick in his mouth.

"I'm not the one getting secret letters," Becky said, rearranging the spools of thread.

The doctor placed his hand on his daughter's arm. "Still haven't settled yourself to the fact that he's married to someone else, have you?"

Becky put down the two spools of thread she held and hung her head but didn't respond.

"I know it's hard, sweetheart. But you must accept it." He slipped his arm around her shoulders and pulled her toward him.

She burst into tears, hiding her face in her father's coat. He closed his arms around her. After a moment, she regained control. Her father fished a hanky from his pocket and gave it to her.

"I'm trying. It's hard, Father. Oh, so very hard," she admitted, wiping her eyes. She blew her nose, then straightened up. The bell over the door jingled as the door opened.

"Good morning, Josiah, what can I do for you?" Becky asked.

Her father patted her shoulder and slipped into the back room.

"Did I just see Sam Chesney in here, Becky?" Josiah Quint asked.

"You did. What do you need." She stiffened. She'd had more than enough conversation about Sam Chesney.

"What was he doing here?" Josiah made eye contact.

"Buying nails."

"Oh."

"Do you need something or you just come to check up on Sam?" Becky asked, narrowing her eyes.

Josiah colored a bit. "No, no. I do. I need some flour, a pound, I reckon, and yeast."

"Baking bread?" she asked, walking to the big flour sack.

"Tryin'," Josiah said, grinning.

"I'm sure my mother would be happy to give you some advice," Becky said, measuring the flour.

"Thanks. I'll stop by on my way home." While Becky filled his order, he leaned against the counter. "So. You still stuck on Sam Chesney?"

Becky stopped moving. "He's married, or haven't you heard? And how is that your business who I'm stuck on?"

"Dunno. Figured if you ain't stuck on him no more, you might get a mite stuck on me."

Becky blushed as red as the crimson ribbon. "Why Josiah Quint! You flirtin' with me?"

"Might be. Might be."

She shoved his purchase over the counter toward him. "Here. Go peddle your love eyes somewhere else."

"Aw, Becky. Don't be mad. Can't help it if I like you, can I?"

"Try, Josiah, try." With that, she raised her chin, glared at him and disappeared into the back of the store.

SAM AMBLED BACK TO the Wilcox home. The information about the letters confused him. Who could Violet be writing to? He had never seen her with anyone. Maybe she had an aunt she was fond of who lived somewhere else? But the idea of her writing to a man tied in with her cool disposition lately. Could she have feelings for someone else, someone he didn't know about?

He shook his head for a second. Ridiculous! She'd just delivered his child. No way could she be thinking about anyone else. Women didn't do that, did they? No, it must be some distant relative she was corresponding with. If that was true, why did she keep it a secret?

Thinking about the situation made him uneasy, so he decided not to press the issue. Violet was simply overwhelmed, he thought. With the baby, the farm work, and him working so hard he wasn't around all the time. Well, a young woman could get flustered. She'd bounce back in another week or two, he figured.

When he arrived at the house, the aroma of stew permeated the air, making his stomach growl. Hope Wilcox was a darn good cook. There were visitors in the living room. Mrs. Austin with William and Matthew had come to call.

"See what the Austins brought," Abiel said, pointing to a basket of fresh vegetables and sweet rolls.

There was tea and a plate of tarts on the table. Sam sat down and ate, listening to the chatter of the women. How they went on about his son! Sam looked forward to the days when the boy could help with the farming, like he had helped his father. He sighed. Too bad George hadn't lived to see his grandson.

Sam, Violet, and Zachary stayed another week. The warm May days grew blustery. Sam checked the sky. Dark clouds were heading their way.

"We'd better leave tomorrow. Looks like we're in for a storm," Sam said.

"All right. I'll get Zachary ready."

"Let's leave early," Sam said.

Violet nodded and took the baby in for his nap.

"Sure will miss having the little one here with us. But I see what you mean. Storm's a comin' all right. Best you be safe in your house," Abiel Wilcox said.

Sam awoke when Violet got up to feed their son. He checked the sky again. The clouds had thickened.

"I hope we can make it home before this hits," Sam said.

Violet nodded. When she finished feeding the baby, Sam slipped his arm around her shoulders. He leaned in to kiss her, but she turned away.

"What?"

"Not tonight."

"Not any night!"

"Shh. Keep your voice down," Violet said.

"What's wrong, Violet? Did I do something?" he asked, taking her hand and raising it to his lips.

She looked away, avoiding his gaze. "No, Sam. You haven't done anything. I'm just tired. The baby keeps me very busy."

"Oh. I see. Then when he's not so demanding, you'll come back to me?"

"Let's not worry about that now," she said, glancing out the window. "We'll have a lot more to worry about with this storm coming and the planting so new."

Sam slid back in bed. Violet had touched on something that had been on his mind ever since he saw the clouds. His planting was new, too new. The seeds wouldn't have taken root and if the storm was severe, much of his work might be washed away. He lay back in bed, his brows drawn together, as he searched his brain for a way to save his work from what might be a devastating lashing from Mother Nature.

BY THE TIME SAM, VIOLET, and the baby got underway, light rain had started. Abiel loaded them in the Conestoga wagon. Sam rode behind in his wagon pulled by Amos. Both wagons bumped over the uneven road. The bumpy ride made the baby cry. Even though the babe was in the wagon ahead of him, the sound made Sam's teeth hurt. He hated that his child was unhappy, but there was nothing to be done.

By the time they reached the house, the rain had picked up. Sam ran inside with the child, hoping to step between raindrops. Violet followed. Abiel carried in their valises, then bid a hasty goodbye.

"I wanna get back before this gets worse," he said.

"I understand," Sam said. "Safe travels."

Exhausted from the trip, both Violet and Zachary fell asleep. Sam was left on his own to rustle up supper. Hope had packed plenty of food, so Sam didn't worry. He brought in more logs to dry out inside and started a fire with the ones that were already there. The house took on a chill that seeped into Sam's bones. He made sure Violet and the baby were well covered, then he sat with a plate of stew and buttered bread by the fire to warm himself.

Thunder crashed overhead. From time-to-time, he went to the window to see how the storm progressed. He didn't need to do that as he could hear the pounding on the roof of his house by the angry rain.

His biggest field was at the bottom of a hill. He prayed the water rushing down wouldn't take his seeds and seedlings with it. But the way it was coming down, he figured his plants would end up in the next county.

Being by himself, he didn't bother to light an oil lamp or a candle. He simply added more logs to the fire and stretched out on an animal fur in front of the fireplace. Wind howled as it blew by, itching to make its way through the crevasses in the logs of his home. He felt an occasional draft when a gust managed to get in. While he'd expected the storm would bring warm air, he'd been mistaken.

He set a small fire in the bedroom fireplace to keep Violet and the baby warm. Quite a bit after sundown, Sam crawled into bed next to his wife. The storm still raged, but Sam was tuckered out from worrying, traveling, and chopping wood. He fell asleep quickly.

A loud crack of thunder woke all three. It was pitch black outside, except for the shine of a cold moon. Zachary cried and Violet fussed over him.

"Do some... Sam. Do something!" she cried, rocking the child, who would not be consoled.

"What do you want me to do? Go out there and yell at the storm? Tell it to quit makin' noise?"

She looked contrite but didn't reply.

Sam threw the covers down and went to the living room window. The sound on the roof had not abated. He looked out the window and saw giant puddles forming by the house. Grabbing a jacket, Sam ripped open the door and ran outside barefoot. He stood in the rain and faced his field. Inside, Lucky barked, so Sam let him out.

Together, man and dog picked their way through the rain-drenched fields. Sam sank ankle-deep in the mud. Rivulets of water ran down the hill and across his field. Row after row, once carefully plowed and planted, had turned to mud puddles. Seeds and tiny plants floated in the small rivers rushing to level ground. Followed by a soaking-wet dog, Sam tromped through field-after-field. With no concern for his own wellbeing, he stomped through the rows that he'd counted on bearing vegetables in the fall harvest.

As his hopes and dreams rushed past him in the muddy troughs, the rain kept beating him, pounding on his head, shoulders, and back with no let up. He'd never seen so much rain, so furious and destructive.

Shading his eyes from the persistent drops, he turned to stare at his house. Water rose by his front door. Soon it would cover the floor inside if he didn't do something. But what could he do? How could he stop the rain?

Lucky barked his query. Shaking the water off his coat, the dog gave him a curious stare.

"I know, boy. You don't know what we're doing out here, do you? Well I don't either. Come on," Sam said, racing back to the house.

He opened the door to see a small puddle crawling across the living room floor. Water had crept in underneath the door, where it just missed connecting with the doorframe. Frantic to stop the flow, Sam searched for anything he could find to stuff into the cracks.

He came upon a bag of rags Violet used for cleaning. He grabbed them and his own clothes and dropped to his knees. Lucky huddled down near what was left of the fire. Sam stuffed frantically. When the flow had stopped, temporarily, he tended to the fire, adding more logs until it blazed again. He picked up the fur rug, and with one remaining rag, wiped Lucky down.

He used a washrag to wipe himself down. Once he was dry, he put on a shirt and his jacket and huddled with his dog by the fire. In fifteen minutes, he stopped shaking. No sound came from the bedroom. Sam figured the baby must have gone to sleep. In stocking feet, Violet crept out of the back room into the living room.

Sam faced her. "We're done for."

"What?" She drew near the fire and warmed her hands.

"We're finished. All the seeds have washed away. There's nothing left."

Violet's hand covered her mouth.

"Yep. That's right. Done. Finished," Sam said, then sneezed.

WHEN THE RAIN STOPPED, Sam ventured out with Lucky by his side.

"Don't be gone long. Supper is almost ready," Violet said.

Mist covered the fields. Occasional droplets fell, splashing on his nose. Sam stood riveted to the path in front of the house. He looked all around at each field. There was almost no grass visible in the two big fields at the bottom of the hill. All he saw was brown, both fields were mudholes.

Weeds, sticks, and stones had been washed down the hill, propelled by the powerful rain. The debris had traveled over the one field that hugged the hill to one closer to his house. As hard as he looked he couldn't discern sprouted seedlings from grass.

"Doesn't matter," he muttered to himself. It was true. It didn't matter which was grass and which were his plantings because there was no way to get them back into the ground. The rubble had spread out in some places and piled up in others.

Desperate to find some areas where his plantings were undisturbed, he walked the fields. Sinking ankle deep in mud in some places, Sam continued on. Despite the wind and the water soaking his pants and traveling to the rest of him. The mist chilled him. Still, he continued onward.

The field to the south of the house had fared better because it didn't have the hill adding speed to the pouring rain, creating deep rivulets and mud slides. He figured about one third of the south field remained intact and might yield some crops.

Eager to bring Amos out and plow the ruined fields again, hoping there would be enough sun and rain to give him a late harvest, he realized he could never get Amos through the mud. And what if he did? No one could plant in wet mud. It was unstable. He had no idea when the land would dry out enough to be replanted. Looking at the pools of water in the middle of two fields, he reckoned it might be as much as a week before he and Amos could plant again. He'd used up all his seed, he'd have to get more. He had no money for seed. He barely had enough to feed them. He'd been counting on the Wilcox's generosity and his grandmother's, too. But now he had no idea when he could ever repay them. Could he replant and reap enough to feed his family until next year? He shook his head.

"Doubtful."

They'd have to move in with the Wilcox's until Sam could get back on his feet, if he ever could. Not easy to recover from such a big blow. He'd no idea what his father would have done since he'd never lived through a squall like the one that just left Fitch's Eddy.

Disheartened, he didn't notice how the clouds and the mist had turned even colder until his body shivered. Pushing tall weeds out of the way, man and dog trudged home through the mud, sticks, and stones. Sam entered the house, took off his soaking shoes and jacket, and padded over to the fire. He added two logs. Lucky curled up next to the fire. Sam sat on the floor, idly petting his dog. With eyebrows drawn together, he watched Violet put a meal on the table.

There was rabbit, potatoes, carrots, squash, and onions. There was half a loaf of bread and some fresh goat cheese. The smell of the food cooking whetted Sam's appetite. He also detected a slight aroma of cinnamon. He loved the way Violet added a few spices to her cooking to make meals of the same ingredients a touch different to the tastebuds.

He sat at the table. She poured cider.

"Well?" she asked, sitting down and picking up her fork.

"Fields are ruined. I'd be lucky to get a couple of acres plowed again. I don't know how Ol' Amos would do slogging through the mud," he said, filling his fork.

"Mud?"

"Yep. That's about all there is on a good portion of our land. Mud. Just mud. Dirty stinkin' mud." He put the fork in his mouth.

"What are you going to do?"

"I'm gonna go into Fitch's Eddy, buy more seed, harness up Amos and re-plow any parts of the fields that dry out enough."

"But you can't plant now. You'll never get a harvest."

"Got no other choice. We'll have a late harvest. Real late. But maybe enough to feed us until it's time to plant again," Sam said, slicing a potato in half with his fork.

Violet's eyes got wide. She jumped up from the table. "We'll starve!"

"No, no we won't. If we have to, we can stay at the Inn. My grandma will help us."

"I don't want to move back in with my parents or your family. I like being independent."

"Well, honey, there may be nothing we can do about it. Sit down. Finish your meal. We both need all the strength we can muster," Sam said.

They ate in silence. After dinner, Sam had a sneezing fit. He added more logs to the fire, checked their supply, much of which was still water-logged from the rain and brought more logs inside to dry out. A shiver ran up his spine.

"I'm going to bed," he said.

Violet stood at the sink tidying up after their meal. "Fine," she said, tight-lipped, her beautiful skin pale in the faint light.

Lucky followed Sam into the bedroom. Sam stoked the fire there and added more wood. The baby slept peacefully. Sam stopped to look at his son. He was beautiful with not a care in the world. He smiled. How wonderful to be that young and have nothing to worry about except growing up!

His father's wisdom came to Sam in a rush. "Dad would say, tomorrow's another day, another chance for success." Although he didn't feel hopeful, Sam clung to that little shred of hope and bundled his chilled body into the bed.

Later when Violet stood by her side of the bed before climbing in, he heard her mumble.

"Starting over may work for you, Sam, but not for me," she whispered. Half asleep, he heard her. He didn't know what she referenced, but her cold tone gave him chills.

Chapter Fifteen

June

The next day when the raging storm had ended, Abiel Wilcox drove his Conestoga wagon to the Chesney farm.

"I'm taking you home with us. Hope insisted. And now that I see what a mess the farm is, I think she was right. Pack up. When the land dries out, you can decide what to do," Abiel said.

With shoulders sagging and head down, Sam approached the wagon. "Take Violet and the baby. I'm sick and I don't want to bring that to your house."

"All right, Sam," Violet said, climbing into the wagon. "Pass Zachary to me."

Sam did as she wanted and stood in the doorway and watched them drive away.

Violet looked back once. Sam looked so pathetic, standing there, his shoulders drooping, his face tired. Even Lucky didn't seem to have much energy. Violet felt a pang of pity for her husband. He'd have to find a way to overcome this setback without her.

If she played her cards right, he'd be replanting alone, and she'd be on her way to a new and better life. She let out a breath. Relief at leaving this hateful life behind flooded through her.

She'd kept her word. More or less. She'd tried as she'd said she would to her mother and grandfather. She never promised to stay forever. And now that the baby was born, she needed to carve out the life she wanted. And it didn't include Sam Chesney.

Remembering the argument she had with her grandfather, she'd been vindicated.

"But Grandpa, a farm wife? Me? Are you serious?"

"Violet, dear, if you don't marry Sam, you will bring disgrace down on the Wilcox family."

"What do I care about the Wilcox family? Do you know what you're asking me to do?"

"Yes. And if you don't do it, your disgrace will be with you forever," Abiel had said.

"And no decent man will ever want to marry you. Is that what you want, child? To be an unmarried mother with no polite explanation?" Hope had put in.

"I'll make up a husband. Tell people I'm a widow," Violet had sniffed.

"Then we'll have to move to a new town. We can't stay here if you birth a bastard child," Abiel fairly shouted.

"So? We'll move!"

"Elijah Fitch is paying me to be the Sheriff of Fitch's Eddy. Where else can I get a decent job that will pay for our living? Do you want to take in washing?" Abiel asked.

Violet looked at her soft, pretty hands. "No."

"Or sewing? Staying up into the late hours, sewing by the light of a candle? Do you want to do that?"

"No, I don't."

"Then you'll do as I say. It's your own fault. Never should have left you alone for one minute with that no-account, Zeb Gates," Abiel said, pacing.

"He's not a no-account," she protested.

"Left you high and dry to take the blame, didn't he?" Hope looked over her glasses at her daughter.

She couldn't argue with her mother on that point. And she had hated Zeb, but only for a while. She forgave him when she remembered he didn't know she was with child when he left town. She'd imagined things would have been different if he had known. After all, she herself hadn't known until it was too late and he'd left.

"It's the only way, child," Abiel had said, his tone softening. "You know I only want the best for you. Sam Chesney is a fine young man. Comes from a good family. He'll take care of you."

Violet turned up her nose at Sam Chesney. Naïve, often tongue-tied, and maybe slow-witted, she had thought. Not bad looking, but he'd expect her to feed animals and do dirty chores. Ruin her pretty hands! Just the thought had made her nauseous.

Yes, Zeb had deserted her. And now that was about to change. She hoped she'd be free to live the life she wanted.

She took one last look at Sam and the farm. Her gaze swept over the devastated fields. The massive puddles, the ruts and gullies where the rain had gutted the land and upended Sam's crops.

Sympathy rose up in her chest. Sam Chesney was a good man and didn't deserve this nasty turn of Fate. She tamped down her sympathy. But there was no reason two people should suffer from the capricious maliciousness of Mother Nature. No, she would not stay with Sam and work herself to the bone anymore, especially with no assurance of an easier future.

She'd tried to love him but failed. She felt a strange affection and sympathy for him but that was all. Yes, he had taken good care of her, was a good father, and smarter than she'd first figured. An honest man, he didn't see the dishonesty of others around him. That would be his downfall.

When they reached Fitch's Eddy, Violet settled herself and Zachary in quickly. Then she made tracks to the general store, hurrying as fast as she could. There must be a letter there for her.

When she barged in through the door, Becky stood behind the counter, counting onions and carrots. She looked up when the bell over the door tinkled the arrival of a customer.

"Oh. Violet."

"Hi, Becky. I'm here to collect the mail."

"All right," she came from behind the counter and disappeared into the back.

Violet paced nervously for a few seconds, then stopped and tapped her toe. It must be there. The letter. The one thing that could save her life.

Becky returned with a piece of white paper in her hand.

"I do have some mail for you. Something for your grandfather, and a letter for you," Becky said handing the pieces to Violet.

As she took the papers, she sensed the rush of heat to her face. Yes, it was the letter she had hoped for. At least she thought it was but wouldn't truly know until she read it.

"Thank you, Becky," Violet said and turned to go.

"Wait. How did your farm fare during the storm?" Becky asked, her brow furrowed.

Poor Becky. She'd lost Sam and yet she still cared for him. Violet spoke up.

"Not well. We were wiped out. All the fields were destroyed by the rain. There's nothing left."

Becky gasped. Her hand went to her throat. "Nothing left?"

"No. It's sad. Very sad. After all Sam's hard work." Violet shook her head, then remembered she held a most important letter in her hand. She scooted out the door and scurried home. Once in the house, she checked on the baby, who napped. She flung herself down on the bed and tore open the letter with eager fingers. It read:

Dearest Violet,

Good news! I have secured the job of postmaster in a small town south of Hartford. I am living in a boarding house now but have made plans to purchase a small house. Our time has come. I'm returning to Fitch's Eddy in a fortnight. Be ready, my darling.

Love,

Zeb

She wanted to jump for joy, scream out his name, but dared not. No way would she let her mother and grandfather in on her plans. She counted out the days. A fortnight meant he'd be there tomorrow! Goodness, there was so much she needed to do.

Happiness flowed through her. She spent her remaining energy gathering her things and putting them in one place. She'd have to return to the farm to scoop up her possessions there – and Zachary's. By the time she finished, she was tuckered out. She fed Zachary and then climbed into bed. Sleep came quickly.

SWEATY, SAM AWOKE WITH the sun. The fever had left him, however, he still had no energy. He dragged himself out to the barn, hoping the chickens had laid a few eggs. He was rewarded. Between the three hens he gathered enough for a hearty meal. He returned to the house and made breakfast for himself and Lucky. They ate, he dressed and man and dog went to inspect the ravaged land.

Rutted with trenches made by the pounding rain and the run-off from the hill, he spotted seeds scattered, sometimes over a couple of feet of land, sometimes clumped together in piles. Very young plants had been ripped up by their roots. He picked up some, wondering if they could be replanted. The seeds, bloated and waterlogged, were no longer worth planting. Some had started to sprout. Sam dug a shallow hole in the mud and dumped them in, hoping it wasn't too late.

As he and Lucky slowly examined every foot of his property, they discovered a few patches where the plantings were intact. Some small stretches had been protected from the punishing rain by trees overhanging the turf.

The hot June sun beat down on him. He had no idea how much he'd be able to harvest. He hoped enough to keep himself, Violet, the baby, and Lucky until he could plant winter crops in the fall. It would be weeks until he could judge how much he could reap from those precious patches that had been saved.

Still feeling sick, he drank a tankard of cider and crawled back in bed. The knock of wagon wheels against the rocks and ruts in the road woke him. He slowly walked to the window. Who could possibly be coming to see him? It couldn't be Violet, she wasn't due back for another two weeks, at least.

He rubbed the sleep out of his eyes, splashed water on his face, dried off and stepped outside. A small Conestoga wagon pulled up. A man got out. Violet sat up in the seat next to him, holding the baby.

"My name's Zebulon Gates," he said extending his hand.

Sam shook it. "Sam Chesney."

"I know. Look, no reason to postpone this any longer, I've come to take Violet away to live with me. We came to gather her things. And to return your baby to you."

Shock filled Sam. He weaved a bit, almost losing his balance. "What?"

"You heard me. I'm taking Violet. She's going to divorce you and marry me."

"Violet – what is he saying?"

After settling the baby safely in Zeb's arms, she alit. As she approached, she avoided his gaze, and reclaimed baby Zachary.

"Is what he's saying true?" Sam asked.

"I'm afraid so, Sam. I'm sorry. Really, I am. You've been wonderful. But I love Zeb. I've always loved him. We're going to Wethersfield, near Hartford. Can I get my things?"

Sam stepped aside. Violet handed him the baby.

"Pretty babe," Zeb said.

Sam cradled Zachary, who cried until he rocked him. Then he settled down.

Violet and Zeb hurried to the house, loaded up their arms, then carried everything to the wagon. Sam stood, cooing with the baby and trying to get his head around what was happening. Violet was leaving him. While he would be helpless without her to take care of the baby, he could manage his life without her.

He'd grown affectionate toward her, but his heart still belonged to Becky Rhodes. And now he had little Zachary to build a future for. He'd probably have to return to the Inn and his grandmother's care. His head spun with ideas, questions, problems, and possible solutions.

On her last trip to the wagon, he managed to grab her arm. "Wait. You owe me some answers. Why didn't you tell me before? Why did you marry me?"

Zeb stopped. "Come on, Violet. It doesn't matter. None of that matters now. Let's go. We have a long trip." Zeb took her hand.

"Wait, wait. I do owe him an explanation," she said. Taking the baby from Sam, she continued, "I'm not leaving the baby."

"What?" Zeb's eyebrows rose. "I'm not raising another man's son." He set his jaw firmly.

"That's part of the answer," she said, facing Zeb. "That's not Sam's baby. That's your baby, Zeb."

His jaw slacked as he stared. "What?"

"No. This is my child," Sam said, reaching for Zachary. Violet held him tight and swung away from Sam. The baby fussed.

"No, Sam. I'm sorry, but I was with child before you and I..." Her voice dropped off.

"Why didn't you tell me?" Zeb interrupted. "I would have come for you sooner."

"I didn't know until after you left. I didn't know where you were. As far as I knew you were gone forever. I had no way to reach you. If I had known where you were, I would have told you."

Zeb stood still. "I'm so sorry," he said, his voice low as he reached for Violet.

Totally betrayed by his wife, Sam refused to give up the baby. "You're not taking my child," he said, ripping Zachary from Violet's arms. Zeb took a menacing step toward him, and Sam raised his fist.

"Sam, you must believe me, Zachary is not your son," Violet said, anger flashing in her eyes. "I am taking him."

At a loss for words, Sam's heart broke at the idea of losing Zachary. As long as Violet claimed he wasn't Sam's, there was nothing he could do. Anger replaced sadness in his chest.

"Vicious woman! You tricked me," Sam said, his voice dripping with venom.

"I had to. Grandpa forced me. They didn't want the disgrace. Neither did I. You made me respectable." She moved toward Zachary. Sam stepped back with the child still in his arms.

"Please, Sam, don't fight me. I'm sorry you have to lose him, but he's mine and Zeb's. I was with child when you and I started courting."

"So he didn't arrive early?" Sam asked.

"No, he didn't. If you don't believe me, ask Dr. Rhodes. He knew."

"Seems everyone knew but me," Sam said. Emotion choked him.

"And me," Zeb said. "You've had a long time with my son. Since he's mine, I want him."

Zeb took a step toward Sam.

"Don't come any closer! Legally, he's my child. My last name is on his birth certificate." Sam set his jaw, his eyes cold.

"Don't do this, Sam. I'm sorry. I lied to you. It was mean. It was unfair. Be mad at me, but don't keep Zachary from his real father," Violet said, softly. She gestured to Zeb to stand back.

"Please, Sam," she said, inching closer.

The baby cried in earnest.

"He needs his mother," Zeb said.

"Shut up!" Sam hollered.

"Please, Zeb. Let me handle this," Violet said. She moved closer to Sam and Zachary. "Let me have him, Sam. He's crying. He needs me."

Sam couldn't argue with her words. Deflated, he quietly passed the child to Violet. The baby immediately quieted down.

"Take good care of him," Sam said, barely able to choke out words.

Violet handed the child to Zeb and hugged Sam. "We will. I promise you, we will."

"I promise, too," Zeb said. "Thank you."

Anger bubbled up in Sam's chest. "Get out of here before I get my shotgun," he growled.

With that, Violet burst into action. She jumped up into the wagon, Zeb handed her the child and vaulted himself into the driver's seat. He clicked the reins and the horses took off.

With tears streaming down his face, Sam stood watching them until the horizon swallowed them up.

TWO WEEKS LATER, JULY

Engulfed in depression, Sam wallowed in sadness. The life he'd worked so hard to create had vanished in an instant. Between the storm and Violet's betrayal, Sam had been left with nothing but a useless farm, with acres of untillable mud.

His fever returned. With barely enough energy to feed himself and Lucky, Sam did nothing but eat and sleep. Day after day, he didn't gather the energy to figure out how to move forward. At times he wondered if his family and friends in Fitch's Eddy knew what had happened to him. The shame of it, the humiliation kept him from venturing into town. He simply couldn't face his family, nor keep from shooting the heads off what remained of the Wilcox family.

While he'd grown accustomed to distance with his wife, he missed the child. Sometimes at night, he'd dream he heard Zachary crying. Then he'd wake up with a start, bolt out of bed and look through his empty house for the infant. Then he'd remember, stumble back into bed and fall into a dead sleep.

One day, Amos lowed continually. Sam wondered what the ox had picked up on. He swore Amos could foretell a storm. Midnight grew jumpy and so did the chickens. Sam figured a fox had been snooping around. He brushed off his gun and sat by the barn, ready to defend his creatures.

After two weeks of moping, Sam knew he had to do something. He rose early and took Lucky out hunting. One fortunate event from the rainstorm was the size of the pond nearby. Sam figured it had doubled in size since the storm. And there he spotted half a dozen juicy ducks paddling around, innocently seeking their breakfast. He took aim.

Lucky retrieved the two birds Sam had bagged. Sam stuffed them in his satchel, and he and his companion returned to the farm. The animals had calmed down some but still appeared jumpy. A lot of squawking drew him to the chicken coop. One chicken was gone!

Damn! Sam had been right all along. It had been a fox, and he'd figured out how to get into the hen house, He made off with one of Sam's chickens. Sam dropped the ducks in the kitchen, fed Lucky, then set about fixing the hen house so no fox could ever get in again.

He brought his own meal outside and ate by the barn, keeping his rifle near.

"Could things get any worse, Lucky?" Sam asked between bites of stale bread.

The dog licked Sam's hand, then curled up on the ground next to his master.

When the sun set, Sam prepared the duck, put it in a pot with two potatoes and a few carrots. He smeared a piece of bread with goat cheese.

"There must be more bread in the root cellar, Lucky," Sam said, walking toward the cellar. The previous farmer had dug a root cellar near the house. Sam had enlarged it, working on rainy days when he couldn't plant. Accompanied by his dog, he hurried down the stairs to take stock of what food he still had.

Since he had been eating from the stores of the root cellar for the past two weeks, there was no longer a large horde of vegetables, bread, and butter there. He didn't worry about meat. He and Lucky could bag ducks, and even a fish or two from the pond. But he needed the squash, potatoes, carrots, and onions to keep body and soul together.

There were only two whole loaves of bread left. He'd have to go back to town soon and replenish his food supply. He dreaded the idea of returning to the shame Violet had stained him with. He figured by now everybody knew about her leaving and taking the baby. Was it his fault? Probably not. But what a fool he had been to think a beautiful woman like Violet Wilcox would agree to marry him and become a farmer's wife. And now everyone would be talking about it. His face colored at the thought of the shame awaiting him.

He ate outside. Looking up at the majestic sunset, it looked off. The sky had turned a strange color, with a greenish hue crowding out the usually brilliant shades of orange, pink, and yellow.

"Looks like maybe another storm is coming, Lucky," Sam said, chewing the last bite of bread.

Again he heard Amos lowing. As he stood to check on the animals, another sound met his ears. It was the rattle of a wagon traveling fast toward the farm. He looked up. Benjamin Fitch manned the wagon, flapping the reins. The horse galloped full out toward the house.

Sam moved toward the wagon. It came to an abrupt stop.

Benjamin hollered from his seat.

"Get in the wagon! Get Lucky in the wagon! You have to leave!"

"What?" Sam asked.

"Now!" Benjamin hollered, louder than before.

Chapter Sixteen

"Tornado's coming!" Ben yelled.

"What?" Sam asked, drying a dish.

"A bad storm. Look at the sky. Rain's coming. Big rain.

Benjamin dismounted. "Postal carrier came from Pennsylvania. He was drenched. He told us about the storm there. My father called it a dust devil. But the carrier said it's bigger than that. Stronger than that. He was just able to ride ahead of it."

"I have to get the animals to shelter," Sam said, dropping the dish towel and shoving the dish in the cupboard.

"We can take Lucky but that's all," Ben said.

"I have Midnight, and two hens and a rooster left. And Amos."

"We can take only Lucky. There's no time to put the chickens in a cage or convince Midnight to get in the wagon. And no room for Amos. We have to go now!" Ben tugged on Sam's sleeve.

Sam sheltered his eyes with his hand and stared off into the distance. Although he couldn't tell how far away the darkening sky began, it moved closer at a rapid speed. The sky was darker than he had ever seen before.

"Get in, Sam. Now!" Benjamin ordered.

"No. I'll take the animals down to the root cellar," Sam said.

"It's your funeral. I'm leaving before it's too late." Ben mounted the wagon.

"Thank you for coming, Ben."

Ben tipped his hat and circled his horses back. Giving them full head, they took off at a gallop. Sam wondered if they could smell or sense the coming storm. Amos lowed loudly and plaintively. Midnight bleated.

Sam rushed over to the barn. He gave the ox a pat on the nose. "I'm sorry, boy. There isn't room for you in the root cellar," Sam said.

He gathered up each chicken and ran to the root cellar. After depositing them, he blocked the entrance with a wooden crate. Then he tethered Midnight.

"Come on, girl. Not safe for you out here." He pulled on the rope, but the goat wouldn't budge.

"I know you're scared. Come on. We're gonna hide from the big bad storm," he said, but the animal didn't move. She dug her heels into the soft earth and bleated louder.

The wind had picked up. Sam glanced to the west. The sky just over the hill grew dark gray. Huge rain drops fell at random, then the pace increased and pelted him and the stubborn Midnight.

"Come on, girl! We gotta go!"

Still, she stood firmly rooted and bleating. Frustrated, Sam gave up. He picked her up, hauled her over his shoulder and carried the squirming, kicking goat to the entrance to the root cellar. He put her down and shoved her rear end until she stumbled her way down the stairs.

Looking around, he'd lost sight of his dog. Fear grabbed him.

"Lucky!" he hollered, then turned about face and yelled again. "Lucky! Lucky!" He prayed the storm had not taken his companion. Shortly after yelling, he heard a corresponding bark.

Racing like the wind, the dog flew at his master. Sam caught him, hugged him tight, and raced down the stairs.

"You're safe, boy. You're safe," Sam said, putting the dog down on all fours, petting and hugging his faithful animal.

"Stay," he ordered before climbing the stairs to assess the storm's progress. He turned west again. A furious wind picked up debris and caught it in a funnel. Sticks, rocks, roots, and anything else on the ground swirled faster and faster. Some of it came his way. The wind threw dirt in his eyes and mouth. He sputtered and spit, but the wind simply threw more. All he saw through eyes blinded by grit was a cloud of swirling flying debris, a dusty cloud obscuring anything beyond a foot or two. It was like a giant dust wall.

It came so fast he could do nothing. He covered his face and head with his arms, but the wind found his eyes and mouth anyway. For a second the wind dropped. Sam opened his eyes and saw it – a huge funnel cloud ripping across the landscape. The sky was as dark as midnight. The silence gave way to an ear-splitting roar as loud, he imagined, as if he'd been standing next to an angry lion. He covered his ears.

He watched the stools and tools he had left on his front stoop fly off, swirling high up in the air. The funnel cloud launched them then engulfed him, lifting him slightly off the ground. Panicked, he reached for the railing, pulling himself back until his feet were firmly planted on the steps. His breath came in gasps. Sam ran down the stairs and ducked under cover of the root cellar, pushing Midnight to the back with the chickens. He stood at the bottom step, barely able to abide the deafening sound and watched the funnel come straight for his house.

He heard the crushing and crunching of tree limbs. With one huge crack, a limb came off the elm tree right outside his house. It swirled around and went smashing through his window. He witnessed large limbs break off trees and be pitched at his home. Then the cloud came straight overhead. Midnight rushed to the front stopping next to Sam. She nudged her head under Sam's arm and buried her face in his armpit. Lucky stood guard by the other side of Sam.

"Steady girl. It's all right. We're safe down here," he said, stepping back a bit and petting her forehead.

The chickens squawked and ran in circles in the back of the cellar. Careful not to put his head out too far, where it could get hit by flying tree branches, Sam managed to watch some of the destruction of his farm.

The furious swish of leaves and splintering of wood met his ears. Without thinking, he moved forward two steps. As his sight line rose above the ground, he witnessed the elm tree being yanked up high into the air, two giant limbs ripped from its trunk, by the massive funnel. The tree crashed down on his roof, smashing a giant hole. The top fell into the kitchen, a detached limb shattered the glass window. The wind sped a smaller branch, torn loose from the tree, at him. It came so fast, he only had time to duck part way. The branch glanced off his head, sending him backward down the last two steps and into his goat.

He bounced off Midnight and onto the dirt floor and then everything went black.

SAM AWOKE TO THE NUDGING of his dog. Lucky licked his face and pushed on his cheek with his muzzle. He stirred. Dizzy, he rolled over and tried to sit up. A shooting pain in his head pushed him back down on the dirt floor.

"Ouch! Damn!" He rubbed his head and drew away a bloody hand. Some blood had already dried in his hair, matting it down. Gingerly, he poked around until he found a cut. It wasn't large, but big enough to bleed profusely.

He tore his shirt off and wrapped it around his head. The roaring had stopped. The sky, still a dark gray, had lightened. Slowly he sat up, grimacing in pain. The ground beneath him was damp from the rain. He had no idea how much time had passed, but it seemed to be late afternoon.

He shaded his eyes with his hand and looked up. The sky had cleared considerably, and he could see the sun attempting to break through. He clung to Lucky and pushed to his feet. Shaky, he leaned against the wall while he got his bearings.

He found a cask of cider and scarfed it down. The liquid bolstered him. His legs stopped feeling like rubber and grew sturdy. He got his balance back. Still leery, he kept one hand on the rail for support as he made his way up the stairs, one step at a time. Lucky and Midnight followed.

"Amos!" he said aloud, suddenly aware the poor ox had to make it through the storm on his own. Sam reached the top and looked around. His house, half destroyed, roof on the front caved in by the falling elm tree, caught his attention.

Tears clouded his eyes. This would be the last straw, the last remnant of his dream of life on a farm. Searching the land, he saw the stools, tools, and tree branches scattered far and wide. Slowly he approached the barn. A section of the roof had been peeled back like one might peel an orange. A persistent lowing acted like music to Sam's ears. Amos was alive! He prayed the ox had not been hurt and rushed inside as fast as his battered body would carry him.

There was Amos, pushing against the back wall as if his life depended on it. Sam petted the big creature on the nose and looked into his frightened eyes.

"It's all right, boy. The storm is over. It's safe to come out." He spoke softly and tugged gently on the harness, and the ox slowly followed him outside.

Midnight sought a pile of hay that had not been scattered and took a mouthful. Amos followed.

"Come on, Lucky. I hope the food in the house hasn't been ruined," Sam said, rushing toward the front door.

Ripped from its hinges, the door lay on the ground. Sam picked his way over shattered glass shards, twigs, leaves, mud, and stones lying on the floor of the front room.

"Stay there, Lucky. Stay!" Sam commanded. He found bread that had been thrown up into the tree poking through his roof. Jumping, he grabbed the loaf and a dish and joined his dog. They plopped down on the ground by the pump. Sam filled the bowl with water and offered it to Lucky, who took a big drink. Then he fed the animal some bread. After he ate and drank, he pumped water for Midnight and Amos. Then he stuck his head under the pump and cleaned out the cut on his skull. After finding a piece of cloth, he rewrapped his head.

Scrounging around he found enough food for himself and the dog. The air had cleared. Sam saw stars shining in the night sky. He and Lucky crawled into bed and fell asleep. They slept through the night, waking up to the noise of several wagons approaching.

"Sam! Sam!" shouted a woman. It was Abigail, his mother, standing feet spread, hands on hips with her daughter, Lizzie, on one side, and her young son, Jem, on the other.

Sam pushed to his feet and smiled. Abigail, Caleb, his grandmother, Benjamin, Sarah, her baby, and Elijah Fitch sat in their wagons eyeing him. Never had he been so happy to see his family before.

"Are you all right?" his mother asked.

He nodded. "By the grace of God," he replied. He made his way through the destruction and piles of debris to the root cellar and retrieved the chickens.

"DIDN'T YOU GET WRECKED by that tornado?" Sam asked.

"It missed us. Not by much, but enough. The town wasn't touched," Elijah said.

"Lucky for us all," Benjamin said.

"Darn right," Caleb put in.

"Let me take a look at your head," Martha said, approaching him. After poking around, making Sam yowl in pain several times she said, "I think he needs stitching. We best take him to Doc Rhodes."

Everyone agreed. They loaded Sam, Lucky, the goat, and the chickens into Caleb's wagon and started out.

"But I'm comin' back once my head's stitched up. This is my home. I need to fix it," Sam said.

"Devil of a business getting that tree out of your kitchen," Elijah Fitch said, shaking his head.

"I've got a good saw. Benjamin, will you help? I think with three of us, we can clear it out. Don't know about fixing the roof, though," Caleb said.

"We'll work out something," Elijah said.

Sam climbed in the back of the wagon with his animals. "Sure is a miracle Fitch's Eddy was spared," Sam said, almost to himself.

Caleb dropped off his wife and children, then rode on to the general store and dropped off Sam and Lucky.

"Much obliged, Caleb," Sam said. "Will you take the animals?"

"Of course. We'll save supper for you," Caleb said, then gave the reins a shake.

Sam stopped before entering the store. Shame filled him at the idea of facing Becky. He prayed she would be on an errand. Deserted by his wife, the baby ripped from his arms, the farm destroyed – he had nothing. How she would laugh at him and congratulate herself on turning down his marriage proposal.

Color heated his face. Yes, she'd been smarter than him. She'd avoided being surrounded by destruction. He stepped up to the door and opened it slowly, peeking around to see if Becky was there. She stood behind the counter with her back facing him. The tinkle of the damn bell over the door gave him away. She whirled around,

"I'll be right with..." she stopped mid-sentence, her mouth hung open.

"Hi, Becky," Sam took off his hat and twisted it in his hands. "Is your father here?"

"Sam!" Her eyes grew wide, she clasped her hands together in front of her chest.

"Yep. I need a little doctorin," he said.

She threw back the piece of counter that served as a door, and rushed forward to meet him. "What happened?"

"The storm," he said.

She touched his hair. "You're bleeding!"

"Got hit by a branch. It's probably stopped by now."

"Did that tornado get you?"

"Wrecked everything," Sam said, his voice low.

"I'm so sorry. Yes, my father is here. Let's get you back there right away," she said, taking his arm.

They pushed through the door to the makeshift surgery,

"Well, Mr. Chesney. Haven't seen you in a while. How are you?"

"He's not so good, Dad. He's been cut," Becky said, easing Sam to a stool.

"Let me take a look."

Sam shot Becky a meaningful glance.

"Rebecca, maybe you'd better wait outside," Dr. Rhodes said.

Sam nodded. "I'll be fine, Becky. Thank you."

"Of course," she colored slightly, then left.

The doctor poked around, making Sam hiss in pain.

"Sorry, son. I don't mean to hurt you, but this needs to be cleaned out and stitched up. I'll have to shave your hair."

"Whatever you have to do."

Half an hour later, Sam was done. He reached into his pocket for some coins.

"No charge, Mr. Chesney."

"Much obliged."

"You lose much to the tornado?" Dr. Rhodes asked while he put away his needle and thread.

"Everything, Doc. Everything." Sam didn't know which hurt most, what he'd lost or the cut on his head. He wondered if all of Fitch's Eddy knew Violet left him and took the baby. Probably.

"You need to rest. That'll heal up pretty quick. If it doesn't, come back. You had a pretty good bump on the head, take it easy for a while."

"All right. Thanks." Sam headed for the back door. When he got outside, Becky darted out right behind him.

"Were you going to leave without saying goodbye?" she asked.

"I guess."

Becky's eyes filled. "You don't even want to talk to me?"

"Sure I do. But I've got a lot to do. A lot to forget. I don't want to face Fitch's Eddy yet."

She stood by silently, wiping tears from her cheeks.

"Does everyone know about Violet and the baby?" he asked, wincing.

She nodded. "You know how it is. Gossip travels like the wind in this stupid town."

"I figured."

"It's not your fault. You didn't do anything wrong. That evil woman. She's a liar and a fake."

"She did what she had to do to protect herself and her child."

"How could anyone live with you and not care a whit about you?" He faced her.

"I couldn't," she said, her voice soft and low.

"Thanks, Becky." Sam said, taking her hand. He pressed it to his lips for a moment. "Best be getting to the Inn. Grandma and Ma will be worried."

"I understand. You take care now," she said, managing a small smile.

Sam ambled down the street. Lucky barked and pushed through the Inn door. He raced to his bowl and took a huge drink. It had been a dry and dusty ride. Then he jumped up and licked Sam's face about a dozen times.

Sam laughed. "Down, boy. Down," he said, easing the dog to standing position. Grateful for the nonjudgmental love from his dog, he patted the beast on the head, then went to the table.

"There you are! What did Doc Rhodes say?" Martha asked, settling her fists on her hips.

"He said to rest. But I got a lot to do."

"Sam Chesney! You eat your supper then right to bed with you!" Martha said.

He opened his mouth, but Martha spoke up. "Not a word out of you. You listen to me. We need to get you all well again."

"My life is over, Grandma. Doesn't matter what I do," Sam said.

"Stop that whining and feeling sorry for yourself. You still got land and a house to take care of. We're gonna get you well, then we'll get you right again." She ushered him to the table.

Lizzie and Jem were eating their dessert. Sam welcomed the company of the rambunctious children. Their antics always made him smile.

After the meal, he fell into bed and was asleep immediately. Nightmares of the tornado plagued him, waking him several times. Sweat poured off his face and neck as he recalled the terror facing that monster. Having no idea how he'd begin to climb his way back, he welcomed sleep.

BY MORNING, SAM'S ORDEAL had caught up with him. Lucky woke him at daybreak with his wet tongue. Sam cracked open his eyes for a moment. A headache gripped him. He went back to sleep.

He spent the day in bed sleeping, only getting up for meals. Lucky stayed by his side. The hushed voices outside his door traveled to his ears.

"Not like him, lying in bed all day," his grandmother said.

"Hush, Martha! The boy was injured. Give him time to heal," Abigail whispered. "And lower your voice."

"Did you talk to Doc Rhodes?" Martha asked sotto voce.

"Yes. He said Sam's got a bump on his head that'll take time to heal," Abby said.

"All right, then. But if he's not better in a day or two, I'm getting' Doc Rhodes down here," she said. The swish of her skirts indicated she moved away.

Sam smiled. Maybe he didn't have a wife to tend to his wounds, but he sure had family who cared. He closed his eyes and went back to sleep.

Three days passed before Sam could stand without being dizzy or felt strength return to his body. Restless, anxious to get back to his house and start rebuilding his roof, he tried and tried to get up but failed. He barely had the energy to dress and get to the table for meals.

"This came for you," Martha said, handing Sam a package.

"From whom?" he asked, pulling something out of the pouch.

"Becky Rhodes," she said. "I'll be back later." Martha swept out of the room.

"By golly," Sam said aloud to himself. "Becky." He smiled as he pulled out a hardback copy of "Gulliver's Travels." He opened it and started reading.

Sapped of strength by the end of the day, he'd eat supper on a tray Martha brought. Bored with long days and the inability to rise and work, he read and slept for three long days. On day four, he stood, dressed and went to the table for breakfast.

"I see you're better today," Caleb said, taking a drink of tea from his mug.

"Yes," Sam said, wolfing down the food on his plate.

"Well, well," said Martha, taking his plate for a refill.

Abigail leaned over and kissed her son on the head. "I'm so relieved."

"Caleb, can you take me home?"

"Yes."

"I need to get to work on my house. Raccoons probably moved in. Maybe even bears by now."

Abigail laughed. "Imagine finding a bear sitting at your kitchen table!"

"Not funny. It could happen."

"After breakfast, I have to start the fire, then we can go," Caleb said, lifting a forkful of eggs to his mouth.

"Fine. I have to do something before I leave, too."

He finished his food and pushed away from the table. With Lucky by his side, he trudged up to the general store, hoping Becky would be there. When he opened the door, disappointment settled in his chest. Doc Rhodes was behind the counter.

"Glad you're here, Sam. I was just about to stop in and see how you're doing. Let me take a look," he said.

"Sure, Doc. Thanks. Where's Becky?"

"I'm here," the young woman said, appearing from the back room.

Sam nodded. The doctor came from behind the counter. He examined Sam's cut and the bump.

"It's healing well. I'd like to give you a fresh bandage though. Step into the back, Sam."

He followed directions. The doctor changed the bandage.

"You'll be good as new in another three days or so. Be careful not to bump it."

"Yes, Doc. Thanks," Sam said, pushing to his feet. He went out and stopped at the counter. The doctor took his bag and headed out the front door. Finally, Sam was alone with Becky.

"Thank you for the book. I couldn't get up or do anything and was as sore as a mongoose."

"You're welcome. I thought you'd enjoy the story."

"Did you read it?"

"I did. Loved it," she said, pulling a bolt of fabric down from the shelf.

"Me, too. I appreciate you doing that. I mean...uh," Sam looked at his hands and shifted his weight. "Becky, I... you...we..."

She laughed. "Sam Chesney, I don't think I've ever seen you so tongue-tied. Spit it out!"

He never expected anything from her, but he had to speak his piece. She probably thought he was the lowest thing on Earth. Other people's opinions had never stopped Sam speaking his mind in the past, no reason to start now.

"I still love you, Becky." The words rushed out of his mouth. He took her small hand between his large, calloused ones. "My farm ain't worth much. I have nothing to offer you. I'm still married, though Violet said she would get a divorce. But I've never stopped caring about you." He put her palm on his cheek, then kissed it.

Sam dropped her hand and turned to leave.

"Wait!" she said, pulling on his hand. "Wait. Don't go."

"Go ahead. Tell me you were right and I was wrong."

"I don't want to, Sam," she said, her voice soft. She cradled his work-weary paw between her soft and delicate ones. "You weren't wrong. You just had a lot of bad luck's all."

Sam gave a rueful laugh. "Bad luck? Pickin' a girl who was a liar and a cheat?"

"Well, maybe that wasn't a good move. But you're so honest you think everyone else is, too."

"I've learned my lesson."

"The rest was dumb luck. Being in the path of that tornado? Just bad luck."

"And the rain storm? My dad would've known better than to plant all the crops I did at the base of a big hill. He would have known that one big rainstorm would wipe out my seeds. He wouldn't have waited as long as I did to plant, neither. He was smarter. Much smarter than I am."

She still held onto his hand. "So what are you going to do?"

"I dunno. I gotta go back and see what's left of my house. See if critters have moved in already."

"Oh, Sam. The house is wrecked?"

"Yep. Roof caved in by a big tree. In the front. Kitchen is open to all the raccoons, coyotes and bears around."

She gasped and covered her mouth.

"It ain't my house. It belongs to Elijah Fitch. So I don't get to decide whether to fix it or tear it down."

"You'll have to rebuild it if he says so?" she asked.

"Yep."

"Do you still want to farm?"

"Nope. I'm not suited to it. But I have to see what's gonna come up and harvest whatever I can to pay Mr. Fitch back."

"Then what?"

"I don't know," Sam said, shifting his weight and not daring to make eye contact. "I don't have much to offer you, Becky, but I'd be mighty obliged if you'd give me another chance."

She let go of his hands, fussed with her apron and didn't meet his gaze. "I don't know, Sam. I mean, you have no plans now. You're married. I just don't know."

A small smile brightened his face. "All right. But that's not a 'no, is it? You're still considering?"

She smiled back. "Yes, I'm still considering. Let's see if your luck changes."

"If you're behind me, I know my luck will have change," he said, raising her hand to his lips again.

"Oh, Sam. You get so romantic at the most awful times!" She laughed.

The bell over the door tinkled, and Catherine and Charity Bloodgoode walked in.

"Well, I declare, Charity! If it isn't that no-good Sam Chesney. Not even finished with one wife and already moving in on another woman!" Catherine said, raising her eyebrows.

"Go mind your business, you dried up old prune," Sam said.

Becky laughed.

"Well, I never!" Catherine huffed.

Sam was out the door before another word was uttered. If he wondered what the people of the town thought of him, he now had a pretty good idea.

Chapter Seventeen

Sam got in the wagon next to Caleb. Lucky jumped into the back. As they rode, Caleb opened the conversation.

"So what are you gonna do now?"

"I dunno." Sam looked out over the open landscape as if the answer lay carved in the side of the mountains in the distance.

"Continue to work the farm?"

"I don't see how I can. With my paltry harvest, I won't make enough to feed myself. I owe whatever crops I get to Mr. Fitch."

"You have nothing?"

"Yep. Nothing," Sam said, in a low tone, emotion closing his throat.

"Would you consider coming back to the smith shop?" Caleb asked, giving the reins a little jiggle.

"Work for you again?"

"Yep. I'm over bein' mad you left. You were a right good smithy. Have a knack for it." Caleb kept his eyes straight ahead.

"Really?" Hope sprang forth in Sam's chest.

"Yep."

"I would be mighty grateful."

"I've been working night and day to do your job and mine. And it ain't workin' out too good. I'm running behind. And your mother is complain' I'm too tired to help with the chores at home."

"When would you want me back?" Sam couldn't believe his ears.

"As soon as you can."

"First, I have to fix the house. Then it's gonna be a couple of months until I can harvest anything. If there's anything to harvest," Sam said, wringing his hands together.

"So you'll come as soon as the house is fixed?"

Sam nodded.

"How long do you reckon it'll take to fix it?" Caleb asked.

"Depends. I ain't got lumber for the roof. And it'll take me maybe four or five days to cut up that damn tree and haul it outta the house."

"So you figure?"

"Two weeks? Maybe Mr. Fitch will give me the lumber on credit," Sam said.

"Maybe. After all, it's for his house," Caleb said, loosening the reins.

Gratitude put it mildly. He could have kissed Caleb, if his stepfather wouldn't have slugged him for it.

"I'm grateful."

"Good. You ain't leavin' again?"

"Doubt it. Except for the harvest."

"It's all right. I can get along without you for a week or two," Caleb said, smiling.

As they came around the bend, Sam's eyes widened. There was a wagon parked by his farmhouse.

"Who's there?" Sam asked.

"I dunno."

Sam shaded his eyes. He heard the sound of sawing. As they drew closer, he saw the tree had been removed. It lay in huge chunks on the front lawn. Benjamin and Josiah sawed the tree trunk into logs.

"Holy Hell!" Sam said, jumping down from the wagon and running the rest of the way. Lucky leaped out and ran after his master.

"What are you doing here?" Sam asked.

"Thought we'd give you a hand. Clearing that dang tree out was too big a job for one man," said Benjamin.

"Especially one that's been cracked on the head," Josiah added. "Look in the wagon, Sam. Mr. Fitch gave me some boards to bring down here to repair the roof."

Sam had no idea where he'd get boards for the roof. Now that problem was solved. Along with the challenge of clearing out that huge tree.

"You two...I don't know what to say," Sam stuttered.

"How about 'thank you'?" Ben said with a grin.

"Thank you, thank you, thank you so much!" Sam offered his hand to each friend.

Caleb called from the wagon, "I best be going. The fire's on in the shop."

"Thank you, Caleb," Sam called.

"I think you're in good hands," his stepfather said and turned the horses around.

"I ain't got nothin' to eat. Let's go hunting," Sam said.

Sam's friends put down their saws. The three young men shouldered their rifles and headed for the woods with Lucky trailing close behind.

SAM AND BEN EACH BAGGED a duck and Josiah got a rabbit. The young men returned to the house with Lucky trotting along. Sam cleaned up the leaves, twigs, small branches, and debris still cluttering up his kitchen. He removed the broken pottery and bent mugs, too.

"Doc said I can't do any hard work until my head heals. But I can cook," Sam said.

"Hey, it's all right. I'd rather nail boards than cook any day," Benjamin said.

"You're spoiled!" Josiah said, slapping his friend on the shoulder. "You have that fancy French lady prepare all your meals."

"And you eat at the Inn," Benjamin shot back.

"True. Sometimes I cook for myself," Josiah said.

"Yeah? Well, since Violet left, I've been cookin' for myself all the time. So this ain't no hardship for me," Sam said.

While Josiah and Benjamin laid the boards across the beams then applied nails, Sam lit the fire in the kitchen hearth and prepared the game. He retrieved some of the remaining vegetables in the root cellar and cooked up a mighty fine stew.

Benjamin poked his head in. "Sarah sent some victuals for you," he said, one arm laden with pouches filled with bread, pastry, vegetables, and a jug of cider slung over his shoulder.

"God bless her!" Sam said, helping Ben unload the food.

Sam doled out the stew and, before sunset, the young men sat down to eat.

"Sawin' makes me hungry," Josiah said.

"Me, too," Benjamin said, digging his spoon into the stew.

"Sorry about Violet leavin'," Josiah said, refilling his mug with cider.

"Yeah. What a dirty deal for you, Sam," Benjamin said.

"I don't really miss her. But I miss the baby," Sam admitted.

"Women. More trouble than they're worth," Josiah said.

"Not all women," Benjamin said.

"I understand why she did it, but she played me for a fool. I bet everyone in town is talking about me, how stupid I am," Sam said, shaking his head.

"Not exactly," Ben said.

"What do you mean?"

"Well, yeah, they're talking about you," Josiah said. "But they're laying blame on Violet. They're saying you were honorable and that it's all her fault."

"That's a relief," Sam said, shoving a spoonful of meat into his mouth.

"Did you like being a father?" Josiah asked.

"I did. Yeah," Sam said. He stopped eating as emotion trapped words in his throat.

"I love it. I've got the sweetest baby girl in the whole world. And she smiles bigger for her daddy," Benjamin said.

Sam slapped him on the shoulder. "Stop braggin'. How is my niece?"

"Cutest person in all of Fitch's Eddy."

"So what are you going to do now? Go back to farming?" Josiah asked.

"Nope. I ain't got the knack for it my father did. I made some big mistakes he would never have made. I have to harvest whatever crops there are and pay off what I owe Mr. Fitch."

"You think you still got some plants left?" Benjamin asked.

"I do. There are a couple of patches that didn't flood. But only a couple. I hope your father will take my harvest and cancel my debt."

"He's pretty tough. I'll talk to him," Benjamin said.

"Thank you."

"You still married?" Josiah asked.

"I am. But not for long. Violet wants to marry the father of her son. So I guess she'll be getting a divorce right soon," Sam said, slipping a piece of duck meat to Lucky.

"You got your eye on anyone?" Josiah asked, cutting himself another slice of bread.

"Kinda soon for that, don't ya think?" Sam asked.

"Never too soon for a man to be hound-dogging a woman," Benjamin said with a laugh.

"Do you think Becky would accept your proposal this time?" Josiah asked.

"I doubt it. I don't have anything to offer her."

"You'll have a job. What more could she want?" Josiah asked.

"Maybe a house. Some land. Some money in the bank. Ain't got none of those."

"You will have, you will," Benjamin said, patting Sam on the back.

The men slept in bedrolls on the floor. The next morning, they arose early, ate and set to work. By sundown, the roof was fixed enough to live in.

"Don't look pretty, but it'll keep the rain out," Josiah said. .

"Yep. It's fine," Benjamin said.

"Sure is. Thank you for your help," Sam said.

"You'd do the same for me," Josiah said.

The men ate the rest of the stew, then Josiah and Ben climbed up on Ben's wagon and rode back to Fitch's Eddy.

At sunset, Sam sat next to Lucky. He listened to the crickets and frogs from the nearby pond, the sounds of a peaceful night. Although he was alone, he didn't dwell on it. His biggest problems of the moment were solved. He thanked God for his friends.

Then he thought about where his life would go next. Maybe it wouldn't be so bad to go back to living in Fitch's Eddy. If his buddies had told the truth, sympathy of the town folks was with Sam. If he lived there, he might have another chance with Becky. He'd figured out that if he'd decided to stay living in town, Becky would probably be his wife now. He added that to his list of regrets.

"Lucky, how can one man make so many bad decisions?" he asked his dog. Lucky gave one bark, smacked his tail up and down a few times, then settled down again. Sam reached over and scratched him behind the ears.

"You're right. I don't know either." He again thanked God for Caleb's offering him a job and for his grandmother taking him back at the Inn.

THE NEXT MORNING, SAM and Lucky walked the farm. He inspected every inch he'd planted. There were sprouts in some patches.

"Looks like we'll have some crops to harvest after all."

He pumped water for Amos. Midnight and the chickens were still in Fitch's Eddy at the Inn.

"I know you love it here, Lucky, but we have to go back. Most of the topsoil run off during the storm, washed down field to who knows where. Too late to replant."

The dog trained sympathetic eyes on his master.

"Caleb's right. I'm better at smithing than I am at farming."

Tired from the exertion and healing, he and Lucky ate an early dinner and went to bed. Each day, Sam felt stronger. Watching his plants grow gave him some solace. But everywhere he looked, he missed having a family. The empty cradle reminded him of his loss. At night, when he closed his eyes, he could see Zachary's smile and hear his giggle.

Sure he didn't have a strong connection with Violet like he had had with Becky. But she'd pitched in and done everything she could to help the farm succeed.

The more he thought about her, the more he understood what a predicament she had been in. How the dishonor of being an unwed mother would have made her family outcast. Violet wasn't strong enough to have weathered that. She was a gentle soul.

The more he pondered on what happened, the more he realized that her seduction of him and subsequent lying had probably not been her own idea. He remembered how awkward it had been between them. He reckoned her mother and grandfather must have had something to do with the deception.

Once he saw the truth, Sam's sympathy for Violet grew. She had been in the wrong place, living as his wife. Just like his trying to farm had been the wrong place. Nobody had seen Zeb Gates for months. She had no reason to think he'd come back for her, make an honest woman of her. Heck, Sam guessed Zeb didn't even know she was with child.

Bad decisions by Violet also helped put him in this position – alone with nothing good ahead except hard work and loneliness. Two weeks after the tornado, Sam had regained his strength. He packed up Amos and his few belongings in the wagon along with Lucky and drove them back to Fitch's Eddy.

It was time for him to return to smithing. He smiled as he drove, wondering what projects Caleb had. He'd loaded up the bent mugs. Soon as he had a free minute, he'd fix them at the smith shop.

"Lucky, what do you think Papa would think of my failing to be a farmer?" Sam asked. The dog barked.

"Yeah. I agree. I think he'd say smithing is better because you're not begging Mother Nature not to destroy your life."

After he crossed the bridge over Morgan's Creek and before the bend, he stopped and turned around. One last look at the farm, before he left, not to return until harvest season. He sighed.

When he pulled into Fitch's Eddy, he headed for the Inn. People were out and about, running errands, working, and stopping to gossip.

"Sam Chesney! You back for good?" asked Mrs. Austin.

"Yes, ma'am," Sam said.

"I heard you got a new goat," Young William Austin said.

"I did."

"Can we see her?" his brother, Matthew, asked.

"Sure can."

"What's her name?" Williams asked.

"Midnight. Follow me," Sam said.

Zacharia Lee waved. So did the shoemaker, Thomas Whitfield. Even Ol' Zeke, glued to the chair on the front porch of the general store greeted him.

Relief flooded Sam's body. He didn't realize how much he'd missed the people of Fitch's Eddy. Friendly neighbors lifted his spirits.

Martha, his grandmother, stood outside. She flagged him down.

"Put Amos in the barn. Then come inside. I have soup ready."

Aromas of bread baking and chicken soup simmering greeted Sam. His stomach turned over.

"Sure thing, Grandma," Sam said. He pulled around to the back of the Inn, unhitched Amos and guided him into the barn.

"Baa!" came from Midnight. She pushed up against him and he stopped to pet her. The Austin boys raced around back. They stopped short.

"She's beautiful," Matthew said.

"Hello, Midnight," William said, slowly approaching the goat.

Midnight nuzzled Sam, then turned her gaze on the young boys and bleated a greeting.

Sam went inside.

Martha hugged him. "Welcome home, son," she said.

"Thanks, Grandma. It's good to be home," he said. And meant it.

MID JULY

Uptown at the general store, Becky, her mother and father sat down at the table for their evening meal. They ate roast chicken, buttered squash, baked potatoes, and freshly baked bread. Doc Rhodes and his wife, Virginia, drank beer. Becky preferred cider. The Rhodes family had a higher standard of living than most folks in Fitch's Eddy because they ran the store.

"We're running out of that lace trim, Ma," Becky said, slicing off a piece of chicken.

"Write it down, dear. I have to place an order tomorrow. We're out of flannel, too," Mrs. Rhodes said.

"We don't need flannel, Ma. It's summer."

"Yes, I know. But it will take about two months before it arrives. We need to be ahead of these things," she said.

Becky nodded.

"I see Sam Chesney has returned," Doc Rhodes said. "They say he's moved back into the Inn and is here to stay."

As blood rose to her cheeks, Becky cast her gaze down to her plate

"Well, Rebecca? What do you think of that?" her mother asked, taking a sidelong glance at her daughter.

"Doesn't concern me in the slightest," Becky lied.

"Hah!" her father said, then laughed. "Come, come, my dear. Let's be honest."

"I don't know what you mean," she lied again.

"Daniel, don't tease her. This thing with Sam's marriage and everything has been hard enough on her," Virginia said, stabbing a piece of squash with her fork and putting it in her mouth.

"I'm just asking what you're thinking, Becky." Doc buttered a piece of bread.

Silence.

Both parents glanced at her. Virginia patted her sweaty forehead. Becky raised her gaze to meet her mother's, then she pushed away from the table.

"I'm not hungry," she said. Once she was on her feet, she hurried out the back door. When she hit the grass, she ran as fast as her feet would carry her. She kept running until she reached the pond, her secret meeting place with Sam.

She sank down on the soft grass and sobbed. She wiped her face with her apron. A gunshot alerted her. She scooted over to the tall elm tree and hugged the trunk, getting out of the way of the hunter.

"Why Becky Rhodes! Fancy meeting you out here. You hunting?" Josiah Quint asked.

"No. Just getting some fresh air." She picked a blade of grass and tickled her palm with it.

"I see. Looks like you been crying," he said, narrowing his eyes.

"You're mistaken. Sweat."

He laughed. "All right. If that's what you want to say. Been thinkin' about Sam Chesney?"

She looked up sharply. "What do you know about it?"

"I helped Sam rebuild his house. Your name came up," Josiah said, shouldering his gun and sinking down next to Becky.

"Oh?"

"Yep. I asked him about you."

"And what did he say?" Becky picked several more blades of grass, attempting to appear uninterested.

"Why don't you ask him?" Josiah smiled.

"He's not here and you are," she said, smooth as glass.

He laughed. "You're quick witted, Becky. I'll give you that."

"So?"

"Fine. He didn't really say nothin', just that he didn't have nothin' to offer you now."

"Oh." Disappointed, she raised her gaze to his. "He's said that before."

"Didn't say he didn't care for you none. Seemed to me like he still did, but didn't want to say," Josiah said. He checked the barrel of his gun, then refilled the empty chambers.

"Just like Sam."

"So do you still care for him?"

Becky glanced out to the field. "What if I did? He's married."

"He said he'd be getting out of that. Maybe soon."

She turned abruptly to face him. "He did?"

"Yep. Said Violet'd be looking to marry the father of her baby as quick as she could."

"Makes sense."

"So what would you do if he was unmarried?"

"It wouldn't be up to me," she said, once again searching the grass for fat blades.

"Hah! That's what all the girls say. But it's always up to them. If you told Sam you'd marry him if he was free, well, I'm guessing I'd be brushing off my Sunday meeting suit real quick."

Becky laughed.

"Yep. I'd guess he'd marry you as quick as a fox gets into a hen-house."

"You don't know."

Josiah nodded. "I do. Sam and I are friends. And I know half the men in this town are in love with you. But Sam got there first."

"You're talking through your hat."

Josiah pushed to his feet. "You go ahead and think that. But I know what I'm talkin' about. Sam's as in love with you now as he ever was. And if you were to give him a sign, he'd propose again in a heartbeat. But don't believe me. It'll be your funeral. And the two of you will dance around each other and go on being unhappy for years and years until you're old and dried up."

She looked up at him.

"Don't let time get away from you. Get off your high horse and be happy."

The quacking of ducks drew Josiah's attention. Becky opened her mouth, but Josiah spoke first, in a whisper.

"Shh," he said, as he crept quietly toward the pond.

Becky watched him steal away. She leaned back against the tree, pondering his words.

Chapter Eighteen

L *ate July*
     When he returned to smithing, Sam rose early to make the fire
in the shop. The cooler early morning air made the smith shop more
comfortable. By three o'clock when it was hotter than blazes in town,
they'd let the fire burn out and go home. Sam liked this schedule because it was similar to his farming routine. Sometimes he'd hunt in the
afternoon or take a swim in the pond.

Often after leaving the blacksmith shop, Sam would stop off at the
general store and help Doc Rhodes build an icehouse. Doc bought a
two-acre parcel of land behind his property from Elijah Fitch and decided to increase his business by having an icehouse...to sell ice and ice
cream! He'd even ordered tin ice cream cups from Caleb.

The small icehouse went up quickly. Town folks didn't believe
they'd be able to have ice in the summertime. Doc paid Sam for his
work and offered him a cool drink afterward. He'd sit at a small table
Virginia Rhodes had added to the store so she could serve food and
drinks.

Sam lingered over his drink, taking his time and searching for
things to talk about with Becky. He'd also check the post, hoping his
divorce papers from Violet would arrive. He held himself back as best
he could, always afraid some other man in town would snatch her away.

"What's selling this week?" he'd ask Becky.

"Ribbon. Lace. Cotton." Becky wound some lace around a stiff
piece of cardboard and placed it on a shelf.

"Some special reason?"

"Ladies getting dresses ready for the Harvest Festival."

"Oh, yeah. Forgot about that."

"I didn't."

"You makin' a new dress, too?" he asked, taking a sip of his beer.

"I might be," she'd said, raising her gaze to meet his.

"You going with someone?" he asked, pretending to look innocent.

"Nope."

"I'd ask you, but I'm still married."

Becky stood up straight and faced him. "I don't care that you're married. You are by law. But you ain't got a wife living with you. So it's almost like you're not married," she said.

"If you go with me, people will talk," Sam said.

"So? They talk now."

"About what? I ain't done nothing."

"About you whiling away your summer afternoons sitting here in the store, talkin' to me."

"Oh. That."

"Yeah." She laughed. "The Bloodgoode sisters give me their opinion on your scandalous behavior every time they walk in the store."

"Really?"

"Would I lie to you?" Becky put the bolt of cotton back on the shelf.

"No. Guess not. And it doesn't bother you?"

"Those two jealous bitties? I don't care a whit what they think." She returned some spools of thread to the small display shelf.

Sam took her hand between his. "Good."

"Don't you have something to do?" She slid her hand away from his.

"Not since the icehouse is finished," Sam said.

"Here," Becky handed a small package to Sam. "This came for your grandma. I think it's a package of needles. We're plumb out."

"Thanks," Sam stuffed the package in his pocket. "Best be getting home," he said.

"Yep." She turned her attention to the other items in the day's post.

Sam turned toward the door.

"Wait a minute!" Becky called.

"What?"

"Was that an invitation to the Harvest Festival?" Sam sensed color in his cheeks. "I guess so. I mean...yeah. If you'll go with me."

"I'd be honored," she said, skipping around the counter. She pulled him to her and kissed his cheek.

The heat in his face intensified. "Shucks," he said.

"Just so you know where I stand," she said. "Now go on home. Your supper'll be cold."

He put his hat on, brought her hand to his lips and hurried out the door. Lucky raced out, too, trying to keep up with his master.

END OF AUGUST

Sam spent his mornings in the blacksmith shop, his afternoons working for Doc Rhodes – helping him raise another building on his new land. He put his money in a special jar in his room at the Inn. The nest egg grew slowly. A man with money in his pocket had more options in life. So he saved every penny.

He couldn't gather the fruit of his labors for another few weeks. He didn't expect much, but there would be some harvesting to do. He'd struck a deal with Elijah Fitch. When he finished the work on the roof and delivered him one third of his crop, Fitch would cancel his debt. Relieved, Sam set out with Ol' Amos every Sunday to the farm to work on the roof.

Fixing the house was hard, dry, sweaty work. At the end of each day, he'd take a walk around the property to check on the progress of his crops. There were large patches where grass fought with weeds for sunlight and nutrients, but no crops. Small patches of land away from the hill showed fledgling plants taking root, expanding, and fruit blossoming in the sun.

He made a mental note of where the four patches containing crops were compared to the rest. Much of the land, damaged by the heavy rain and flooding, was rutted, dried mud with ragweed struggling to get a foothold. It would take a lot of work to clear the land of grass and weeds, level it, and replant. He heaved a sigh of relief that he wouldn't be the one doing it.

He enjoyed watching the plants get bigger week after week. Once he finished his roof work for the day, he'd set out on a blanket on the grass near Amos and take a snooze. Working seven days a week exhausted him, but he had a goal, so he forged ahead.

By the end of the second week in September, he had the details of the roof completed and all the damage inside cleaned up, repaired or replaced.

At dinner, Sam shared his plans.

"When the vegetables are ready to be harvested, I'm gonna take the wagon and Ol' Amos and head down to the farm."

"You goin' by yourself?" Martha asked, pushing away from the table. She ambled out to the kitchen for another loaf of bread. She passed by Lizzie turning the spit. Martha stopped to train a sharp eye on the rotating meat.

"I reckon that's about done, young lady. You can go to the table. Caleb?" Martha called.

He left his seat and picked the spit up then set it on the kitchen table. He cut the meat off the iron piece and sliced it.

"Thank you, Caleb. You're such a help," Martha said, patting his hand. "You get the first slice." She piled the meat on a platter, and he carried it to the table. She served him the first piece, then passed it around.

"How long you figure it'll take you to pick everything?" Abigail asked.

"I dunno," Sam said, stuffing a piece of meat in his mouth.

"You going alone?" Caleb asked, cutting a piece of meat into smaller pieces and placing some on Lizzie's plate and some on Jem's plate.

"Yep."

"Mighty hard work for one man," Martha said.

"Won't be that many plants bearing fruit. Won't need more than me," Sam said.

"Squash won't be ready for another few weeks. So, I'll go down and pick the carrots, onions, and potatoes first."

"Saving the squash for last?" Caleb asked, tearing off a piece of bread.

"Yep." Sam buttered more bread and took another slice of meat. Just talking about the work awaiting him sparked his appetite.

Caleb said, "I hope you have a bumper crop. Even if it wears you out."

"Thanks. Me, too."

SEPTEMBER

The weather had turned hot and dry in August, and that continued into September. Sam shaded his eyes with his hand as he stared up at the sky. The sun was as hot as it had been for the past two weeks and there wasn't even the tiniest cloud visible. He took a swig of cider from a jug on the seat next to him, then he pulled a bandana from his pocket and tied it loosely around his neck to catch the sweat.

Ol' Amos trudged slowly along the stony road to the farm. He hoped the heat wouldn't kill the beast. Sam had prayed for rain to break the suffocating, crushing heat but his prayers had not been answered.

"How you doin', Amos? You all right, buddy?" Sam asked. Might as well talk to the ox since there wasn't anyone else. They rode along with

Sam chattering away. Every once in a while Amos would make a low grunt or moo in response to Sam.

When they arrived at the farm, Sam pumped water for Amos and himself. He stuck his head under the pump and let the cool well water refresh him. It was almost sunset. Too late to start harvesting. Still, he could take a gander at the fields and see how the crops were doing.

He chugged a mug of cider and set out to examine the vegetables. The onion beds were his first stop. When he saw that the onion tops had browned and flopped over, he recognized the sure sign the onions were ripe for picking.

He examined the potato beds next. There were tall plants with leaves turning brown, which meant the potatoes were ready to be harvested. He remembered his father showing him how to pluck the plants up and pull the potatoes off. Along with the memory of what to do came the picture in his head of how hard and exhausting it would be to yank potato plants up out of the ground one-by-one.

"I was just a child then. Won't be so hard now," he said aloud to himself.

Next, he checked on the carrots.

"Pick the ones that have a width where the taproot meets the greens of about as wide as the first joint of your thumb, son. They should be sticking up out of the ground." His father George's words echoed in his head.

Sure enough there looked to be plenty of carrots ripe for picking in the two good-sized carrot beds.

A cool breeze swirled around him. The sky grew dark. The rumble of thunder and the streaks of lightning across the sky preceded a thunderstorm. Sam took off running. He arrived at Amos's side as a loud crack of thunder startled both of them. Amos lowed loudly. Sam guided him into the small barn.

Huge drops of rain splashed on his head. Instead of running into the house, Sam stood and welcomed the coolness and water. Rain started slowly but quickly became a torrent. Would this powerful storm injure the crops? He shrugged his shoulders. Nothing he could do about it.

Once he was completely soaked, the cool wind blowing against him made him shiver. How just like the crazy Catskill weather to be hot and dry one minute and wet and cold the next. He went inside and changed into dry clothes. He fixed a cold supper of meat, cheese, and cooked squash and sat by the window to watch the storm. As the sun disappeared, the lightning lit up the sky. While this storm grew angry and powerful, it couldn't compare to the one that wiped out his farmland. The sound of the rain pounding on the new roof lulled him. As Sam grew sleepy, he saw the storm growing weaker, the thunder more distant and the lightning less frequent. He crawled into bed, pulled up the covers and fell asleep. He'd face the results of the storm in the morning.

SAM AWOKE TO A BRIGHT blue, clear sky. The storm had cleaned the air and cooled the wind. Eager to get started, but wondering how muddy the fields would be, he prepared some buttered bread and went out to inspect the land.

While he'd be kneeling in some mud, the good news was that the rain had softened up the earth, so pulling the plants up would be easier. He raced back to the house, pumped water for Amos, took him to a grassy area for his breakfast and entered the house.

As he prepared breakfast, he heard hoofbeats.

"What the?" he wondered aloud. "Who could that be?" It could only be someone coming to see him, for there was no other farm, town or even an outpost nearby.

He stepped into the doorway. With red hair flying, Becky Rhodes came galloping down the road on her palomino horse, Goldy.

"Becky?" Sam asked himself. Then he called out, "Becky! Becky!" She waved. Sam ran to meet her. He grabbed the horse by the harness and helped Becky dismount.

"What are you doing here?" he asked, hiding his joy at seeing her.

"Nice! Is that a gentlemanly way to greet a lady who's come all this way to help you harvest your crops?" She pulled her mouth down in a mock frown.

"You what?"

"You heard me, Sam Chesney." She retrieved two baskets tethered to her saddle bags.

"You came to help me? It's a dirty job. And even more dirty today after the rain we had last night."

"Yep. That's right. Soon as I heard you'd be here all alone to do this, I made up my mind to help," she said.

"But you'll get dirty and muddy."

"Hush! We're wasting time."

"Food first," Sam said, taking her arm and escorting her inside.

When they finished, they each took a basket. Sam directed them to the fields with crops. First they pulled potato plants up from the ground and snapped off the potatoes attached to the plant. They quickly filled each basket.

"I'll take them to the wagon," Sam said, picking up Becky's basket. "It's too heavy for you."

"No, it's not," she insisted, snatching the handle from him. But when she tried to lift it, she grunted. "Oh my goodness! Who knew a few potatoes could be so heavy."

"It's a lot more than a few," Sam said, taking charge of the basket. He marched over to the wagon and emptied the baskets out. When he returned, she had uprooted three more plants. Together they toiled.

"What are the Fitch's Eddy folks gonna say when they find out you came down here by yourself?"

"I don't care what they say."

Sam put down the plant he'd just picked. "Why? Why are you here?"

Her eyes grew moist. "Don't you want me here?"

He took both her dirt-covered hands in his. "Of course I do. But I don't want you to be hurt by gossip."

"Nobody I care about is going to hurt me."

Sam looked down at their hands linked together. "This is the nicest thing anyone's ever done for me, except Benjamin and Josiah rebuilding the roof."

"You deserve it."

"I love you, Becky. I've never stopped," he said, his voice quiet.

She eased one hand from his and rested it on his cheek. "Dear Sam. And I still love you."

His head snapped up. "You do?"

"Of course. You didn't think I'm so unfaithful that I would stop caring for you because we couldn't be together, did you?"

"Yes, I did. I thought you hated me."

She laughed. "I could never hate you."

"I broke your heart," he whispered.

Her eyes filled, she cast her gaze to the ground. "Yes. But I understood why."

"I'm sorry. So very sorry. It was a mistake."

"I know. But you had to try it," she said, raising her eyes to his.

"I'm glad you understand. I'm not a farmer. I'm a blacksmith," Sam said, his voice heavy.

Becky smiled. "I don't know. These potatoes look darn good."

Sam laughed. They went back to harvesting.

When they finished, they headed over to the carrot patch. Becky rubbed her knees.

"You don't have to do this," Sam said.

"Wait! I know!" She ran into the house and returned with a blanket. She folded it several times, then put it on the ground and knelt on it. "I know it'll get dirty, but we can wash it."

"Good idea."

Halfway through the carrot patch, they broke for supper.

Although a cool breeze blew, the sun still beat down on them.

"Darn hot for October," Sam muttered.

"Let's eat," Becky said.

On their way to the house, Becky stopped by Goldy and fished in one of her saddle bags. She pulled out a meat pie and dishes containing pudding.

"You brought supper? Wonderful," Sam said as his stomach protested being empty.

They sat at the kitchen table, eating. Becky brought Sam up-to-date on all the Fitch's Eddy news.

"Is the house finished for the carpenter and his family?" Sam asked, taking a forkful of the delicious pie.

"Just about. Elijah Fitch announced that they were delayed in their travel here, but they're coming in time for the Harvest Festival."

"Oh?"

"Yes, the carpenter, his wife, and five children," Becky said, taking another helping of pie.

"Five children!"

"Four are his own, and one is adopted," she said.

When they finished eating, they resumed their work on the carrot patch. They finished a bit before the sun would slide down for the night.

"Becky, you have to go home," Sam said, dumping a basketful of large carrots into his wagon.

"Why? You have onions and squash left to do."

"I know. But you can't be here overnight," Sam said, pumping water for her horse and Amos.

"Why?"

"People will talk," Sam said, pumping water over his sweaty head.

"I don't care." She stepped up to the pump.

"But I do." He pumped, and she splashed water on her face and neck before scrubbing her hands.

"Becky!"

"Sam!" She put her fists on her hips, her legs spread to steady herself.

Sam grabbed her by the waist and pulled her up against him. His mouth came down hard on hers. He kissed her with all the pent-up love and desire he felt. She melted against him, all resistance and attitude faded away.

When he let her go, he put his hands on her upper arms, picking her up and setting her down then stepping back until six feet separated them. "That's why."

Stunned, and red-faced, she touched her lower lip. "Because you wanted to kiss me?"

"Because I want more than just kissing you. I'm only human, Becky. If you were to spend the night here, well, I don't know how far we'd go."

"Sam, are you accusing me of having no self-control?"

He laughed. "No. I'm the one with no self-control. Why tease each other? Let's wait until we can be together for real."

"All right."

"Good. Now let me help you," he said. He gave her a leg up. "Thank you for being here, helping me."

"You're welcome. When are you coming back to town?"

"As soon as I get the onions and squash harvested."

"In time for the Harvest Festival?" she asked, picking up the reins.

"Yes. You going with me?"

"Yes. I'll meet you at the dance," she said.

"No, I'll pick you up. Your parents all right with you going with me?" He raised his collar against the late afternoon wind.

"I'll talk to them."

"Good. Thanks for helping me. Now hurry. You must get home before dark."

"You're welcome." She blew him a kiss then rode off, heading north on the road to Fitch's Eddy.

Sam prayed Violet's divorce papers would arrive soon. He didn't know how much longer he could control his desire for Becky Rhodes. Smiling, he went inside and to bed. He needed rest and to rise early to finish his harvest and return home. When he wondered about the greeting they'd get at the Harvest Festival, his brow wrinkled.

Chapter Nineteen

S am packed up his few remaining belongings in the house and added them to the wagon. He hitched up Amos and climbed onto the front seat. Lucky ran alongside. He turned once to feast his eyes on the better-than-expected output from his farming. It wasn't nearly enough to sustain the small farm, but he'd be able to pay off Old Man Fitch and have a reasonable amount left over to add to the Inn's supply, and maybe sell some, too.

"Looks like we got a mess of vegetables, Old Boy," Sam said to the ox. "Let's go home."

A few puffy clouds broke up the brilliant blue of the sky. Around midday, the October sun heated the air to an uncomfortable level, but by late afternoon, it quickly cooled down. Sam buttoned his jacket against the fall chill in the air.

The cooler temperature made it more pleasant for Amos to trudge home, pulling the extra weight of the crops. When he rounded the bend toward town, his heart sang. People were out putting up lanterns, setting out fresh fall flowers, pumpkins, and even hanging up quilts for the Harvest Festival.

Gratitude filled Sam's heart. After the trials he'd faced, he needed a celebration, and this would be the perfect event. He drove up the main street and turned left, maneuvering behind the Inn and coming to a halt halfway between the barn and the root cellar. He hopped off Martha's wagon and unhitched Amos, who made a beeline for the trough filled with water.

Martha came out the back door. "Sam! You home for good?"

"Yep, Grandma. And look at all the vegetables!" Sam spread his arms out.

Her eyes grew wide. "Lordy! Are these all for us?"

Lucky barked.

"No. A third belong to Mr. Fitch.

"Let's divide them up," Martha said. "Lizzie! Jem! Come here. I've got a job for you."

"Mr. Fitch might want to pick his own vegetables," Sam said.

"Pish tush. We'll give him the best-looking ones and that'll have to do. I got cooking to do. Let's get this done. The children will store our share. This is mighty fine, Sam," Martha said, patting him on the back.

"Thanks, Grandma."

"Bet a lotta work went into gettin' these."

"Darn right," Sam said. He separated the vegetables into groups by type and then took one third of each group and swept it to one side of the wagon.

"Your daddy would be proud," Martha said, her eyes filling.

"I don't know about that. He'd probably have three times as much."

"This is fine. It'll be a big help this year. That storm wiped out some of our garden as well as your farm," Martha said. "You goin' to the Harvest Festival tomorrow night?"

"Sure am. Becky's coming with me," he said, pride shining through his voice.

"Becky? Becky Rhodes? Goodness gracious! Glad to see you two finally getting together."

"Me, too," Sam said with a chuckle. He piled Mr. Fitch's bounty in the two baskets and left them in the wagon.

Within twenty minutes the children had the vegetables safely stored below ground. Martha returned to the kitchen. Sam went to his room and looked around for his father's old military uniform. He wore that to all fancy occasions. It was nowhere to be seen.

"Grandma, where's Papa's uniform?" he asked.

She chuckled. "I figured you'd be home for the Harvest Festival and wantin' to wear that. So I cleaned it and gave it a good pressing. It's hanging in my closet. Go on up and get it."

He kissed her on the cheek. "Thank you, Grandma!"

"Sam, we're running behind this year. Could you go out to the orchard? The apples are so ripe, they're falling off the trees and the bees, raccoons, and birds are getting 'em."

"Sure. Mr. Fitch is sending Charles to pick up his share. Will you see that he gets it? It's the two baskets here," Sam said, pointing. "Thanks. I'm going to pick apples." He tucked a ladder under his arm and made tracks to the nearby apple orchard.

AFTER FIXING THE EVENING meal, Martha set a spell in her rocking chair on the front porch of the Inn, sipping a cool drink.

Abiel Wilcox wandered by. He stopped and took off his hat.

"Good afternoon, Mrs. Chesney."

"Afternoon," Martha said, not making eye contact.

"May I say you're looking lovely today?" He gave a little bow.

"Horsefeathers, Mr. Wilcox. I been working all afternoon over a hot stove."

"I beg to differ."

"Take your soft soap somewhere else." She sniffed, directing her gaze to the shoemaker's shop where they were hanging a wreath made of fall leaves.

"Are you accusing me of lying?" Abiel bristled.

"Call it what you will. It's soft soap. What is it you want, Mr. Wilcox? Get to the point." Martha pulled her shawl a little tighter around her shoulders.

"I was hoping you'd accompany me to the Harvest Festival."

"Waiting until the last minute to ask me, aren't ya?"

"You haven't been very friendly since Violet left," he said, clearing his throat.

Martha narrowed her eyes. "Got that right. That was a dirty deed you pulled."

"I don't know what you mean, Mrs. Chesney," Abiel said, shifting his weight and casting his gaze at the ground.

"You know darn well what I mean. What you pulled on poor Sam." Silence.

"I got eyes. I got a good head on my shoulders. I've seen every kinda flim-flam going. Don't think for one minute you fooled me," Martha hissed.

"Good day to you," Abiel said, turning to leave.

But Martha grabbed his arm. "Don't you be goin' nowhere. I ain't finished. I know all about the deal you cooked up. Your granddaughter was already with child when she started keeping company with Sam. T'weren't his child she gave birth to," Martha said, narrowing her eyes.

Abiel's face blanched.

"You put her up to trickin' him. Poor naïve boy. He fell for it. Being the honorable young man he is, he did the right thing."

"I'm sorry..."

"No use apologizing. Harm's been done. But you'd better get those divorce papers right quick. Sam's got a fine young lady who likes him. But he can't marry her until he's uncoupled from Violet."

"I'm expecting them any day now."

"Better be. Or I'll be telling the whole town what you did to my grandson," Martha snapped.

"I'll bring them over as soon as they arrive. I promise," Abiel said, his hands shaking.

"Yeah? You better. A promise from a snake like you isn't much good."

"I had to do it. I had to save Violet's reputation," Abiel said, hanging his head.

"At the expense of my grandson. Shame on you! And she ended up running off with that Zeb fella anyway. I'm guessing he's the true father?"

Abiel nodded.

"Get those papers. And until you have those? Get outta my sight, Mr. Abiel Wilcox," Martha spat with venom.

He rushed off.

Toting a bushel basket full of ripe, red, juicy apples, Sam joined his grandmother. He placed the basket on the ground and sat on a stool next to her.

"Want one, Grandma?" he asked.

Martha perused the barrel bursting with color and the aroma of ripe apples.

"Don't mind if I do," she said, plucking a fat, juicy one from the basket.

Sam looked down the street. "That Abiel Wilcox?" he asked.

"Yes. That scoundrel. Snake," Martha said before taking a big bite of the fruit.

"What did he do?"

"Never you mind. It's over. Said he'd be rushin' those divorce papers over as soon as they arrive."

"Good. I need to be free," Sam said, taking an apple for himself.

Martha took the last two bites, then slipped the core back in the bushel. "Will you throw that out for me?"

"Sure," Sam said, taking a bite. "Best crop in years," he commented.

"Probably all that water from the big rainstorm," Martha said, licking her lips.

"At least it was good for something," Sam said.

THE NEXT DAY.

Sam gathered more apples, then got out of the way while his mother, Abigail Tanner, made an apple pie for the apple pie contest. Sam cleaned and loaded his gun for the rifle competition. Strains of clarinet, flute, fiddle, and banjo floated into his room. The sounds made him want to move. He stepped a bit lively as he took down his papa's uniform and got dressed for the occasion.

His mother and grandmother fussed in the kitchen. Martha was entering her nut bread, and Abigail was entering her pie in the food competitions. He heard Martha grumble about Giselle, the Fitch's French cook, who always entered at least one fantastic baked confection and usually won.

Sam chuckled to himself. He loved them and they worked so hard, but there was something about Giselle's baking that left others in the dust.

The Harvest Festival started at two in the afternoon and ran until ten at night. The pie judging and the rifle competitions were held early in the day. Dancing started about four. At half past, Sam trudged up the hill to the general store. When he entered, both Doc and Mrs. Rhodes were behind the counter.

"Good day, Dr. Rhodes, Mrs. Rhodes. Is Becky ready?" Sam asked.

"I believe so," Virginia said. "Becky! Sam is here."

Becky floated out from the back room. She wore a stunning dress. The bodice was scoop-necked and made from a lavender, green, and white small calico print. It had sleeves that puffed from shoulder to elbow. The skirt was a white dotted Swiss, with a big ruffle across the bottom of the same calico print as the bodice.

Sam gasped. "Oh my...you look beautiful!"

She twirled. Her long red hair had been twisted into a chignon.

"You made that dress?"

She nodded.

"You will be the most beautiful woman at the dance," he said, offering her his arm. She slung a wrap around her shoulders, hooked her hand through his elbow, and they ambled out to the street.

As they approached the old meeting house where all Fitch's Eddy events were held, except the few at Elijah Fitch's elegant, lavish home, Sam's nerves kicked up.

When they entered, all talking ceased as every eye in the room zeroed in on Becky and Sam. He swallowed and felt her tighten her grip on his arm. The silence grew, engulfing the room, making him sweat. Suddenly, out of the far corner came a strong familiar voice.

"Sam! Brother, dear. And beautiful Becky! How nice to see you. Sam, it's been forever since we were last together. Come see your niece, my lovely babe. You too, Becky."

It was Sarah, his sister, coming to their rescue. Her welcome left no room for anyone to say anything untoward. After all, Sarah was now a Fitch, kind of like local royalty. So no one dared denigrate her brother in her presence. Benjamin stepped forward to keep the attention away from Sam and Becky. "Gentlemen, play your instruments. Let's have a dance. It's the harvest. Let's celebrate!"

The band played a lively jig. Sam took Becky's hand and joined in the dance. When the band took a break, Becky and Sam grabbed mugs of cider and plopped down on a bench with Sarah and Benjamin. The baby slept in a crib nearby.

"I'm hungry," said Sam.

"Me, too," Becky said.

Along with Benjamin, they wandered over to the food table. Josiah Quint joined them there.

"Becky, I swear you are the prettiest girl here. If Sam hadn't already claimed you, I'd make my pitch."

"Josiah, you settle down? Hard to believe," Sam said, chuckling.

"Every man grows up eventually," Becky tossed off.

"That's right," Josiah said, grinning.

Plates were filled with roast duck, beef, and chicken, stewed or roasted. There was an abundance of roasted vegetables: potatoes, squash, carrots, corn, turnips, and onions – all filled a long table barely sturdy enough to hold the lavish offerings. There was a small table just for different kinds of bread and butter. And for dessert there were apple pies, pumpkin pies, squash and pumpkin pudding, chocolate pudding, pear tartes and sweet cinnamon rolls all on display on a separate table.

Josiah had won the rifle shooting contest. Abigail won the pie contest, Giselle won for her tarte and cinnamon rolls, and Martha won a special mention for her nut bread. Sam didn't care that he lost the rifle contest. He figured he'd won the best woman in Fitch's Eddy and that was prize enough.

Sam and Becky left early to take a detour on the way home. They swung by the tree near the pond that had always been their meeting place. With the sun down, it was cold out. They sat on a log. Sam put his arm around Becky and drew her to him. She snuggled into his shoulder.

"I'm not a single man..." he started.

"Yet..." she added.

"Right. Yet. But I will be, soon, I hope. So I just want to ask. I mean I know I have no right..."

"Sam! Sometimes you can be so frustrating. Just spit it out!"

"All right, all right. When I'm single again, will you marry me?"

Silence blanketed the couple.

"Well?" Sam asked, his voice shaky.

"Of course I will. But we'll live here, in Fitch's Eddy?"

"Yes. I'm going to stay with smithing. Caleb thinks we might be able to open a second shop. And that would be all mine."

"Oh, Sam! Your own shop?" Becky threw her arms around him. He seized the opportunity to kiss her with all the love in his heart.

They picked their way home through the field, guided by the light of the harvest moon. Once at the store, Sam gave Becky a gentler kiss and bid her goodnight. On his way back to the Inn, he stopped in again to the meeting house because the party was still going on.

Elijah Fitch buttonholed him. "I saw the share of your harvest. Mighty fine looking."

"It's all right then?"

"Yes. Your debt to me is canceled."

Sam stuck out his hand. Fitch took it. The band stopped, then played an introductory chord.

"Look, Sam, It's our cabinetmaker," Elijah said, then moved forward.

Josiah sidled up to Sam.

Elijah put two fingers in his mouth and gave a big whistle then clapped his hands.

"Hear ye, hear ye. The newest residents of Fitch's Eddy have arrived. It's Micah Edwards, his wife and children. He's a cabinetmaker who's going to put Fitch's Eddy on the map!" Applause reverberated off the plain wood walls. People went over to shake Micah Edwards' hand and introduce themselves.

"This is my wife, Ruth. And my sons, Harry, and Gideon. And my daughters, Lucy, Charlotte, and Caroline," Micah said.

Sam glanced at Josiah who stared at Caroline Edwards, a brown-haired, brown-eyed beauty. His mouth hung open.

"What?" Sam asked.

"We have a new most beautiful woman in Fitch's Eddy," Josiah said and then gently rolled the words over his tongue, "Caroline Edwards.

THE END

Epilogue

"**M**arriage is not for me," Josiah said, sharing a mug of beer at the Inn with his friend, Sam Chesney.

"That's what they all say until they meet the right one," Martha Chesney said. "Then it's bang! Married in three shakes of a lamb's tail." She laughed.

"I mean it."

"What about that new girl, Caroline Edwards?" Sam asked.

"I spoke to her, and she ignored me."

"Really?" Sam raised his eyebrows.

Caleb and Abigail burst through the door in time for the evening meal.

"You joining us, Josiah?" Martha asked.

"Yes, ma'am. If it's not too much trouble."

"No trouble at all. You're like my second grandson," she said, placing a plate in front of him.

Caleb and Abby took their places. "Who ignored you, Josiah?" Abigail asked.

"Tell me and I'll give them a stern talking-to," Caleb said, frowning, as he filled a mug with cider and handed it to his wife.

"He's trying to make it up with that new girl, Caroline Edwards."

"I spoke to her, she smiled but never said a word," Josiah said.

"Maybe that's because she's a mute," Caleb said, taking a piece of bread before passing it on.

"Mute?" Josiah asked.

"Means she can't talk," Abby explained, taking a mouthful of cider.

"Oh, I didn't know," he said.

"Some people are born like that," Caleb said.

"And some get like that after something really bad happens," Martha explained.

"Sit, Martha," Abby said. "Let me get the food."

"Don't mind if I do rest these old bones."

Josiah refilled Martha's mug. "Tell me more, Martha," he said.

Stay tuned for book 4 in the Catskills Saga – "Josiah's Discovery".

Made in the USA
Monee, IL
21 April 2025

16137633R00138